GRAFTON HOUSE

John Vialet

Published by BookLocker.com, Inc., St. Petersburg, Florida.

Printed on acid-free paper.

BookLocker.com, Inc.
2018

First Edition

Dedication

For Joyce, and with thanks to Don Tingle
for his invaluable encouragement.

PART ONE: FRIDAY, JULY 1, 2011

CHAPTER 1

On this particularly pleasant July afternoon, a surprising number of people and vehicles were milling around and above the Newport mansion known as Grafton House. Surprising because Grafton House was the home of a Harvard think tank, and its occupants did most of their thinking indoors.

The Center for Inter-American Policy Studies is basically a source of funds for research by Harvard scholars. The Center got its funds from Alma Grafton, the widow of Alphonse Grafton, Harvard 1886. The Center's vague title allowed Harvard to fund almost any research that Harvard wanted to fund. And Alma's Newport mansion, Grafton House, was a delightful place to house the Center and its thinkers. So delightful that the Center is usually called Grafton House.

A MEDEVAC capable search and rescue helicopter from the Coast Guard's Castle Hill station hovered noisily over the mansion. The pilot examined the terrain below her, looking for a good spot to land. She saw a very large building sitting in the middle of a huge expanse of green lawn. Two tennis courts, a swimming pool, and a parking lot were located at the rear of the building. The mansion was situated at the top of a small hill. A driveway led down hill from the mansion to Ocean Drive.

Two police cars were parked on Ocean Drive blocking the entrance to the driveway. A third police car and a large red fire truck were parked halfway up the hill. And at the top of the hill, a red emergency light swirled silently on top of an ambulance. A small group of people stood next to the ambulance. Behind them, a much larger group of people had gathered on the steps by the entrance to Grafton House. Above the entrance, a large green banner said "WELCOME TO THE GRAFTON HOUSE SUMMER CONFERENCE ON INTERNATIONAL MIGRATION PATTERNS AND POLICIES."

Three emergency medical technicians emerged from the entrance to Grafton House pushing a gurney toward the ambulance. Karim Pandit, a junior Grafton House research assistant was half sitting up on top of the gurney. An oxygen mask covered Karim's face. He feebly waved his hand at Andy Eads, the Grafton House executive director, as the gurney slid into the ambulance.

A worried looking woman carrying a cell phone, large purse, and black briefcase got into the back of the ambulance with Karim. "I'll call you from the hospital when we get there, and tell you what's happening," she said to Andy. "Thanks, Teresa," Andy said. "I appreciate it. And would you call the Coast Guard station at Castle Hill and tell them we don't need a MEDEVAC helicopter. The ambulance is all we need."

"He'll be OK," the chief fireman said to Andy. "We think he ate something he shouldn't have. Something that disagreed with him. Could be anything. They'll figure it all out at the hospital. We get that a lot in the summer time. Food goes bad quick when it's this hot, you know." The fireman shook his head.

"I think that must be what happened to Karim," Andy Eads said. "Food poisoning. We had a lobster dinner last night for all the new staff, and the people who've come in early for our conference tomorrow. There was too much to eat last night, so we put the leftovers in the refrigerator. They must have spoiled. I think Karim was in there this afternoon snacking on the leftovers." Andy smiled. "Our young staff have healthy appetites."

Suddenly, a striking woman with long black hair appeared in the Grafton House doorway. She wore short pink shorts and she was barefoot. She stood in the doorway for a couple of seconds. Then she began to run down the hill towards the entrance gate. "They murdered him," she cried. "Islam and Muhammed killed Karim. I knew they would try, and now they have! "

"Who's that," the chief fireman asked Andy Eads.

"That's Dr. Gardiner," Andy said. "She's our newest senior staffer. Brilliant, but I'm afraid she's overly concerned about the negative side of the Muslim religion."

"That's interesting," the fireman said. "She said she knew 'they' were going to murder him. She said 'Asa Lom' and 'Muhammod' killed him. What did she mean by that? Are they on your staff?"

"I think what Dr. Gardiner actually said was 'Islam and Muhammad.' Islam is what Muslims call their religion, and Muhammad is the man who founded that religion. The one they call the Prophet Muhammad. That was about 1,400 years ago. So he certainly isn't on our staff.

"Anettka has very strong opinions about the Prophet Muhammad and the Muslim religion. Negative opinions. She thinks the religion treats women badly. Not just radical Muslim groups like al Qaeda, but the religion as a whole. She's not very interested in terrorism, although I think she sees it as part and parcel of treating women badly. I'm afraid she blames Muhammad and the Muslim religion as a whole for problems they really didn't cause. Although a lot of American politicians seem to agree with her. In my opinion, she's being simplistic. Anyway, I'm pretty sure she used the word 'they' to refer to Muslims. As I said, she doesn't like them very much, even though she used to be one herself. She really shouldn't say things like that, but there it is."

"My mother-in-law was like that," the fireman said. "She thought the Pope ruined the Catholic Church. Not this Pope, but the nice old guy who ran the Church back in the Sixties. I liked him myself. But my mother-in-law thought he was a limb of the devil. She used to say he was a Communist, because he got rid of the Latin. I don't think she had any idea what a Communist was, but she knew it was bad. She wouldn't go to church, either. Said the priests were all Communists and queers. I think she thought the two things were connected. Frankly, she was a little nuts."

The fireman took off his helmet, and wiped his forehead with a red handkerchief. "These things are kind of hot in the summer," he said. "Is that kid a Muslim? Don't they have a rule against eating lobster, stuff like that? Maybe that's what the lady meant."

"I don't think so. We have a number of Muslims on the staff, and they all eat lobster when we have it. They won't eat pork, but they're fine with lobster. No, I think Dr. Gardiner was just blowing off steam."

"Maybe," the fireman said. "But I think you probably should go speak to her before Lieutenant Graves does. Which he's definitely going to do. Calm her down. Because Sam's definitely going to ask her who she was talking about. Because saying somebody's been murdered, or is gonna be murdered makes cops get nosy. Just a word to the wise."

Several policemen stood talking quietly among themselves by the police cars on Ocean Drive. Another policeman was standing by the police car parked halfway up the driveway. He was looking down the hill, watching three people standing by the entrance gate.

"That's Sam Graves," the Chief Fireman told Andy. "He's the Deputy Police Chief."

The gate was a hundred yards away. It was much further than Andy could see clearly. But identifying the three people wasn't hard, despite Andy's miserable eyesight. The small figure jumping up and down and waving its arms dramatically was obviously Anettka Gardiner. Harold Cummings, the Grafton House groundskeeper was certainly the tall figure standing next to her -- no doubt patiently listening to Anettka's complaints. A third person, tall, wearing a skirt, so perhaps a Scot but probably a woman stood motionless behind Harold. That must be the woman from Harvard University's research center management office, Andy thought. She's here to evaluate us. But I can handle that.

"Thanks," Andy said to the Chief Fireman. "I appreciate your advice. I'll do that. But now I should probably tell everyone to go back to work." He nodded towards the large group of staff who had gathered n the broad steps leading up the entrance to Grafton House to watch the activity. A few of the younger staff were sunning themselves on top of the stone lions on each side of the steps, but most were standing or sitting on the broad steps themselves. As far as Andy could tell, they all looked happy: pleased with the opportunity to be out in the Newport sun for a few minutes.

For the most part, they were talking quietly, but a small young woman with a mop of curly red hair was heatedly addressing a burly man with a red beard. They looked related, but Andy knew they weren't. "That's just bullshit, Jack," the young woman said in a loud voice. "You know that. You just won't admit it." A group of junior staff watched them with interest.

Andy Eads mentally scratched his head for a moment and came up with the young woman's name. Tobie something. Tobie Shakespeare? No, Tobie Shaw, he decided. One of the Grafton House computer nerds. He watched Jack Chrysler try to calm the young woman down. <u>Pax vobiscum</u> Jack, he thought. Lots of luck with that one. Better you than me.

On the other side of the group on the stairs, another knot of junior staff respectfully surrounded a man in a white seersucker suit. The man's head was very large and completely bald, and he wore dark sun glasses. "But Dr. Khan," a young woman said. "Don't you think that Dr. Gardiner's views are authentic, even if they're wrong-headed in some respects?"

Suleiman Khan waved a hand dismissively. "Authenticity," he pronounced, "is hardly a justification for fatuity. Dr. Gardiner needs to get a grip on herself and her bizarre fantasies."

"Suleiman! Jack! Everyone!" Andy said. His lecturer's voice, shaped by years of speaking to large halls filled with dozing college students, effortlessly rose above the noise of the crowd. Everyone turned to look at him. "I think everything's pretty much over with here, folks," Andy said. "The EMTs think it was food poisoning, probably from some bad lobster. They say he'll be fine once they get him to the hospital. So, we should probably all get back to work now. I know it's a nice day, but we've got a lot of work to do before the conference starts and we need to keep plugging away at it."

There was a murmur of disappointment from the crowd. Some of them had obviously been hoping for a dramatic turn of events that would allow them to take the afternoon off. But the staff dutifully began to disperse and go back to their offices inside Grafton House. Suleiman Khan nodded curtly at Andy and walked slowly away, leaning slightly on his cane. Jack Chrysler said something quietly to Tobie Shaw, who smiled tentatively, and then came over to where Andy was standing.

"One of us needs to talk to Anettka," Andy said.

"Why?" Jack Chrysler asked.

"I guess you didn't hear her, then. She was making a scene before you got here. She told the cops that Karim was murdered. A lot of nonsense about Muhammad and Islam being responsible. She was freaked out. I don't know what got into her. I think she and Suleiman had been arguing. I'm not sure. Anyway, I'm pretty sure the police lieutenant over there is going to ask her what she meant. And we need to calm her down before that happens."

"What's this 'we' stuff, Andy? She's the one who needs to calm down. Not us. And she will too, you know that. She's too smart not to."

"Alright," Andy said. "I thought there wouldn't be any harm in asking. I'll do it. Talk to you later."

The firemen were getting into the ambulance, and about to drive off. Andy walked over to the ambulance and leaned in the window. "Thank you, guys," he said. "We appreciate your help a lot. I'll come over to the hospital myself as soon as I can get away this afternoon."

The ambulance slowly began to drive down the hill to the entrance gate, and Andy followed it on foot. When the ambulance got to the entrance, one of the firemen poked his head out a window and spoke to Anettka and Harold. Harold smiled but Anettka looked angry. The young woman with them looked curious. The ambulance drove off through the entrance as Andy reached the bottom of the hill.

"I'm Andy Eads," Andy said to the young woman. "I'm the director, and you must be Dr. Snow from University Hall."

"How do you do," Phoebe said. "I hope this isn't a bad time for me to arrive." Melanie was right, she thought. He is an attractive man. Beautiful blue eyes. I wonder how old he is.

"Not a bad time at all," Andy Eads said. "Not at all, not at all. There's always something happening here in our little group. I think of us as a laboratory, as a matter of fact, an experiment in social relations. I'm afraid that Dr. Gardiner thinks I make too much out of that metaphor."

"For God's sake, Andy," Anettka said.

Andy paused. "Harold," he said. "Would you mind taking Dr. Snow up to her room while Dr. Gardner and I have a chat. And then I'd like you to drive me over to the hospital to see how Karim is doing. I sent Teresa with him to take care of the paperwork, but I should look in on him and make sure he's alright. And if we've got time, maybe we can drive by Pinewood and see how my father's doing."

"I'll be back around six," Andy said to Phoebe. "There's a lot I'd like to tell you about our work here. Perhaps we can meet for drinks on the veranda. I'll give you a ring when I get back."

"Of course," Phoebe said. "Whatever works for you. I know you've got your hands full right now. I'll be fine."

"Thank you," Andy said. "I appreciate it." He paused and waited until Phoebe and Harold got back in the Lincoln and drove up the hill. Then he turned to Anettka and said, "Let's sit over here on the wall." He led the way to a low retaining wall that flanked the entrance gates. Anettka looked rebellious.

"Karim's going to be OK," Andy said. "The firemen are pretty sure it's food poisoning. But I think you need to get ready for the police lieutenant over there. I'm pretty sure he's going to ask you what you meant just now about Karim's being murdered.

"I told one of the firemen that you were just blowing off steam. That you had strong views about Islam and the Prophet and... well, I didn't use the word metaphor, but I tried to suggest that you didn't mean someone literally tried to murder Karim. But that's what you said, and people heard you. So I'm afraid you're going to have to explain yourself to the police lieutenant who's walking towards us right now as a matter of fact." Lieutenant Graves was a tall man with short grey hair. He appeared to be somewhere in his fifties. He wore a starched white Cuban style shirt over khaki pants, and his skin was very black. He looked formidable.

"Shit," Anettka said in a low voice.

"I don't think I introduced myself before," Andy said to the policeman. "I'm Andy Eads, and I'm Director of Grafton House. And this is Dr. Gardiner, who's a senior member of our research staff. Dr.

Anettka Gardiner. Her husband's Paul Gardiner, the America's Cup winner a few years back."

"How do you do," the policeman said. "I'm Lieutenant Sam Graves. Mrs. Gardiner probably doesn't remember but we were introduced last summer at the Redwood Library book fair. I had the privilege of serving in your husband's platoon in Vietnam, Mrs. Gardiner."

Anettka smiled warmly. "Of course I remember, Lieutenant. I particularly remember how pleased my husband was to see you. He said you were the best Marine in his platoon. He's usually so reticent, and he was so warm when you appeared."

Lieutenant Graves nodded but did not return the smile. "I'm sorry to bother you," he said, "but I'm afraid I have to ask you about some things you said just now." He reached into his back pocket and produced a slip of yellow paper. "I think you said something like 'They've murdered Karim.' Or Karim's been murdered.' And something about "Islam and Muhammad murdered him,' or 'killed him.' Something like that. It would be very helpful to us if you would explain what you meant when you said those things."

Anettka stood silently for a moment, obviously thinking. Then she said quietly, "I'm afraid I was angry and talking through my hat, Lieutenant. I had just been having a heated argument with another member of our staff, Dr. Khan, about religion. He is a Muslim, a follower of the Prophet Muhammad. I was brought up in that same religion, but I no longer subscribe to it. In fact, I believe it's a deeply flawed religion, responsible for many of the world's problems. Karim, the young man who was taken ill, is a former Muslim like me. I happen to know he has been under severe pressure from his family to return to their religion, and in fact to return to Jordan. That's where he's from. I myself have been under such pressure in the past. When Karim collapsed just now, when I saw him unconscious, I jumped to the conclusion that he had had a heart attack. A stroke. Something fatal. And I'm sorry to say I behaved hysterically. I didn't think. I just reacted. And ranted. I'm sorry. I didn't mean to cause a problem."

"I think I see, Mrs. Gardiner," the police lieutenant said slowly. "I know how upset people can get when they're arguing about religion. And I'm sure it was alarming when the young man collapsed. So I think I can say that we don't have a problem here. Particularly since the young man appears to be on the mend from his food poisoning. Thank you for your time."

"Thank you, Lieutenant," Anettka said. "I appreciate your courtesy."

"Thanks, Lieutenant," Andy said. "Please let me know if there's anything further we can do to help you on this."

All three Newport Police Department cruisers had drawn up beside them while they were talking, and the Lieutenant got in the first one. The cars drove off and Andy and Anettka watched them as they drove away.

"You did a good job just now," Andy said. "I think the Lieutenant was reassured. And that's good. But is that all there is to it? Have you left anything out that you didn't tell the Lieutenant? Anything that you should tell me? In confidence, of course."

"Yes," Anettka said. "Yes, there is. I think Suleiman has been pressuring Karim to go back to Jordan. That was what we were arguing about. He has been working on Karim's guilt feelings about being an apostate, about rejecting his parents' religion. You know Suleiman. Better than I do for sure. And you must know he is a master of psychological warfare. He hates me because I reject his evil religion, and he hates anyone strong enough to free himself from the bondage of a madman's fantasy. He would like me dead, to shut me up. And he feels the same way about anyone who dares to speak out against Islam."

"So when you thought Karim was dead, you really did mean that Islam had murdered him." Andy examined Anettka's face. It was slightly flushed.

"Yes," Anettka said. "I realize that sounds extreme, but I also think it's true."

"I'm sorry about that," Andy said. "I know it's difficult sometimes, but my goal is to make Grafton House a community where we can disagree strongly about ideas but still care for and love one another. Perhaps I'm naïve, but I do think that's possible." He looked earnestly at Anettka. She shrugged.

"I no longer believe that," she said. "I'm sorry to disappoint you."

"Everything OK?" They turned and saw that Jack Chrysler had driven up in a red Mini Cooper convertible, "I'm driving into town to see how Karim's doing," Jack said. "Do you want to some with me?" He looked at Anettka.

"Harold's going to drive me in later," Andy said. "But you guys go ahead. I know Karim would like to see you."

"I haven't got any shoes on," Anettka said. "And I'm not presentable in my shorts."

"Hop in," Jack said, " I'll take you back up to the main house and you can change if you really think you need to."

"I'm supposed to be a respectable married woman," Anettka said. "Even I know that." But she got into the passenger seat of the Mini Cooper.

Andy watched the Mini Cooper cruise back up the hill and drive around back to the residential wing of Grafton House. Jack's red hair, Anettka's black hair and the red convertible driving up the green hillside make a pretty picture, Andy thought. A painting by one of the French Impressionists, he decided. I hope they aren't getting in over their heads, Andy thought. I really do hope they aren't.

CHAPTER 2

"Andy Eads," Melanie Ferguson had said reverentially to Phoebe Snow. Melanie was Harvard's Assistant Dean for External Research Center Management and Phoebe's boss. Melanie paused and took a sip of Evian water from the plastic bottle on her mahogany desk. "Andy Eads," she continued, " is the key component, the dominant factor in the Grafton House management system." Melanie was a devoted advocate of the "systems" approach to human resources management.

"What you have to understand," Melanie had said, "is that Andy Eads is a very late bloomer. When he was 35, everyone assumed that he was going to be famous. Super famous. Accomplish great things. Fantastic things. But he didn't. He made full professor in the Government Department at 32, which of course is amazing. And his first book was seen as a breakthrough -- something about the horrible effects of U.S. aid to military governments in Latin America. It's still supposed to be the best book on the subject. But after that, nothing seemed to work for him. He had tenure, so he couldn't be fired. And he produced a couple of books that no one was interested in. I've heard rumors that he had a serious drinking problem for a while, and wound up in rehab. Marital problems. Three ex-wives. The usual stuff. And frankly, he didn't do much for the next thirty or so years. Until he was in his sixties, I think. But then, about five years ago, the Director of Grafton House, Wolfgang Froelich -- a wonderful man -- died. Age 92, playing tennis with his granddaughter. And when that job opened up, Andy Eads asked if he could have it. Well, of course he could. The 'Gov' Department was delighted to have a new full professorship vacant. And that was what Grafton House was really set up to do. Be a dumping ground -- well, that's too harsh -- be a happy hunting ground for faculty who weren't pulling their weight as much as they should." Melanie smiled, clearly pleased with her trenchant analysis.

Phoebe's boss was renowned within Harvard's administrative staff for being "hard nosed." As a graduate student at Harvard Business School, Melanie Ferguson had specialized in human resources management. In Phoebe's private opinion, Melanie was a drama queen, for whom every day was a three act opera. Still, it had to be admitted that Melanie was extremely competent, and a whiz at statistical analysis. She was 42 and single and very successful. Phoebe sometimes wondered if she was going to turn into a bad imitation of Melanie. God, I hope not, she thought.

"What we had there when Andy Eads arrived," Melanie went on, " was an under-performing think tank." She impatiently pushed one very red fingernail through her curly blond hair. "All of Harvard's external research centers suffer from the same basic problem. They're separate foundations, separately financed by their own endowments. So they're relatively independent, and only partly under the control of Harvard's academic departments. They tend to 'go native:' go off on odd tangents if we're not careful. That's why we're here to provide some oversight."

I know that, Phoebe thought. Why does Melanie always have to pretend that I'm a newcomer? She nodded to make it clear that she understood the point.

"Grafton House got started the way a lot of Harvard's external research centers got started," Melanie went on. "A rich widow gave Harvard a big chunk of money to study her husband's favorite subject. Which was bananas in this case. Alphonse Grafton was fascinated by bananas. Some people said he was obsessed with bananas. He made his money in the 1890's in the banana trade down in Central America. A very rich man by the time he was forty. He was a wild and wooly bachelor for many years but eventually he married a young woman from Honduras. A much younger woman named Alma, which means 'soul' in Spanish I think. Alphonse married Alma in the 1930s. He was seventy-one. Alma was twenty-two. He brought her back to the States, built her a very big house in Newport, and after a couple of blissful years of marriage he died. Leaving Alma a very rich woman. Despite the Depression. Alphonse had been very prudent with his investments.

"After her husband died, Alma developed an interest in bananas. Her husband had grown them and imported them and made lots of money at it. He was well known in the banana business because of his success in developing varieties of banana that could survive the long voyage from Central America to the United States. This is his biography," Melanie said and showed Phoebe a large red leather-bound volume. She opened the book at a bookmark and read aloud.

"'Prior to the arrival of the first North American entrepreneurs in Central America and their establishment of a scientific banana cultivation and trading system, the primitive fruits of the indigenous banana tree were much smaller than our modern banana. The original native banana was fragile, and grew in bunches of widely varying sizes, so that shipping them to the United States in bulk was difficult and costly. A major obstacle to efficient shipping was the curved semi-circular shape of the primitive banana. Each tiny fruit curved back upon itself, and in bunches the yellow fruits resembled a native witch doctor's angrily clinched yellow fist, according to one explorer.'

"'Grafton's principal contribution to the North American banana trade was his development of a much larger and less curved banana, which grew in regular sized bunches of uniform dimensions. This was a key innovation. It allowed shippers to pack banana bunches closer together, which saved space and substantially reduced shipping costs. As P.F.J. Skithering, one of Grafton's fiercest competitors, admiringly commented, "You've simply got to give Al credit. He took the bend out of the banana, by God!"'"

Melanie closed the book with a thump. "I'm not sure if that's really true," she said. "About the bend I mean. I read another book that attributes the invention of straighter bananas to someone else. It doesn't matter. Alma decided to devote the rest of her life and her fortune to exploring the ins and outs of the banana. In memory of her beloved husband. And since Alphonse was a graduate of Harvard – Class of 1886 to be precise – she decided to give Harvard a lot of money to study the banana. In memory of Alphonse. This was in 1959, Dwight D. Eisenhower was the President. Alma stayed on at Grafton House after we set up the Center. She lived in one wing, and the Center was set up in the other two wings. Very cozy, I'm sure. Periodically, Alma would tour the house and bring cookies and milk to the staff. She died in 2001, a happy woman by all accounts."

Melanie paused and blew her nose with a Kleenex. "It must be some kind of allergy," she said. "I never get colds in the summertime. Anyway, to begin with, Grafton House doesn't really study bananas. It never has. That was what Alma wanted, and that's what Harvard's lawyers told her the new institute would do. But they were lawyers, after all, and they set up the foundation so that Harvard could study anything it wanted to as long as there was some remote connection to the banana.

"You have to remember that this was in the Eisenhower Administration. John Foster Dulles was Secretary of State. It was the height of the Cold War. Saber rattling by the Soviet Union. Castro overthrowing Batista in Cuba. So the U.S. was scared to death of communists getting a foothold in Latin America. National defense was a top priority for every segment of society, including Harvard. And someone in the Government Department had a bright idea. Why not use Grafton House to study our relations with Central and South America? Starting with the foreign policy implications of the banana trade with Central America?

"Alma thought that would be just fine, and signed the requisite check. It was a respectable sum, even by today's standards, and it allowed Harvard to spin off a number of marginal faculty members who weren't performing up to Harvard standards, but had families and needed jobs to support them. And who had a few good friends in Harvard's administration.

"It was a sweet deal. Good pay. A nice historic New England town to live in and raise a family. No real responsibilities except to hold a few seminars and conferences, and of course publish books. Over the years, we moved a number of underperforming staff off to Grafton House, where they proceeded to live the good life and study various topics vaguely related to U.S.-Latin American relations. I think one woman actually wrote something interesting about the banana trade, which made Alma very happy. Otherwise, very little of note took place. Nobody made any headlines, but it was generally agreed that the Alphonse Grafton Center for Inter-American Policy Studies was a respectable think tank. Not very productive, but respectable." Melanie made a small moue of disgust. "Until Andy Eads arrived five years ago."

"What happened then?"

"You have to give him credit," Melanie said. "He's really transformed the place. He decided that what Harvard needed was a center to study U.S. immigration policy, and he proceeded to turn Grafton House into exactly that. I've put together a dossier which you can read later, but what it boils down to is this: Andy got rid of the old staff -- pensioned them off -- and recruited a new group of scholars who wanted to study immigration policy. He's been absolutely catholic in his recruitment policy. He hasn't tried to hire people who agree with him. He doesn't appear to have any political axe to grind. What he seems to want is controversy. Controversy that -- he says -- will force scholars to refine their arguments and ultimately clarify the issues for everyone. So he's hired scholars with wildly different views on immigration. Liberals who want to let everyone in. Conservatives who want to keep everyone out. Free market types who want to import cheap labor from abroad. Union types who want to keep cheap labor out and protect American workers. Tree-huggers who want zero population growth -- two babies per family max and absolutely no immigration -- to stop global warming and protect the wild turnip. Traditional value types who want to make English the obligatory national language. You get the picture. Lots and lots of fierce arguments and competing points of view. Exactly what Andy Eads wanted.

"And of course, Andy's vision of the Center's potential was absolutely on target. Grafton House researchers are making major contributions to all sides of the current political debate over illegal immigration from Mexico. Under Andy's leadership, Grafton House has accumulated the intellectual heft needed to put the current crisis into the overall immigration policy context. To show that both legal and illegal immigration are complex mixtures of economic and moral issues."

Melanie paused and took another sip of Evian water from the bottle on her desk. Phoebe wished she had some coffee.

"Which brings us," Melanie went on, "to the little problem we're having with the junior staff at Grafton House. Well, not that little. As I said, there are strong ideological disagreements among the senior fellows. That's what Andy wanted, and Harvard's fine with that. But some of the junior staff have apparently decided that Andy is biased against U.S. citizens. They think he unjustly favors foreign staff because they're cheap and docile. Which is ridiculous, to be frank. Andy isn't interested in saving money and he certainly doesn't want people to be docile. Far from it. Nevertheless, some of the junior staff have filed a formal claim of bias with the University. And Harvard's legal counsel asked us to look into it. Which we would have done anyway, of course.

"The junior staff are mostly graduate students finishing their dissertations, with a sprinkling of post-docs. About half of them are foreign, or foreign-born US citizens. The rest are native born -- U.S. citizens. The staff who are complaining appear to be mostly native-born Americans who also have conservative views on immigration policy. Not all of them, I suppose. Frankly, I think that a good part of what's going on reflects the hysteria over Al Qaeda and terrorism that's gripping the country right now. Some of the foreign born staff are Muslims and this seems to freak out the conservative juniors. Anyway, the bias claim hasn't drawn that much public attention, but it's become a hot topic on some of the conservative blogs. And it's starting to show up on the conservative talk show circuit. 'Left wing Harvard eggheads are coddling radical Muslims and discriminating against native (by definition Christian) Americans.'"

Phoebe winced and Melanie nodded. "You get the picture."

"Only six of the junior staff have actually signed the bias claim," she went on, "but a lot more of them appear to be upset about the matter. We don't want that. And things could get out of hand if we don't play our cards right.

"So we decided, here in External Research Management, I mean, Dean Dillon and I decided to send you down there to look around. Spend a couple of weeks and get the lay of the land. Tell us what's really going on with this bias allegation. Talk to the junior staff about how they feel about the issue. See if there are any other issues that haven't come up yet but could become a problem. Come up with some ideas about what Harvard should do. And this is a good time for you to go. Grafton House is holding a summer conference on immigration policy the week starting on the Fourth of July weekend. So that's what we want you to do."

"OK," Phoebe said. "I can do that. It sounds interesting. Not too complicated."

Melanie laughed. "Sorry," she said. "I'm afraid it is a little complicated." She took another drink of water. "I said this bias claim has some obvious ideological overtones. We want to keep those from getting any more traction among the junior staff. The basic problem is the Grafton House management team. The word 'team' doesn't really describe them very well. Andy Eads has two assistant directors. They're supposed to help him run Grafton House. As far as I can tell, they don't do anything except cause trouble. Nothing useful. At all. However, they're both eminent scholars, and they see themselves as beacons of truth and illumination. One of them is a former Jesuit named John Chrysler. He calls himself Jack. He's a charmer. Very cute. Well actually, Andy Eads is a charmer too. He's also very cute. But older, the Teddy Kennedy type, but in good shape. Lots of hair, big shoulders, and a flat stomach. He must be well into his seventies by now, but he's still attractive."

Melanie looked pensive. "A flat stomach and lots of hair. It's odd how well that works for older men, isn't it? But I digress. Jack Chrysler got his law degree from Yale, and worked for one of the Ralph Nader litigation groups down in Washington. His views on immigration policy are simple. He wants to let everyone in. No restrictions on immigration. Welcome immigrants from Mexico and Central America with open arms. Tear down the fences at the border, abolish the Department of Homeland Security's immigration arm, that sort of thing. He's big on the Golden Rule. The nuts on right-wing talk shows love to piss and moan about him, and he's a favorite whipping boy for anti-immigration groups. Conservative Catholic groups hate him, too. He gets lots of publicity, which Andy of course loves. He's a guru for the foreign graduate students on the Grafton House junior staff. He's made it clear he thinks the bias claim is bogus. Of course a lot of the American-born junior staff think so, too.

"The more conservative junior staff also have a guru, Dr. Suleiman Khan. Dr. Khan is the other assistant director, and he's definitely the most eminent scholar at the Center. He's the author of a seminal book on international migration. We published it."

Melanie handed Phoebe a copy of the *Economist Magazine*. The magazine's cover showed a photo of a book entitled, *International Migration: Global Patterns and Underlying Dynamics*. By Suleiman Khan. "He was awarded the Sveriges Riksbank Prize in Economic Sciences for the book. That's a really big deal. It's called the economics Nobel Prize."

"I'm pretty sure he's not supportive of the kids filing the bias claim," Melanie continued. "He's a Muslim himself. He's a naturalized American citizen, originally from Pakistan. He was born a Muslim, but as far as I know he wasn't particularly religious for most of his life. But three or four years ago he had a personal epiphany and became a devout Muslim.

"He certainly doesn't sympathize with the anti-Muslim statements we keep hearing from right wing politicians these days. But he's definitely a conservative on immigration policy. Doesn't want to let anybody into the country who doesn't have a PhD in engineering. He thinks the brain drain is a blessing.

"And of course he thinks Jack Chrysler is a fool. But the person who really freaks him out is Anettka Gardiner. She's Andy Eads's most recent recruit to the Grafton House senior staff. Suleiman hates Anettka, and she seems to hate him. They don't even pretend to get along and that's a real problem for Andy."

Melanie paused and blew her nose. "Anettka is really one of a kind. Sui generis, as my favorite teacher used to say. "

"To begin with, she's a very serious scholar. She has a PhD from Oxford, and we – I mean Harvard – published her thesis." Melanie poked around in her desk drawer, pulled out a slim volume with a yellow cover and handed it to Phoebe. "It's your cup of tea. Mostly mathematics. It's an analysis of the German guest worker program's effect on economic productivity. I tried reading it but it's frankly incomprehensible. But you shouldn't have any trouble with it. It's the reason Andy recruited her for Grafton House.

"Anettka's from the Middle East herself. She's a Pakistani, too, and she's very critical of Islam's treatment of women. She published an essay in the *New York Review of Books* about her own personal experiences. Suleiman Khan detests Anettka and hates her book. He thinks Anettka is evil, and has made no secret of his feeling that she should be punished for her criticism of Islam and the Prophet. I forgot to mention that Anettka included a couple of the Danish caricatures of the Prophet Mohammed in her NYRB piece. Dr. Khan has received some publicity, but not as much as Anettka or Jack Chrysler.

"Gardiner is Anettka's married name. After she got her PhD at Oxford, she went back home to Pakistan to teach. When she got home, her parents tried to make her marry some guy she didn't want to marry. She said she wouldn't, and her brothers threatened to kill her unless she married the guy. Apparently that's considered standard operating procedure over there. So Anettka got out of Dodge. She left Pakistan in the middle of the night, flew to London and claimed refugee status when she got there.

"So Anettka's a handful. She's very smart. She's a genuine scholar. And she's definitely a feminist. Think Henry Louis Gates combined with Gloria Steinem. Her piece in the NYRB was a huge success. She's been on television, and NPR discussing her experiences. She's drop-dead gorgeous by the way, with a tony Oxford accent. And at least one Islamic group has threatened to kill her. Maybe two. I'm not sure. She's actually pretty interesting, and as you can imagine, she's generated a lot of publicity for Grafton House. Mostly positive publicity on talk shows, but a few anonymous death threats from what appear to be radical Islamic groups. Obviously, those are worrisome.

"She's married to an investment banker named Paul Gardiner. He's New York society, spends his summers in Newport sailing large boats, and-- most importantly for us -- he's on the Harvard Board of Overseers. Very rich. Much older than she is. There are rumors that she's trying to radicalize the foreign student contingent at Grafton House. God knows what that means. Maybe she's been telling the staff that women and men should have equal rights. Be very careful what you say to her."

Melanie paused and looked slightly embarrassed. "So what we want you to do, among other things, is try to figure out how we can prevent the rivalry among Jack Chrysler, Suleiman, and Dr. Gardiner from spilling over into relations between the foreign staffers and their U.S. counterparts. And we don't want to upset Dr. Gardiner's husband. At all. I know that's a little vague, but you'll get a better sense of it when you've been there for a while."

She paused again. "There is one more thing you should be aware of," she said. "You must have heard about the incident at Eliot House last week. The murder of the drug dealer, I mean."

"The one where they knifed the guy in the Eliot House courtyard? Sure. It was all over the news on TV."

"That's the one," Melanie said. "We're not sure, and we hope we're wrong, we really do, but it looks like the girlfriend of one of the suspects is on the Grafton House staff. The junior staff. The cops think her boyfriend and his partner learned about the victim -- he was a local drug pusher in Cambridge -- from our staffer, and they think she may have set up the guy who got stabbed. Arranged for him to go to Eliot House to deliver some drugs and told her boyfriend when the guy would be there. Her name is Shaw -- Tobie Shaw. She's a statistician, really smart. From Boston. The thing is her boyfriend isn't just a doper. He's some kind of anarchist nut, part of a nut group that believes society is corrupt -- rotten to the core -- and needs to be demolished. Violently. Bombs and stuff like that. They plan to abolish materialism and replace it with communes. Not Muslims, though, thank heavens. We're pretty sure about that, because we know they're strongly in favor of 'free love.' The cops can't find this guy or the other one either; they've both disappeared. One of the detectives on the case here in Cambridge thinks that the reason for the killing was to get funds for this guy's group, to finance its activities. They think he may be planning to do something nasty at Grafton House. Maybe blow up the immigration conference. That kind of thing. Get publicity for his cause. So that's the icing on the cake. As far as we know, there's nothing concrete, nothing whatsoever, that connects the killing at Eliot House to Grafton House, but still you should be aware of it."

Melanie smiled. "I know that's a lot to absorb at one time. Go through the dossier and give me a call when you finish it. We can discuss where the systems approach is likely too take us. I think you'll enjoy this assignment. I know I would."

Maybe I will, Phoebe thought, when I figure out how all the pieces fit together. God knows I need something new to think about.

CHAPTER 3

Settled in the driver's seat of his red Mini Cooper, Jack Chrysler baked in the late afternoon sun and waited for Anettka to change her clothes and reappear. I should have put some sun block on my nose, he told himself. And worn a hat. I'm too old to be this stupid. He rubbed his eyes with his left hand. Stupid in more ways than one. I'm too old to behave like a lovesick swain. No you're not, a cynical voice within him said. No I'm not, he admitted to himself.

This was not the first time Jack had been in love. In the seminary, he had harbored a secret crush on the daughter of the seminary caretaker: a red-haired young woman with large breasts and merry eyes. Later, as a young priest in a suburban Chicago parish, he had spent a tumultuous summer in love (secretly) with a young teacher in the parish nursery school. He left the priesthood at the age of thirty-seven because he no longer believed in God. Well, to be technical about it, he still kind of believed in God. He just didn't believe in most of the stuff in the Nicene Creed. So it really wasn't appropriate for him to continue to be a priest. (At least not in the Roman Catholic Church. Some Episcopalians might have let him do this, but not most of them.)

Even so, he might have stayed in the priesthood anyway, except for the celibacy thing. He had a profound yearning for a life in which he could legitimately fall in love with a woman and make love to her. And he couldn't do that and be a priest. Or at least an RC priest.

His first effort in that direction was not a success. A few months after leaving the priesthood, he met and then married a former nun. He was lonely, and she was attractive, and they both had a desire to remain connected to the Church. But he was shy and she was inhibited and sex turned out to be a disappointment. Worst of all, he was still lonely. The marriage broke up when he fell in love with a fellow academic — a buxom Latina named Carlotta who taught ecology — at the university where he taught ethics. Their affair was tumultuous: a romantic extravaganza, replete with exhausting but interesting ethical dilemmas. It ended abruptly when Carlotta fell out of love and wisely returned to her patiently waiting husband, a successful orthodontist. (Carlotta had beautiful white teeth.)

In the ten years since Carlotta, Jack had had a series of semi-serious girlfriends. A few had been in love with him, but he had not been in love with any of them. So now, his obsession with Anettka was a surprise. He had not planned to fall in love with her. He knew it was a terrible idea. There was absolutely no conceivable way in which it could work out happily. And there were a plethora of absolutely horrifying possible outcomes.

Still, there it was. He was in love. IN LOVE. The symptoms were unmistakable. He felt slightly queasy in Anettka's presence. His palms were moist. He was aware of warmish feelings in the vicinity of his underpants. And he could not stop thinking about Anettka Gardiner, Ph.D. (Oxon.). About her beautiful dark eyes and long eyelashes. About her aquiline nose. About the back of her long graceful swan-like neck. About her bosom, which was just the right size. About her long graceful fingers. About her brilliant mind, and sharp wit. She was perfect. Perfect. It made him want to cry. But of course that was impossible.

Anettka knew of course. How could she not know? And she was kind. She had told him she understood, but that their love could never be. Stuff like that. It only made him want her more. Want to be with her. Want to drive with her into Newport to see Karim Pandit. Hoping against hope that he could find a way to put his hand on the back of her slender neck and pull her to him and kiss her passionately. Jack leaned back in the driver's seat of the Mini Cooper and thought about this possibility.

"You should put a hat on," Anettka said," and I should probably just stay here." She stood by Jack's side of the car, looking down at him. She was wearing dark blue trousers and a white blouse, and looked remarkably like a schoolgirl. "I don't think I've done enough work on my presentation for opening day. Why don't you find Andy and take him? That would save Harold from making the trip."

"No!" Jack said in a strangled voice. "I don't want to drive in with Andy. I see enough of him as it is. I want to drive in with you. I really do."

"You've got to promise me two things, Jack, I really mean it. You've got to promise to behave if I do go with you. And you've got to promise to listen to me while I rehearse my lecture. Really listen, and give me some constructive criticism. Don't groan. Either you promise or I stay here."

"I promise," Jack said.

"No crosses count?"

"No crosses count," Jack said. "Is that the way the English say it? In Chicago, we say 'no crossies count.'" He smiled at Anettka, who got into the Mini Cooper and put on her seat belt.

"Who was that girl you were arguing with on the steps?" Anettka asked him. "What were you talking about anyway?"

"Tobie?"

"The one with all the red hair."

"Tobie. Tobie Shaw. She's one of the computer people. Very competent with statistics, data analysis, that sort of thing."

"So why was she looking so upset?"

"I think she's got various things on her mind. Boyfriend trouble. That kind of thing. And she's got this idea about the tall ships. The naval training vessels that are visiting Newport from around the world. She wants us to invite the officer candidates on board the tall ships to the lunch tomorrow. One of them is her boyfriend. She said he's on the Peruvian ship. I told her I didn't think it was feasible at this point in time, but she wouldn't listen to me. She thinks we can do it if we want to. And she's probably right, I'll give her that. Andy probably doesn't want to do it, at least I don't think so, but then I haven't really asked him about it."

"You should ask him," Anettka said. "It might be fun."

They were slowly driving down the driveway towards the entrance gate. As they approached the gate, Suleiman Khan suddenly rounded the corner by the gate and began walking up the hill toward them. Jack tapped on his horn, and waved cordially at Suleiman, but

Suleiman pointedly looked away from them and did not acknowledge Jack's wave.

"He hates me," Anettka said. "And I hate him. He's a bully and a liar. Grafton house should fire him. I've told my husband that, but he won't listen to me. Yet. But he will."

Jack pondered this statement. It was quite likely that Anettka was correct and that Suleiman hated her. Their conflicting views about Islam were more than enough to explain that. As to whether Suleiman was a bully and a liar, Jack was willing to admit that Suleiman was probably a bit of both, but not to an unusual degree. Male chauvinist pig was a more accurate description, but for some reason Anettka shied away from feminist buzz words. It's probably her age, Jack thought. She's from a post-feminist generation. Hers is probably the "X" generation, he thought. Maybe "Y". I need to Google that, he thought.

"I know you don't like Suleiman," Jack said, "but it would really be better if you just stayed away from him. He's a first-rate scholar. Probably the best scholar at Grafton House. It would cause a real mess if you convinced your husband that Grafton House should get rid of Suleiman. Really. I know you don't like each other, but you should just ignore him. I try to as much as I can, and I have to work with him."

"We'll see," Anettka said. "I'll think about it." The Mini Cooper was now passing the Newport Country Club. Anettka opened her backpack, removed a sheaf of papers, held together with a large paper clip, and began to read. "Good afternoon," Anettka said to an imaginary audience, as Jack drove slowly along Ocean Drive. "I'm Anettka Gardiner, and I'm a senior fellow here at Grafton House. My research over the last year and a half has focused on some of the effects of illegal migration from Mexico and Central America on the U.S. economy. In particular, I've tried to measure some very interesting effects that these migrants have had on labor productivity in certain sectors of the U.S. economy.

"For those of you who are not labor economists by trade, let me begin with a definition of the phrase, 'labor productivity.' According to the U.S. Labor Department's Bureau of Labor Statistics, labor

29

productivity relates economic output to the labor hours used in the production of that output. Two Bureau of Labor Statistics programs produce labor productivity and costs (LPC) measures for sectors of the U.S. economy."

Anettka paused. "I'm going to open up with something general like that, for the non-specialists in the audience." Then she fished around in her backpack and produced an eight-by-ten picture of a three-dimensional geometric form. The form resembled a jellyfish. A translucent jellyfish. The form was dotted with arrows pointing toward various mathematical formulae. "I probably should have brought copies of all the slides I'm going to show them." Anettka said. "But this will give you an idea of what they look like. I made them with my copy of Mathematica. When I get into the maths, it's really much easier to understand what I'm saying if you can see a visual representation. Of the maths I mean. On my slides."

Presumably, Jack thought, the labor economists in the audience will understand what she's saying. But then that's always a problem at academic conferences. Academics in different fields speak different languages. I certainly don't speak math. They do. I was never any good at math. He nodded his head judiciously, and tried to stay awake as Anettka plowed through an essentially incomprehensible series of numbers and formulas. Think of something pertinent to say, Jack, he told himself.

Time passed, as it always does, and eventually the Mini drew up in front of the Newport Hospital. Anettka stopped reading and put her sheaf of papers back in her backpack. "How does that sound so far?" she asked Jack.

"I think the slides are a good idea," Jack said. "But if I were you, I would try to come up with a set of non-mathematical conclusions for the non-economists in the room. To be honest, I didn't understand most of what you said. I get it that you think the effects on labor productivity are basically positive. But it would be helpful if you could tell us why without using math."

Anettka groaned. "I've tried," she said. "I really have. I'm afraid it's the two-culture thing that C.P. Snow wrote about. I speak maths, and you don't. And that makes it hard for me to tell you what I've learned. And vice-versa, of course. I'll work on it some more."

"I think you're wonderful," Jack said.

"You promised me not to do that, Jack. I really mean it; no crosses count," Anettka said to Jack as they got out of his car. But Anettka smiled when she said it.

CHAPTER 4

Harold Cummings parked the shiny black Lincoln Town Car in a small paved area marked "Director Only" next to the front entrance to Grafton House. Then he pressed a button on the dashboard, which caused the trunk to open with a hollow, satisfyingly melodic "Kerthunk!" Phoebe had ridden up the hill in the front passenger seat, and she quickly opened her door and got out before Harold could come around the car and open the door for her. She walked around to the back of the car to get her suitcase, but Harold got there first. "I'll get that," he said, and deftly retrieved Phoebe's suitcase. "The front door isn't the quickest way up to the guest suites," Harold said, "but since it's your first visit you should see the mansion the way Mrs. Alma intended you to see it."

Seen up close, the front entrance to Grafton House turned out to have two sets of doors. A revolving door on the right side of the entrance led to the Center's work areas. The formal entrance to the mansion was made through two enormous doors in the center of the entryway. The doors were very tall, perhaps fourteen or fifteen feet high. They were made of frosted glass and encased in a bronze metal framework. Phoebe could see fragmented images of herself and Harold reflected in the metal strips. The images were a bit distorted but quite recognizable. She was almost as tall as Harold, but half as wide. And both she and Harold appeared to have lots of very curly hair. Do I really look like that, she wondered.

The two doors were shut tight. Harold pressed a button discreetly hidden in a plaster detail on the wall by the door and the front doors slowly swung open. "Hydraulics," Harold said. "Eighty years old but it still works like a charm. Mr. Grafton was an engineer by training, and he had all the latest gadgets installed in this house when he built it."

"This is spectacular," Phoebe said. "Really amazing." And so it was. The front doors opened on an enormous corridor almost as long as a basketball court. The walls of the corridor were made of white marble, and lined with enormous paintings in gilt frames. The ceiling was at least twenty feet high, and lined with a series of chandeliers.

" Mrs. Alma called those big lights candelabras," Harold said. "I've turned on all the lights so you can see how pretty it all is, but usually we only turn on the light bulbs in every fourth candelabra. We do our best to save on the electric bill."

In the distance, Phoebe could see a very large room at the end of the corridor. On the right side of that room was a huge winding staircase that led to the upper floors of the house. And in the back of the room was a giant window overlooking Narragansett Bay.

"This is really fantastic," Phoebe said. "You'd never guess it was built in the Depression instead of the Gilded Age."

"It's something else, isn't it," Harold said. "I always get a kick out of showing this to our visitors. There are older mansions in Newport on this scale, but Grafton House is right up there with the fanciest. The funny thing about this house, and all of the others for that matter, is that the people who owned them only used them part time. They were vacation properties. Like the little beach houses that people have nowadays."

"We don't need to climb up the stairs," Harold said. "There's an elevator just before we get into the grand salon. That's what we call the big room at the end of the hall."

At the entrance to the grand salon, Harold paused by the elevator, and pointed toward the rear of the room. The evening sun was shining through an enormous glass window. "As you can see," Harold said, "we have a wonderful view of the Bay from this room." He pushed the elevator call button, and the elevator doors opened silently. "After you," Harold said, and Phoebe and Harold got into the elevator.

When the elevator doors opened, Phoebe saw that they were entering a long hallway, with rooms on either side, "This is where the senior staff stay," Harold said, " I mean if they don't have houses here in town." He paused in front of a door with a large golden door handle, and the letter H on the door.

"This is going to be your room," Harold said. "They call it the Hyacinth Room because of the statue and the wallpaper." He produced a large antiquated looking key, inserted it in the lock, and opened the door. Almost immediately, a large blue grey cat materialized out of nowhere and rubbed its head against Phoebe's leg.

"Oh dear," Harold said. "I hope you don't mind cats. That's Oscar. He's a descendant of Mrs. Alma's Russian Blue cats. A great grandson, I would imagine. It's sort of a Grafton House tradition. The cats wander where they want to. The thought is that they'll keep the mice under control, which may or may not be true." He bent down and patted Oscar. "Now run along," he said to the cat. "We've got company."

"I like cats," Phoebe said. "My mother always kept cats." She pushed open the door and went in, followed by Harold, and at a safe distance by Oscar. Just inside the door, a small marble statue of a nude young man catching a discus stood on a shelf in the foyer.

" Hyacinth?" Phoebe asked.

"Yes," Harold said. Dr. Eads' wife put that there. His late wife, I mean. She was interested in Greek mythology. She passed away several years ago, but the statue stayed."

The room was very large. In one corner Phoebe saw a massive four-poster bed with a canopy on top. "That's what they called a tester bed when I was growing up in Trinidad," Harold said. "People used the top to hang mosquito nets from. And it looks very pretty, too." He put Phoebe's suitcase on a stand by the bed, and opened the blinds on the window.

Phoebe looked around the room with interest. As Harold had suggested, the wallpaper was covered by images of violently blue hyacinth blossoms. The paper itself appeared to be made of some very expensive material that resembled silk. The overall effect was slightly suffocating.

"The wallpaper's a little overwhelming, isn't it," Harold said. "But with the shades up and the light coming in, I think you'll like the room. There are more pillows in the closet."

He paused, and then said "There's a little map on the desk in the corner that shows where everything is in Grafton House. Usually the staff meets after work in the lounge on the first floor just off the Grand Salon. You can leave a message for Dr. Eads on the house phone. The operator keeps tabs on where he is, and she can make sure you find each other. You can call me on the house phone too if you need me. Is there anything I can do for you now?"

"No thank you," Phoebe said. "You've been very kind. I enjoyed the house tour. I've never been in a house like this before, and I certainly needed a guide."

"You're very welcome," Harold said. "I enjoyed talking with you. It's nice to see new people now and then. I hope you enjoy your visit here. There are lots of things going on that will be of interest to you, I think." He started to leave and then paused and turned around to face Phoebe.

"I hope you won't think I'm being critical," he said. "I think Dr. Eads is a wonderful man, and he's made many improvements here at Grafton House. But he's a very good man, an idealistic man. I sometimes worry that he's not fully aware of some of the negative things that go on here. Among some members of the staff, I mean. I'm afraid Dr. Eads thinks the senior staff are just as good-hearted as he is. Which they're not."

"What kind of negative things?" Phoebe asked him.

"I've said too much already," Harold said. "When you meet the senior staff, you'll soon find out for yourself what I mean. Start with Dr. Chrysler, and then Dr. Khan and then Dr. Gardiner. You saw her when we arrived. It won't take you long. But I've talked much too much. I'd better be going now. If you need me, you can always reach me on the house phone." And he turned and quickly left the room.

Phoebe sat down on the bed and took off her shoes. Then she lay back on the coverlet and looked up at the top of the tester bad. The canopy was very white with a small gold medallion in the center. Grafton House is an odd place, Phoebe thought. And Harold Cummings is an odd man. Not exactly a garden-variety groundskeeper.

This will be a good project for me, she thought. I need some quiet time to think about my life. Newport seems like a quiet place and Grafton House looks interesting. I think it would be a good idea if I took a short nap, she thought, and closed her eyes. I'll decide what to do next when I wake up. And then she went to sleep. She did not hear Oscar, the cat, quietly jump up on the bed and lie down beside her head.

CHAPTER 5

Phoebe was sound asleep and in the middle of a complicated dream about flowerpots and cactuses when her cell phone rang. She opened her eyes and was surprised to find herself in a strange room. Where am I, she wondered for a second, and then remembered.

"Feeb," the voice said, "It's Jackie. Where the hell are you, honey? What's happening? I haven't heard from you in ages. Are you alright?"

"Hi, Jackie," Phoebe said. "I'm in Rhode Island. In Newport. In a huge mansion called Grafton House. Their chauffeur picked me up at the train station in Kingston in a big black limousine. You'd love it, dear."

"Newport!" Jackie said. "I'm impressed. Edgar and I spent a week there two years ago. For the film festival. We saw all the big houses. They were simply gorgeous. And we stayed at the Chanler. Very posh, but pricey. What's with the mansion? Are you going to a party?"

"Just work, Jackie. I'm visiting one of Harvard's research institutes. It's in one of the big houses, though. A millionaire named Grafton built the house back in the nineteen thirties. He made his money in fruit. Bananas to be specific. According to his biography, Mr. Grafton put the bend in the banana. Or took it out. I'm not sure which."

"Ewww," Jackie said. "Don't be gross, dear. Vulgarity doesn't become ladies. Although I must say I enjoy it myself, sometimes."

"That's not vulgar, Jackie. It's science. So how are things with you and Edgar these days?"

"Edgar has a roving eye," Jackie said. "I won't say anything more. I try to overlook things, you know. But it can be hurtful. You should know. How about you and Juan Carlos? Have you pulled the plug on him yet? You should, honey. Believe you me. That man is a skunk, if you'll pardon my French. Cute. I'll admit that. Very cute.

He could park his shoes under my bed anytime. But I suppose he only likes girls. Too bad."

"I saw him in New York," Phoebe said. "Saturday. Same old same old. Nothing to report. I'll let you know if there are any developments." I don't want to talk about Juan Carlos, Phoebe thought. I really don't.

"Do I detect a teeny edge in your voice, Feeb? Am I treading on sensitive ground?"

"Nope," Phoebe said.

"Whoops! Sorry about that. I should keep my big trap shut. Don't mind me, Feeb. I apologize."

"It's OK," Phoebe said. "I'll tell you when there's something to tell. Keep in touch, dear. It's nice to hear your voice."

She closed her eyes, and immediately began to think about Juan Carlos. Juan Carlos had called her, out of the blue, three whole months after they had broken up. Three whole lonely months after she had ended their affair.

"I'm going down to New York for the weekend," Juan Carlos had said. "I'm going to be staying at the Pod Hotel, on East 51st Street. I've got two tickets for the Met on Saturday night: Les Troyens with Susan Graham singing Dido. On the aisle. Catherine says she can't come. She's preparing for a big trial on Monday. And I thought, perhaps foolishly, that you would like to come with me."

No! Phoebe's super ego shouted silently. Don't do it! If you go, you'll tell him and you can't do that. Just say no! Tell him no! So Phoebe said nothing for a long moment. I should tell him no, she thought, I know that, but I just don't want to. I miss him desperately, and I want to be with him. Now. And I don't care if that's crazy. I don't care if I have to lie to him about what I did. "Alright," she said in a low voice. "I'll come. I'll be there Saturday afternoon. The Pod Hotel. East 51st Street. There's a ten a.m. Acela from South Station, so I should get to the hotel by two p.m. Two-thirty maybe. Assuming the train's on time, which it usually isn't."

"I love you," Juan Carlos said.

"I know," Phoebe said, and hung up. Then she got up from her desk, closed the door to her office and began to cry. I'm not going to tell him I'm pregnant, she thought. It's my fault that I'm pregnant, and telling him would be dishonorable. Then she cried some more for a while.

Phoebe's affair with Juan Carlos was in almost every respect a classic doomed romance. Phoebe was 30 when they met, and Juan Carlos was 53. Phoebe was single and lonely; Juan Carlos was married, more or less happily to a successful corporate lawyer. Phoebe was the latest in a series of female academics Juan Carlos had successfully enchanted over several decades. He was a first for Phoebe. She had been in love before, of course, with several boys in college and one man – a Welshman -- in graduate school. These attachments had been pleasant, and frequently enjoyable, but not very demanding. But she had never fallen passionately and obsessively in love with anyone until she met Juan Carlos on the first day of her job at Harvard.

Phoebe had drifted into her job with Harvard's administrative staff in the usual way that young people drift into inappropriate jobs. She had majored in math at Wellesley, and she had enjoyed it. When she graduated, she won a fellowship to study abroad. She decided to study math at Cambridge University in England, her mother's alma mater. She found graduate school engrossing and rewarding and soon was recognized by her professors as an exceptionally talented mathematician. She dated occasionally, but she had little time and less patience to spare for the task of finding a satisfactory man. The dweeby mathematics grad students who asked her out were also competitors, and hard to imagine as lovers. At one point she met an attractive medical student, a taffy haired Welshman who looked like her father. He asked her to marry him, and she moved into his flat. But after a few happy months she realized that he bored her, and she moved out.

During her years in graduate school, Phoebe grew increasingly solitary, concerned almost wholly with her work and her career. "You're becoming an old maid," her mother told her. "It's unnatural. Women aren't meant to live alone. You need to put those damned 'maths' books down and try to meet someone. Surely there must be someone out there who would suit you." Phoebe was stung by her mother's criticism, but not enough to change the way her life was organized. She continued her studies, and at the age of 27 received her doctorate in applied mathematics.

When Phoebe finished her doctorate, one of her former teachers at Wellesley encouraged her to apply for a teaching position at MIT. Her specialty was fractal theory, and she was writing a book -- based on her doctoral dissertation -- about turbulence in non-linear systems. The Chairman of MIT's math department hinted that a tenure track appointment might be possible if her book was published and if her teaching performance was satisfactory. But at the age of 29 Phoebe suddenly fell out of love with mathematics. She was bored. She wanted something different, something involving people rather than abstractions and she was foolish enough to let this be known to her colleagues. She made excuses to herself and her publisher about her inability to finish her book on turbulence. And soon enough, the Chairman of the department made it clear to her that she might be more comfortable at another university.

Phoebe had a friend at Harvard: a fellow student at Cambridge University who had taken a job with Harvard's administrative staff. Jeremy was a "baby dean," and he suggested that Phoebe would be a perfect candidate for a job like his. An opening existed on Harvard's administrative staff for someone with a scientific background to help monitor Harvard's external research facilities. Phoebe applied and was immediately accepted.

And on the first day that Phoebe began her new job at Harvard she met Juan Carlos, a.k.a. Professor Juan Carlos Cisneros, the Chairman of Harvard's Urban Planning Department. She was walking up the steps to her new office in Harvard's University Hall and she slipped. Behind her, she heard a man's voice say, "Let me help you." She turned her head and saw Juan Carlos for the first time. He was very tall, with broad shoulders and a barrel chest. And he was middle aged, with short salt and pepper hair. He wore an elegant grey Brooks Brothers suit with a striped tie and a blue shirt, and he had grey eyes. He looked down at Phoebe with a gaze that seemed to penetrate her soul, and she was immediately smitten.

When Phoebe was standing up again, Juan Carlos introduced himself. "I am Juan Carlos Cisneros-Puglisi," he said, His voice was very deep and resonant -- an opera singer's bass-baritone voice -- and he had a slight foreign accent." I am from Peru, but I teach here at Harvard. I don't usually wear suits, but I'm on my way to see the Dean of Arts and Sciences, so I got dressed up."

"I'm Phoebe Snow," Phoebe said. "I work here. Or I'm about to. This is my first day."

"Good," Juan Carlos said. "I am going to a meeting with the Dean of Arts and Sciences. But afterwards, perhaps we could meet for coffee? Around 10 a.m.?"

Phoebe examined Juan Carlos with interest for a second and then said, "Yes. I'm going to be in room 28B." And that was that.

Juan Carlos made it clear to Phoebe immediately that he was married, and that there was no possibility he could ever divorce his wife, Catherine. She was Catholic. He had promised that he would never, never leave her, had given her his word, and divorce was not possible. Phoebe said she understood this. She told him she admired his devotion to principle. In fact, she found it infuriating. It was one of many things about Juan Carlos that she found infuriating.

To begin with, Juan Carlos was a male chauvinist pig, to use an antiquated phrase from the women's liberation movement. Phoebe had ambivalent feelings about the women's liberation movement, but in one regard she thought they were completely correct. Women, she believed, were as capable as men and deserved the same opportunities to succeed. Juan Carlos said he believed this but it was perfectly clear that he didn't really. Once, late at night after they had made love, Phoebe casually mentioned that the former President of Harvard still seemed to stupidly believe that the best male scientists were superior to the best female scientists.

"Wasn't there some research study that proved that?" Juan Carlos said.

"There are pseudo-scientific studies that prove all kinds of nonsense," Phoebe said. "The ridiculousness of it makes my blood boil. What an idiot!" Juan Carlos said no more, but Phoebe knew he wasn't convinced. That made her mad.

So did Juan Carlos' position that he could not divorce Catherine. Principle was all very well, but the net effect of this so-called principle was that Phoebe slept alone most nights. And brooded about how unfair it all was. It made her mad to imagine Juan Carlos sleeping warmly in bed next to his wife, the very image of connubial bliss. Catherine got to give dinner parties to which Juan Carlos could invite colleagues and old friends. Phoebe's social life revolved around secret meetings with Juan Carlos to see foreign movies at the Kendall Square movie theatre, occasional rides in the country on the pillion seat of Juan Carlos' motorcycle, and solitary meals of take-out Chinese food consumed in her bedroom after Juan Carlos had left her apartment and gone home.

All of this irritated Phoebe, but the fact remained that she was smitten by Juan Carlos. He was brilliant: chairman of his Harvard department and an éminence grise in the urban design profession. He was a world famous designer and theorist, with work all over the world. A reflecting pool in Osaka, an urban park in Capetown, a war memorial in Rwanda. And books. Wildly successful books. Two Pulitzer Prizes. One for a book on the future of urban design. The other for a memoir about his childhood in Peru that made the New York Times bestseller list. And frequent essays in intellectual journals, like his famous piece in the London Review of Books about the built society and its potential for beauty.

OK, she was smitten by Juan Carlos' intellect. And she liked sleeping with him. He was sexy to look at and hold, sensitive to her needs, and passionate. She had slept with other men, and sometimes it had been more trouble than it was worth. Making love with Juan Carlos wasn't always perfect, but it was usually very enjoyable. That was another reason their affair lasted almost two years.

Then, one day, she woke up alone in her small apartment near Harvard Square. The window was open to the late April spring weather, and through the window came the cry of a baby. She looked out the window from her second floor apartment, and there, below her window on the sidewalk, a young mother in a bright yellow dress was pushing a baby carriage. A young man walked beside her, carrying a briefcase. I want a baby, Phoebe thought. Now. I can't wait any longer. I will be too old.

That evening, after they had made love and were drinking herbal tea and eating ginger snaps -- her preference, not Juan Carlos' -- she told Juan Carlos that she wanted a baby. He said that was impossible. He said he was married. He said he could not divorce his wife. He could not father her baby. That was the bottom line. He loved her but she could not have his child.

That was her bottom line too. "If you won't divorce, Catherine," she said, "and be the father of my child, then I won't see you anymore." She meant it.

"But I love you," Juan Carlos said.

"Not enough," Phoebe said. And that was that.

Except for one thing. She had told Juan Carlos that she wanted a baby, and he had said he didn't, after they had made love. Which was too bad. Because before Juan Carlos had arrived that evening, she had taken her diaphragm out of the drawer next to her bed, looked at it, and then put it back in the drawer. I'll put it in later, if he comes, she thought -- because sometimes he got held up at work and didn't come -- and then she promptly forgot about it. This is the reason most women take birth control pills, but Phoebe didn't trust them. If HRT caused cancer in older women, she reasoned, using hormones to repress ovulation couldn't be a good idea. Freud would say she didn't really forget to put her diaphragm in, but I think she did. In any event, that was all it took for her to get pregnant. Life is like that sometimes

CHAPTER 6

Walking slowly up the hill towards Grafton House, Suleiman Khan swung his cane and decapitated a flowering shrub by the side of the driveway. Cut her damned head off, he thought, and be done with it. She won't get away with saying those things about the Prophet. Impossible woman. A loose woman; I'm sure of it. Certainly an object lesson about her sex. Give them an inch and they'll take a mile.

That's a stupid boy, that Karim, he thought. He needs to understand that changing cultures is a dubious idea at best. Some of us can do it, of course. I did. But I came from a family with long ties to the West. I could cope with the temptations of the West's so-called freedom. That is certainly at the root of the West's appeal to a young man like Karim. A definite appeal. But he is trying to take a giant step when baby steps would be better for him and his family. And he needs to get over his flirtation with atheism. Women like Anettka are seducers, whores, leading boys astray with seductive ideas that lead only to the gutter. Karim must go back to his family, and give up his foolish ideas about Islam before it's too late. I shall do what is necessary to convince him of that.

Suleiman removed a starched cotton handkerchief from his jacket pocket and blew his nose. Ahead of him, the front of Grafton House loomed up against the blue sky. The building's marble façade was blinding white in the bright sunlight. On the third floor of the building, a series of air conditioning units poked out through the windows of the façade in an orderly row. That floor had formerly been the servants' quarters, but had been converted into office space for the Grafton House staff. As he contemplated this view, Andy Eads emerged from the front door, carrying a small black briefcase. He waved at Suleiman, and walked towards him.

"I'm going into town," he said. "Teresa called and said Karim's doing fine, but I thought I should drop by and see for myself.

Harold's going to drive me. How are things going with your group? As far as getting ready for the conference, I mean."

"Everyone's doing their best, Andrew. I can promise you that. Despite the interference by that woman. Not to put too fine a point on it, she's a menace. You need to speak to her."

Andy looked unhappy. "Yes, well, I'm sorry the two of you are having difficulties. I really think that you're less at odds than either of you believes. Surely there's some room for comity, even if you disagree strongly. As of course I know you do."

"You have a charming faith in the secular verities of Western culture," Suleiman said. "I should not be surprised if you were to quote the Golden Rule to me, now." He smiled broadly. What an unpleasant smile, Andy thought. Genuinely a nasty smile. With an effort, he smiled back at Suleiman.

Suleiman blew his nose noisily, and then said, "If you don't mind, I would like to ride in with you. I think it would be good if I spoke to young Karim." He emphasized the word "spoke" in a peculiar way, Andy thought. Almost as if he were Karim's father. A peculiarly paternal pronunciation, he decided.

"And I have a few errands I would like to do, while we're in town. Just a few, I promise," Suleiman added.

"Well of course you can come with us if you want to," Andy said, "but Jack and Anettka are likely to be at the hospital too. They just drove off a few minutes ago. In Jack's convertible."

"Damn," Suleiman said. "I saw them. That woman is a troublemaker. A woman of very questionable morals. If I am not mistaken, she and Dr. Chrysler are 'playing around,' as they say. I would not be surprised if it were something more than a simple flirtation. Something considerably worse. That would not be a good thing for Grafton House, particularly given her husband's position on Harvard's Board. Perhaps you could speak to Dr. Chrysler about her." He looked inquiringly at Andy.

What a nasty man, Andy thought. Always wanting to speak to other people and tell them what to do. That is not my style, he thought. Not at all.

Sometimes white lies are necessary, Andy decided. "I am sure there is nothing untoward in Dr. Gardiner's friendship with Dr. Chrysler," he said firmly. "Nothing whatsoever."

"Perhaps," Suleiman said. "Perhaps. But I think it best if I remain here. Perhaps Harold can take me in later this evening. Or I can ask one of the juniors to drive me. I fear that the lack of public transport makes this idyllic spot a challenge for someone like me who does not drive. As I have perhaps told you, I have never driven an automobile. When I was advising the High Command in Islamabad, I had a driver. In those days, officers never drove themselves. At least that was true in the Pakistani Army. And then too, I have always lived in cities."

Yes, Andy thought, you have told me all this before. Several times, in fact. It is less endearing than you clearly think it is. But I shouldn't be unkind, he chided himself. I repeat myself at least as much as Suleiman. And of course I don't drive either, which is easy for me because I'm the Director and Harold works for me. Be kind, Andrew, he told himself.

"How are your remarks coming?" he asked Suleiman.

"Very well, very well," Suleiman replied, nodding his head judiciously. "I have been practicing them, with some of the junior staff. I find that a live audience is helpful in assessing the impact of my remarks. And of course, questions from my auditors cannot help but clarify my principal points. Of which, as perhaps you know, there are four."

Suleiman paused and appeared to draw himself up before an invisible podium. Oh God, Andy thought, he's going to give me his lecture again.

"Yes, yes, very good," Andy said. "A really good idea involving the juniors. I think one of the most important things we can do here at Grafton House is to use these occasions, by which I mean the symposium, as teachable moments, learning experiences."

This was an oft-repeated mantra of Andy's, and Suleiman automatically began to look bored. As Andy had intended, he also appeared to rethink and abandon his plan to enunciate his four principal points. Harold Cummings had now appeared with the Grafton House Lincoln, and Andy got in the front seat next to him.

"Good talking with you," Andy said out the window to Suleiman.

"Let me know when you return, Harold," Suleiman said. "I may want a ride down to the village later this afternoon." He turned and began to walk towards the Grafton House front doors.

"Why does he say 'village,' Dr. Eads?" Harold asked with a smile.

"Don't be sarcastic, Harold," Andy said. "Be kind to others. Practice the Golden Rule."

"All right," Harold said. "I'll try. But sometimes it's pretty hard, you know."

"I know," Andy said.

CHAPTER 7

In her very small cubicle on the third floor of Grafton House, Tobie Shaw sat in front of three blank computer screens and contemplated the futility of her life. She had turned off her iPhone to prevent anyone from reaching her. The window in front of her desk was mostly blocked by an ancient air conditioning unit, which rumbled noisily as it produced a trickle of moist cool air.

"Shit," Tobie muttered. "Shit, shit, shit."

As Jack Chrysler had told Anettka, Tobie was having boyfriend trouble, although not of the old-fashioned variety that Jack imagined it to be. Actually, Tobie had three boyfriend problems. Maybe four, depending on how you counted boyfriends.

Problem number one was Wilford "Fat Willie" Thomas, the boyfriend Tobie had tipped off about a planned drug delivery at the Harvard College dormitory called Eliot House. At last report, Fat Willie was in hiding, on the run from the Cambridge police. In an email message sent from the Cambridge public library, Fat Willie had claimed that he was not the one who had knifed Ed Moriarty, Tobie's former boyfriend, the Cambridge drug peddler who had been killed when Fat Willie and his friend George attacked him and stole his drugs. Fat Willie claimed that George was the one with the knife. In Tobie's opinion, this was probably true. Fat Willie was not by nature a violent man. A friend of hers who lived in Eliot House had told her about Ed Moriarty's planned drug delivery. She told Fat Willie about it because she was mad at Ed for selling her some inferior pot. She didn't exactly think about what Fat Willie would do with this information, but she had often thought that if Ed ever got robbed it would teach him a lesson. She hadn't really thought through exactly what kind of lesson it would teach him, and that had clearly been a mistake on her part. Fat Willie was a large and scary man, and Tobie had sort of assumed that if he were to rob Ed Moriarty, he would do it by himself. But Fat Willie did it with his friend George, who was a very different kettle of fish.

George was an MIT graduate student whom Tobie had run into occasionally at parties. He was someone she knew casually, but not really a former boyfriend. And he was nuts, no two ways about it. To begin with he asked people to call him Omega. He said the name Omega captured his preferred identity as someone who wanted to end capitalist society. Young women often did call him Omega, but boys usually refused to. Cambridge graduate student parties frequently attracted young men and women with radical political views, but even in that context George's views were generally thought to be extreme. He had told Tobie about his views one night at a party. Tobie was stoned and thinking about something else, but she could clearly remember that George's life had been transformed by a very special book. The book was by a radical French author, and it was called "The Coming Insurrection." After Fat Willie had told her about George's part in the robbery of Ed Moriarty, Tobie had looked up the book on Google. The book was even nuttier than she had expected. Based on the stuff she read — admittedly not much because it was very boring — the book advocated the violent destruction of practically every aspect of current Western society and its replacement with communes. Free love communes. Tobie was not much impressed with the idea of free love, and violently destroying everything seemed excessive even if you were as unhappy with society as she was.

Whenever Tobie had seen him, George had made it abundantly clear to anyone who would listen that he hated all aspects of bourgeois society and wanted to destroy it root and branch. From what Fat Willie had told Tobie in his email, George had lost his temper when Ed Moriarty refused to hand over his cash and his drugs and had knifed him in a fit of rage.

Fat Willie had gotten involved in the robbery to make money. He had a gambling habit and had accumulated debts that he really needed to pay. George had apparently wanted to raise money for his anarchist agenda. The last time Tobie had seen him, George had spoken admiringly of Germany's Baader-Meinhof Gang, whom he saw as precursors to his own noble cause. Tobie had not known that

Fat Willie would recruit George for the robbery and was deeply sorry that he had done so.

Now Tobie was worrying that the Cambridge police would catch up with Fat Willie and that he would inevitably implicate her in the botched robbery and murder. As a practical matter, it was hard to see how Fat Willie could avoid blaming her if, as seemed inevitable, he were caught. Based on Tobie's TV-based knowledge of police procedure, Fat Willie — who really wasn't very bright — would be putty in the hands of the Cambridge police detectives.

So that was one, or maybe two boyfriend problems. She had enjoyed being Fat Willie's squeeze; he was large and sexy and grossed out her irritating bourgeois parents. (Tobie was Jewish, and a graduate student in computer engineering, and a native of Newton, MA. Fat Willie was an African-American high school dropout from Providence, RI.)

Tobie felt sorry about Ed Moriarty's being stabbed, of course, even though she really didn't want to think that it had been her fault. Maybe a little, but not mostly. After all, she told herself, selling illegal drugs is dangerous and Ed should have been more careful. But since Ed had once been her boyfriend, she decided that his death probably should be counted as boyfriend problem number two.

George — she could never remember his real last name, but it was something Slavic with lots of consonants — George was not exactly a boyfriend, more an acquaintance, but she was very worried about him too. Maybe she should count him as a boyfriend problem. Because George knew that she was spending the summer in Newport at Grafton House. And he knew, or probably knew, that she had tipped Fat Willie off about Ed Moriarty's planned drug delivery to Eliot House. And she had a sinking feeling in her stomach at the thought that George was going to show up in Newport and ask her to hide him. Something like that seemed to happen in most suspense movies. OMG was all she could think when this possibility loomed up in her mind's eye.

Finally, she came to boyfriend, or boy problem number four. Whatever. This was Peruvian Naval Ensign Arturo Cisneros-Stern. She had met Arturo in Peru the summer before, while serving an internship with the Smithsonian Astrophysical Observatory's Peruvian research station. He was tall, dark and handsome, with beautiful manners. And his mother was Jewish, which didn't usually matter to her but still. And he was actually in Newport, at that very moment, in one of the beautiful Naval training school sailing ships at anchor in Newport Harbor. They called them the Tall Ships. And she wanted to see him desperately, and she couldn't figure out how to arrange it. He had emailed her from his ship, but apparently they were under strict orders to remain on board and not go off by themselves into town. Which seemed desperately unfair.

She had asked Jack Chrysler to ask Andy Eads to invite the foreign naval cadets in the Tall Ships to visit Grafton House. She had suggested to Jack that this could be linked to the immigration policy conference, although she really wasn't quite sure how. Still, it seemed like a perfectly reasonable request. There were lots of single people on the junior staff of Grafton House and they would certainly enjoy the opportunity to meet handsome young naval cadets from exotic foreign countries. So she was working on this. There ought to be a hook somewhere, she was certain of that.

She looked at the clock on the wall. It was almost six, time for the daily happy hour in the junior staff common room. I should go, she thought. She put her iPhone in her bag, turned off the lights in her cubicle and left the room. I'll turn my phone on after I've had a drink, she thought. Surely, things can't get any worse.

CHAPTER 8

George Rakylz slowly pedaled his stolen bicycle into the parking lot at Middletown's Sachuest Beach. Most people had gone home, and there were no attendants in the gatehouse, but there were still plenty of cars in the parking lot. "Attention!" a woman's voice said over the public address system. "Lifeguards at Second Beach will be going off duty in five minutes. The dressing rooms and restrooms will be open until 6:30, but there will be no lifeguards on duty after six o'clock."

People were slowly emerging from the rear of a rectangular brown building. There were two doors facing the parking lot, one marked "MEN" and the other "WOMEN". These were obviously the doors to the dressing rooms. George leaned the bicycle against the steps to the building, and carried his bulging backpack up the stairs to the entrance that said "MEN".

"Where's the shower?" he asked a boy standing by the door.

"Outside," the boy said. "The other side of the building. The beach side. It's pretty cold though."

George walked through the dressing room and out the door on the other side of the building. He could see the ocean a few hundred feet away, and people walking up from the beach toward the parking lot. Children were frolicking in an outdoor shower at ground level, and George realized that he would have to wear something himself if he wanted a shower. He retreated to the dressing room. He rummaged around in his backpack, found a pair of swim trunks and put them on. He went outside and stood under the cold outdoor shower for a few minutes. Then he came back into the dressing room, found a razor and some shaving cream in a pocket of his backpack, and shaved himself. He examined himself closely in the mirror. He still wasn't used to seeing himself with a crew cut and without a beard. He hadn't looked this way since he was in high school.

I don't look like a threat to the corrupt capitalist society, George said to himself. But I am. And they will find that out in due time. He examined a pimple on his chin and then squeezed it mercilessly. The pimple popped and a small dot of white pus emerged. Satisfied, he took off his swimsuit and put his jeans back on. He smelled his socks to see if they could last another day and decided he should change them. He found another pair of socks in his backpack and put them on. Then he put his motorcycle boots back on and went outside toward the beach.

The tide was going out, but it was still sunny. George thought about going for a swim and decided against it. I've got to contact Tobie, he repeated to himself, and dialed Tobie's cellphone again. "Hi," Tobie's voice said for the millionth time. "I'm not here right now. You can leave a message after the beep." After which the phone would dutifully beep.

George had not left a message. He was pretty sure that Tobie was not looking forward to hearing from him. It really hadn't been his fault about the mess in Cambridge. The guy was supposed to be an easy mark. Tobie had told them that, and Fat Willie had said it would be a piece of cake. Which of course it wasn't. The guy had refused to cooperate. Fat Willie had asked him for his money, and he had had a hissy fit instead of handing it over the way he was supposed to. George hadn't meant to stick him with the knife. Just frighten him was all. But he had rushed at George like he was going to hurt him. George had simply put out the knife to stop him from attacking him, and the moron had practically stuck himself with the knife. So it definitely wasn't George's fault at all. Drug dealers were the scum of capitalist society anyway. So George wasn't going to feel sorry about it. Shit happens. That's for damn sure, George thought.

Anyway, George thought, I've got the money, plus some good weed. I'll be all right. And if this whole deal works out the way I've been planning it, I can generate some major changes in public consciousness about The Program.

"The Program" was the way George liked to describe his personal vision for the future of mankind. George envisioned a coordinated humanistic effort to tear down the market society and replace it with a fully free cooperative network of anarchist idealist communities. He had been thinking about The Program for three years. The basic concept had come to him in a dream, the night after he attended an Elizabeth Warren rally, and the night before his twenty-third birthday. He was stoned when he was at the Warren rally, and he hadn't really taken in anything concrete. But he definitely came away thinking that the country needed radical changes and young people could make them happen. In his dream, Elizabeth Warren had pointed her index finger directly at him, and told him that he could make her vision come true. So far, George had failed to recruit anyone else to join The Program, but he was optimistic. Destroying the fat intellectual whores at Grafton House was going to be one of the seminal events that was going to inspire other idealistic young people to join The Program. Of that, George was quite convinced.

Now the first step was to get hold of goddamn Tobie Shaw and get her to sneak him into Grafton House. Or at least give him a place to crash for the night. He reached into his backpack and found the long canvas bag that held his TEC-DC9 machine pistol and three 72-round magazines. Then he found the cardboard box containing his own personal handmade Improvised Explosive Device. He patted the box lovingly. He was very proud of his IED. He had purchased a kilo of Semtex and two electrically triggered detonators from an enterprising Nigerian graduate student at MIT. He had burned a very small piece of the Semtex to make sure it was genuine. He had also exploded one of the detonators using a modified CVS cellphone as the trigger, and phoning the CVS phone from his iPhone to activate the trigger. He had tested the system on the Boston Common. The detonator duly went off, making a small popping sound. No one noticed. They'll notice when I hook up the Semtex, George thought happily.

In the final version of his IED, George had packed the kilo of Semtex in a 3.78-liter Hefty Ziploc storage bag. (George was a great admirer of the metric system.) He had buried the detonator in the Semtex and channeled its two electrical connections through a small hole in the Ziploc bag to another modified CVS cellphone. As long as the CVS phone was turned off, the device was not going to explode. But when it was turned on, a phone call from George's iPhone would trigger the detonator, which would make the Semtex explode.

And the best part of all was the command that would make his IED explode when he wanted it to explode. George's iPhone was programmed to make voice-activated phone calls. And just like saying "Mom" to his iPhone if he wanted to call his mother – he rarely did – all he had to do to set off the IED was to say "Shit!" to his iPhone, and the job was done. Boom! That made George a very happy camper. You guys are going to make the world sit up and take notice, he thought, as he patted his TEC-DC9 and his IED. You and I are buddies. We are going to make a real difference. He looked out to sea and was interested to see a rainbow arcing across the pale blue sky. Wow, he thought. That's beautiful. Maybe it means something.

CHAPTER 9

Sitting up in his hospital bed in the Newport Hospital, Karim Pandit peered out the window at the elm tree outside his room. His arm was attached to an IV, and he was uncomfortably aware of the catheter snaking up his urethra into his nether regions. A pretty young nurse with a starched white cap examined the IV and the catheter, patted him on the knee and said "I'm sorry you have to have all these awful things stuck in you, honey, but they're for your own good. Believe me. They'll probably take them out in the morning. We'll give you something that'll let you sleep OK. And look! You've got visitors. Isn't that nice."

Karim quickly turned his head and saw Jack Chrysler and Anettka Gardiner standing by the doorway.

"Poor Karim," Anettka said. "What a horrible day for you. She reached over the bed and patted his hand. "I'm so sorry." Karim looked as if he were about to faint. His large brown eyes had a moist look, and his cheeks were pink. I wonder if he's in love with Anettka, Jack thought.

"Everyone at Grafton House was very worried about you," Jack said. "And very pleased when we found that you were going to be OK."

"I'm dreadfully sorry," Karim said. "I really feel such a fool. I shouldn't have eaten all that stuff. I'm never going to eat a lobster again. UGH!"

"I've never been comfortable with the idea of eating lobsters," Jack said. "Particularly after I saw some live ones. Crawling around in a tank. They look a little too much like bugs. Bugs from outer space."

"I've never seen a live lobster," Karim said. " I don't even like thinking about them. Actually, I feel like I'm never going to eat anything but vegetables from now on!" He banged his fist on the hospital bed for emphasis.

"Watch out, honey," the nurse said. "You're going to knock that IV right out of your arm."

"I'm sorry," Karim told the nurse. He turned his head to look at Jack. "And I'm sorry about my paper not being ready for your seminar."

"That's OK," Jack said. "Your last draft was fine. We can go with that for the seminar. The suggestions I gave you were all minor points. The paper's just fine as it stands. So don't worry." He smiled. "Do you remember that song, " he asked Anettka. "'Don't worry, be happy.' They sang it in the Bahamas back in the Eighties."

"I was in elementary school in the Eighties," Anettka said. She smiled at Karim.

"I was born in 1987," Karim said.

"Ouch!" Jack said. "You guys are making me feel ancient."

"You are ancient," Anettka said, "But Karim and I admire our elders. We envy them their experience and wisdom."

"We do, Dr. Chrysler," Karim said earnestly. "We really do. All the staff do."

"Thank you, Karim," Jack said. "I appreciate your saying that." He paused for a second, trying to think of something else to say and couldn't think of anything worth saying. Anettka got him off the hook.

"We just wanted to come by and see how you were doing," she said. "You look like you're doing just fine, so we'll let you get some rest. We'll see you in the morning back at Grafton House."

Anettka paused for a second. "And don't worry," she went on. "I meant what I told you yesterday. You're doing the right thing, and you're going to be fine." Then she bent down and kissed Karim on the cheek. Jack decided that his initial conclusion was valid. Karim looked blissed out, and was definitely blushing.

"Thank you, Dr. Gardiner," Karim said, "and you too, Dr. Chrysler," he added quickly.

"Goodbye, Karim," Jack said and patted Karim on the shoulder. Karim smiled bravely at Jack.

"Goodbye," he said, and waved his free hand in a gesture of farewell as Jack and Anettka left the room.

In the hall outside, Jack and Anettka stood by the elevator bank waiting for the elevator to come. "That poor boy," Anettka said. "I'm so worried about him. Suleiman has been trying to pressure him to go back to Jordan. He's got Karim half-persuaded that it's his solemn duty. Duty to his family and to his damned religion. All sheerest nonsense, and all pie in the sky, but Karim half-believes it.

"I've told him and told him, that Suleiman is jerking his chain. Making him feel guilty when he has no need to. But I'm not sure I've convinced him, and it makes me mad."

"I think he's in love with you," Jack said. "You do know that, don't you?"

"He's young," Anettka said. "He'll get over it. I don't mind." She smiled. "Men are such romantics," she said. "Always falling in love with unsuitable women. Women are much more sensible."

The elevator doors opened, and Jack stood back to let Anettka get on first. He stood stiffly at her side, and suddenly she leaned forward and kissed him on the cheek. "There," she said, "Don't be jealous." She smells like honeysuckle, Jack thought.

The effect of Anettka's kiss on Jack was immediate. And unsurprising. He put his arms around Anettka and pulled her toward him, and kissed her on the mouth. Anettka did not resist this, and after a few seconds put her arms around him and began to kiss him back. They continued to kiss passionately until the elevator came to a stop on the ground floor and the doors began to open. They quickly let go of each other and moved to opposite sides of the elevator. And there, standing in front of the elevator on the ground floor, and looking directly at them with a searching gaze, was Andy Eads. What a revolting development this is, Jack thought.

CHAPTER 10

At the exact same time, the very same moment, that Anettka and Jack began to kiss each other in the elevator at the Newport Hospital, Anettka's husband Paul reaches down and unbuckles his seat belt. He is sitting in Business Class on Air France 111, which has just landed at Boston's Logan Airport.

Paul's decision earlier that day to leave Paris and fly home, had been sudden and something of a surprise to him. He hasn't told Anettka that he's coming, and he's not quite sure why. But when he woke up that morning in Paris, he was possessed by the desire to a) go back to the United States and b) see Anettka. And without further thought, he put down his cup of coffee, called Air France, and booked a 4:10 p.m. flight to Boston. Paul is rich, but he is also parsimonious, so he booked an economy class fare to Boston. (Not that he was actually going to sit in economy class. People who spend as much time as Paul does on Air France get automatic upgrades to business class, which is a lot more comfortable.)

The question of why he was suddenly flying home had come up earlier that day when Paul had lunch with a college classmate who lived in Paris: Gaston Poirier (known as "Gass" to his classmates). They were eating at McDonald's because Gass was feeling homesick and wanted a Big Mac. Paul had a salad, because he's worried about cholesterol.

"I thought you were going to be here over the weekend," Gass said. "Why are you going back so soon?"

"To see Anettka," Paul said. "I miss her."

"I can certainly understand that," Gass said. "She's a fascinating woman."

"She is," Paul said, and changed the subject. But the truth was, he was worried. And not just about cholesterol.

Let us count the other things Paul is worried about besides cholesterol. Paul is almost sixty-five. At Harvard, he and his friend Gass were greatly amused by the elderly gentlemen returning to the

Yard for their annual college reunions. Now, their own fortieth anniversary is three years in the past. And a surprising number of their classmates hadn't come to that reunion. Because they were dead.

So the prospect of turning sixty-five makes Paul nervous. The very phrase "turning sixty-five" makes him anxious. It makes him think of his mother, standing in the kitchen late at night and tipsily sniffing a half empty bottle of milk. He can hear her saying "Well, no surprise here. This milk is too old and it's turned. Turned sour. Gone over the hill, I'm sorry to say." Paul's mother, Fiona, had a gloomy streak that sometimes surfaced after a glass or two of wine.

Fiona is still going strong at ninety-two, living with her second husband, Max Finkel, on Beacon Hill. She and Max are active members of Beacon Hill Village, the cooperative association of elderly Beacon Hill residents. Fiona and Max deliver groceries to homebound seniors, and are featured on a really cool promotional video for the group. Paul's father, Paul Senior, however, is long dead. He died at age sixty-five during Paul Junior's senior year at Harvard. Then, sixty-five had seemed ancient. Of course his father was dead; what else could you expect at sixty-five if not death? Now, sixty-five is a month away and the prospect isn't pleasing.

Paul's father's death at sixty-five was sudden, congestive heart failure according to his mother. Not surprisingly, Paul is worried about his own heart, which occasionally seems to vibrate in a disconcerting way. He has consulted another of his classmates, a cardiologist at Mass. General, who has recommended that Paul stop smoking, eat less red meat, and take up swimming.

That's why Paul is eating a salad instead of a Big Mac. And why, since arriving in Paris a few weeks ago, Paul has been swimming every morning at the Piscine Pontoise near Saint Germain-des-Prés. The Piscine Pontoise was built twelve years before Paul was born. Paul swam there for the first time at the age of ten when his parents were vacationing in Paris. Paul's father liked the Art Deco style. Paul likes swimming on his back and looking through the glass ceiling to the sunny sky above the pool.

Unfortunately, Paul hasn't stopped smoking. He had promised Anettka that he would stop while he was in Paris, along with his new swimming regime. Promised himself, too. But he hasn't. He's cut back. Way back. But he just can't stop. Which is going to be embarrassing when he gets back to Newport. Because Anettka has stopped too, and will certainly be furious at him.

Which brings us to Anettka. Paul loves Anettka. He really does. I'm not sure if he's still romantically in love with her, but he likes her a lot. He's coming home early from Paris because he misses her. But being married to a much younger woman is not an easy row to hoe.

One of Paul's friends from Groton is a portrait photographer, and as a wedding gift took a photo of Paul and Anettka. Said photo resides on Paul's desk in their (well, really his) apartment in Boston. It's a very good portrait. Anettka looks very young and radiant, and gazes admiringly at Paul. Paul is wearing a gray suit and a red tie and looks distinguished. He also looks like Anettka's proud father. Not good.

Which of course illustrates the problem. Paul is much older than Anettka. Twice her age, to be exact. Among other things, this means they don't have the same memory banks. Paul was a Marine officer in Vietnam before Anettka was born. Richard Nixon and Jane Fonda and Martin Luther King are historical figures as far as Anettka is concerned. She's never heard of Howdy Doody or Annette Funicello! Or the Mouseketeers!

And sexually… Lady Macbeth advises her husband to screw his courage to the sticking point. She's talking about murdering Duncan. That was a bad idea, but her advice is on target. Macbeth is afraid of failing in the attempt, and — in the short run — courage gets him to the sticking point. Sex doesn't work that way, at least not for most men. Courage won't get you to the sticking point.

Much to Paul's dismay, he's found it necessary to take a pill before he makes love to Anettka. You may say, "So what?" and I agree that it's not really that awful, but the fact is, these things interfere with a man's self-image. Cowboys don't have to take a pill before getting on their horses. Marine officers don't need to take a pill before leading their men into an unfriendly rice paddy. (Although, lets face it, some did.)

So the idea of making love to Anettka makes Paul very nervous. Which in turn has a bad effect on his ability to perform what Paul's mother called "the act itself."

To start off with, Paul needs to take his pill an hour before he wants to make love to Anettka. A big dose. Timed carefully so as to take effect at the desired moment. Spontaneity goes out the window. Oddly enough, taking a drink before making love has turned out to be a bad idea. Early in the morning seems to be the optimal time of day, but Anettka is not a morning person.

Moreover, the big pills that Paul has to take have worrisome side effects. They make him feel dizzy, or at least he thinks they do. And he's not sure, but he thinks they make his blood pressure go up. He sometimes looks red in the face, which worries him and also worries Anettka.

All of that is bad for his morale. It makes him feel like he really is falling apart. This is not helped by the latest development along these lines. He has developed a tremor in his right hand. In other words, his right hand has developed a life of its own.

To put it simply, his hand shakes. Involuntarily. Without warning. Clenching his fist or putting his hand in his pocket are the only ways he knows to stop his hand from trembling. Worst of all, Anettka hates it, and snaps at him when it happens. Which is embarrassing. Humiliating. To be avoided if at all possible.

But after all, what is Paul to do? He loves Anettka. He wants to be with her. Sort of. Anyway, he flew back to Boston later in the afternoon. He didn't call Anettka to let her know he's coming. He had planned to do that when he was in the car going to the airport. Anettka would be up by then, he thought. But then he didn't remember to call her. You won't be surprised to learn that he somehow doesn't remember to call Anettka after he gets through Customs and takes a taxi from Logan to his apartment on Beacon Hill. (He enjoys living near his mother. He often visits her when he's not busy and they each have half a glass of sherry. And chat.)

CHAPTER 11

"Let's go by the hospital first, Harold," Andy Eads said. "And then if we have time, we can go by Pinewood."

"OK," Harold said, and steered the Lincoln Town Car down the hill.

"Did you have a chance to talk to Dr. Snow, our visitor?"

"A very interesting young woman," Harold said. "She didn't say much about herself, but she told me she went to Cambridge, in England that is. And she mentioned that she was on Harvard's administrative staff. That her job is to review the work of Harvard's research centers. Like Grafton House. That's why she's visiting us."

"One of the deans called me last week and said she was coming. It's supposed to be routine, but I'm not convinced. All this petition business about me and the foreign students was bound to raise some eyebrows in University Hall. They don't like problems, and they don't like to hear anything that sounds like it could turn into a court case — or a headline in the Boston Globe for that matter. Which I can certainly understand."

"Un-huh," Harold muttered.

"Come on, Harold," Andy Eads said. "What's this 'un-huh' business? What do you think?"

"About what, Dr. Eads?"

"You know what, Harold. About the petition those kids signed. Do you think I'm prejudiced in favor of foreign students? That I'm discriminating against native-born Americans because I want to save money? Or because I'm prejudiced against my own countrymen?"

"No, I don't think that, Dr. Eads. You know that. I think you're the victim of your own good nature. If you were a meaner man, people would be less likely to mess with you. When I was growing up in Port-of-Spain, my father was a very kind man, friendly to everyone. But no one ever messed with him. Because they knew Daddy wouldn't let them get away with it. He was not exactly a mean man, but he could be mean when he had to be."

"And you think I let people get away with things they shouldn't. Is that it?"

"Get away with murder, in my humble opinion. Maybe not yet, but maybe sometime in the future."

"That's a pretty grim assessment," Andy said. "My mother would say things like that. She was Scotch-Irish, you know. Their word for thoughts like that is 'dour.' I miss her sometimes. She was a very pessimistic woman, but she was very cheerful about it. She used to say she was a cockeyed pessimist. I think she was bragging, although she would have denied it." The Lincoln pulled up in front of the Newport Hospital and Andy Eads got out. "I won't be long," he said. "I think you can stay here in front. If anybody asks, tell them I'll be back in a jiffy." He smiled and disappeared into the hospital.

The volunteer at the hospital information desk told Andy where Karim's room was and pointed to the elevator. The elevator door promptly opened. The elevator was large and poorly lit, and at first all Andy could see was a man and a woman standing very close to each other at the back of the elevator. Then the couple moved away from each other and toward the doors of the elevator. As they did, they came into focus, and Andy realized that they were Jack Chrysler and Anettka Gardiner. Oh dear, Andy thought, they look awfully squishy.

"Andy!" Jack said in a falsely cheerful voice. He's pretending to be pleasantly surprised, and making a bad job of it Andy thought. I'm afraid I can guess why.

"Hi Jack, hi Anettka,' Andy said. "How's Karim doing?"

"He seems to be OK," Anettka said. "Very cheerful. I guess it probably was food poisoning after all."

"He looked OK to me too, Andy," Jack said. Of course I'm not an MD but we talked to the resident and he said not to worry. He said Karim should probably spend the night, to be on the safe side, but he ought to be ready to go home tomorrow morning."

"Good enough," Andy said. "I'm just going to drop by for a minute and say hello. Let him know we're concerned about him. I'll see you guys back at Grafton House."

"See you," Jack said. He held the elevator door open for Andy.

"See you," Anettka repeated. The elevator began to make a buzzing sound. Andy went in and the doors closed.

I suppose that was to be expected, Andy thought as the elevator went up. I knew they were very taken with each other. And they're young. Anettka's not much more than thirty and Jack's only about fifty. God knows I wasn't any saint when I was Jack's age. Still, I've got to speak to them about it. Having an affair is one thing, but having an affair with the wife of a Harvard Board member is something else. That definitely would not go over well with University Hall.

The elevator came to a halt, and Andy got out. A pretty young nurse showed him to Karim's room. Karim was watching a soccer game on TV, and he seemed pleased to see Andy. "Hello, Dr. Eads," he said. "I'm doing fine. The doctors say I can go home tomorrow morning."

"Good. Good," Andy said. "I'm glad to hear it." Andy paused. "I did want to talk to you about something when you get back tomorrow. I understand from Dr. Gardiner that you're concerned about...how shall I put it?...the propriety of your staying here in the United States rather than returning to your family in Jordan. I know myself how difficult it can be to change cultures. I came up to New England from a small town in Mississippi to go to college and had a difficult time adjusting."

Andy smiled at Karim. Karim looked embarrassed. "That's all right, Karim," Andy said. "I'm afraid I'm embarrassing you. But I want you to know that you can always come talk to me. I'm not going to tell you what to do. You have to make your own decisions. But I've found that talking to someone else about a problem I'm facing tends to clarify it in my own mind."

"Thank you, Dr. Eads," Karim said. "I didn't mean to bother Dr. Gardiner, but I..."

"She wasn't bothered at all," Andy said. "On the contrary, she thought you were having a difficult time of it, and she wanted me to make sure that I — that we all are doing what we can to help you. You mustn't worry about that." He smiled at Karim again, and Karim mustered a more believable smile.

"I'll let you go back to your game," Andy said. "Who's playing?"

"Milan and Manchester United," Karim said enthusiastically. "They're really good. David Beckham's playing for Milan against his old team. It's very exciting."

"Sounds good," Andy said. "I'll be off now, and look forward to seeing you tomorrow. Goodbye."

"Goodbye," Karim said, as Andy went out the door.

In the corridor outside Karim's room, a nurse was standing by the side of a gurney. An elderly woman lay on top of the gurney, breathing irregularly in sudden gasping bursts of air. Her skin was yellow, and she was clearly very sick. A pair of young doctors in white coats walked by talking earnestly about something incomprehensible. They ignored the gurney and Andy. I hate hospitals, Andy thought as he waited for the elevator. And doctors. And getting old.

CHAPTER 12

When Andy emerged from the Newport Hospital, Harold was waiting in the Lincoln. Andy got in the car, looked at his watch and said, "I think we've got time to go by Pinewood, Harold. I'll just run in for a second and say hello to my father, and then we can go back to Grafton House."

Pinewood, like Grafton House, was a former mansion. It was smaller and older than Grafton House, and it had been tastefully converted into an upscale nursing home for affluent old people. Pinewood had been the first place that Andy had looked at when his father was no longer able to live by himself. Andrew Eads, Sr., like his father and grandfather before him, had lived all his life in Jackson, Mississippi, where he ran the family warehouse and trucking business.

Until the age of ninety-two, Andy's father had gotten along quite nicely with the help of a live-in housekeeper. His eyesight, unlike Andy's, was remarkably good, and his posture was erect. He read voraciously, golfed, and speculated fairly successfully in the stock market. But at age ninety-two all that changed. For no apparent reason except old age, Andy's father developed dementia. Not Alzheimer's, the doctors were pleased to say, but a simple case of dementia.

By then, there were no surviving members of the Eads family in Jackson, or indeed in Mississippi. Andy thought about trying to find a nursing home for his father in Jackson, which would certainly have been cheaper. But Andy's father had plenty of money, and Andy decided that it would be better to move him to Newport. That way, Andy could see him regularly, and keep an eye on how he was doing. A friend recommended Pinewood as being competent and as un-depressing as such a place could be. Andy flew down to Mississippi, collected his father and brought him back to Rhode Island. Where he had been for the last three years.

When Andy arrived at Pinewood, he found his father sitting in a wicker chair on the home's large veranda, watching television. A golf game was in progress, and several other residents were also watching it. "Hi, Daddy," Andy said to his father, who looked up and smiled benevolently.

"Hello there, my friend," Andy's father said. "How are you today?" Andy was not deceived by this seeming normality. His father was calling on a series of rote, essentially robotic conversational responses acquired during his long life. In reality, Andy's father had no idea who Andy was. Certainly not his son. Rather perhaps a late-middle-aged businessman come to try to sell him some overpriced and probably unnecessary equipment for his business. "Good to see you," Andy's father said dismissively. "Thanks for coming by." Then he turned his attention back to the golf tournament on the television set.

Andy examined his father closely. As far as he could tell, his father looked perfectly fine. Hale and hearty, as the phrase goes. Still trim, still erect, still able to watch TV without his glasses. A full head of white hair, and the large aquiline Eads nose. Andy had inherited the nose and the hair but not the eyesight. It must be the combination of my mother's genes with Daddy's, Andy thought.

In the corner, a large male attendant sat watching the TV with his charges. "How's my dad doing, Reggie?" Andy asked him.

"He's doing fine, Dr. Eads, eats like a horse. Behaves himself. A real gentleman. It's a pleasure to have him here at Pinewood."

"Thanks, Reggie," Andy said. "I really appreciate your help." He reached in his pants pocket and took out a folded twenty-dollar bill that he had stored there in preparation for his visit. He shook Reggie's hand, and discreetly gave him the bill. Reggie looked pleased but not surprised.

"Thanks, Dr. Eads. Your dad's a lucky guy to have a son like you."

"I'm lucky to have had a father like him," Andy said. "Goodbye, Daddy, I'll be by next week."

His father turned and smiled again. "Goodbye for now," he said. "You take care now, you hear." Then he turned back to the television set.

It's curious, Andy thought, to have a father who's as old as my father is. I'm by far the oldest person at Grafton House. Suleiman is at least ten years younger than I am and he's probably sixty-two or sixty-three. Harold's about that, too. But almost everyone else is much younger. And yet visiting my ninety-five-year-old father has the pleasant effect of making me feel young — or at least middle-aged. I suppose I still could be considered middle-aged. Barely.

The fact, of course, was that Andy, at the age of seventy-two-and-a-half, was beyond any possible definition of middle age. And Andy knew full well that practically everyone at Grafton House, with the possible exception of Harold Cummings, thought he was old. Period. Not ancient. But old. Old enough to be their grandfather in most cases, and old enough to be practically everyone else's father. Old.

Andy did not find this fact comforting when it chanced to cross his mind. Particularly since he was constantly reminded that getting old has consequences. Like old houses and old cars, old men are a collection of aging parts that are breaking down and wearing out. Rapidly wearing out in some cases, and requiring skilled maintenance and expensive repairs.

Sitting next to Harold in the front seat of the Lincoln as they drove back to Grafton House, Andy contemplated his current physical problems. This was a clear rebellion against the strict rules of behavior forcibly inculcated in all members of the Eads family. His father — indeed the whole Eads family — had assiduously avoided thinking about illnesses of any kind. That was taboo. Had any of his family been able to peer into Andy's mind at this point in time, they would unanimously have told him "You're being morbid!" On the other hand, after many years away from his family (most of whom were dead anyway) and their rules, Andy had found that realistically confronting scary problems helped to put them in perspective and make them a little more bearable. Eyes, ears (particularly the left one), nose, teeth. Andy had other problematic body parts, but those were the ones that currently required the most attention.

His eyes were definitely a scary problem — his scariest problem, he decided for the umpteenth time. The weirdest but least important of his eye problems was the hole in his right eye. Hole in his right retina, to be specific. For various reasons, Andy had never quite figured out what the retina was. Fear probably. But he knew it was a key part of his eye. Probably related to the pupil. Something nasty had happened to the retina in his right eye and produced a hole. That had happened ten years ago. According to Dr. Koenig, the doctor who monitored the hole in his retina, the hole wasn't getting worse. Dr. Koenig thought that the reason he got the hole in the first place was stress. Andy's brother had committed suicide the week before the retina hole appeared. Probably pop psychology, but maybe true anyway.

Further up the terror scale, Andy's glaucoma leered unpleasantly at him. Andy had developed glaucoma about the same time the retina hole appeared. Three eye drops in both eyes twice a day and assorted laser operations had kept Andy's glaucoma from getting worse. Dr. Chu, the doctor who watched over Andy's glaucoma, was very positive about that. But the disease lurked silently somewhere inside Andy's eyeballs, threatening, mysterious and yet another thing to worry about late at night.

Finally, teetering on top of the terror scale was the killer app (as Andy's computer scientist son would describe it), macular degeneration. That should really be in BOLDFACE CAPS: MACULAR DEGENERATION. That was the biggie. It meant that Andy couldn't see very well anymore. The dry kind — not the wet kind — according to his principal eye doctor, Dr. Mansour. Dry was probably better than wet, she told Andy. Dry took longer and you never lost all your vision. On the other hand, you could do something about wet, and dry didn't have a cure. On the third hand, the cure for the wet variety involved sticking a needle in your eye, and that apparently didn't work very well.

He could still see, of course. Just badly. Increasingly badly. Remarkably well given all his other problems, according to his low vision ophthalmologist, Dr. Bhutan. Dr. Mansour went even further, telling Andy that he was remarkably cool and courageous. Which was supposed to make him feel better but didn't. He couldn't drive anymore. And he couldn't read printed material unless it was computerized — he couldn't even read so- called large print books. Which meant that his own very large library, accumulated over a lifetime of reading, was now essentially inaccessible to him. Fortunately, it was possible to read newspapers and magazines and many books on his computer's large screen. And his son Andrew (Andrew Eads III, B.S., MIT, 1989) was — allegedly — investigating electronic devices that could be used to liberate his father's library.

But it had become necessary for Andy to warn people that he wouldn't necessarily recognize them if he passed them in the hall. And he often recognized people by their shape, or their voices, rather than their faces. In other words, he was losing his vision. Not going blind though, he reminded himself.

What was most frightening, if he let himself think about it, was that it wasn't clear how fast he was losing his vision. Certainly it had declined significantly in the past two years. Dr. Mansour had spoken of his being "on the cusp," which seemed to mean at a worrisome turning point but not quite a precipice. But none of his doctors knew — or at least was willing to tell him — if his vision loss was going to increase, or slow down, or even come to a temporary halt. As he always did at this point, Andy told himself firmly, yes, I'm losing my eyesight, and yes, it's probably going to get worse. But I'm doing everything I can to deal with it, and I'm not going worry about it. At least, not right now.

Which let him move on to his ears. Particularly his left ear. His eyes were definitely his scariest problem, but his ears were currently making a play for more of his attention. He had known for some time that he was having problems hearing, but he hadn't worried about it very much. Certainly there had been embarrassing moments in which he had misunderstood things said to him at staff meetings. He had increasingly found it necessary to be cautious in conversations with women. He found soft, high-pitched voices hard to understand. And some very different words sounded the same: free and three, or feather and heather.

He had initially thought it was probably wax in his ears, so he went to an ear doctor, Dr. Pascal, who was in the same building as his dentist. His visit to Dr. Pascal had been horrifying. "What we've got here," Dr. Pascal said, looking judicious, "is two different problems. First of all, you've lost a lot of hearing in the high frequencies area. That's quite common as you get older, and it's why you're having trouble understanding women with soft voices.

"However, your second problem is somewhat different. I think that you may — I emphasize the word may — have a benign tumor in your inner ear that's affecting the hearing in your left ear. A benign tumor. If it's there, it's very small. But if it's there, it's in a very small space. Your discrimination is at sixty percent in that ear. That's why you 're having trouble distinguishing between initial consonants. Are you having any trouble standing up, or falling over, or losing your balance?"

"No," Andy had answered.

"Well, let's wait then," Dr. Pascal had said. "Come back in six months. If your hearing's worse, we'll get you a brain scan. Don't worry about the tumor. I'm sure that if there is one it's benign."

Do I have a tumor in my inner ear? Andy wondered. The idea horrified him. He imagined a small blob of fat getting bigger and bigger and pressing against his brain. Ugh, he thought. Then he shut that mental file. I'm not going to worry about the goddamn tumor, he told himself. Particularly since it's probably not there.

Tumors of course brought his nose to mind. Not that he had a tumor on his nose. But he had had three basal cell cancers and a squamous cell cancer removed from his nose, and innumerable precancerous lesions burnt off his nose and cheeks. With the result that a discolored, white patch – well, a spot really — of skin stretched across the bridge of his nose. Was this a sign of trouble to come? More importantly, was he going to have to stop going out in the Newport sun permanently? I won't think about that either, Andy decided.

And then there were teeth. This year, his teeth had gone berserk. Two root canals, and a crown that stood trembling on the edge of collapse. Andy touched the crown with his tongue and tried to wiggle it. It didn't wiggle, and for once didn't seem to feel odd. I'm not going to think about my teeth now, he thought. Or my bladder, either. He leaned back in the comfortable leather seat of the Lincoln and went to sleep.

CHAPTER 13

When Phoebe Snow woke from her nap, she was initially unsure where she was. She lay on a strange bed, with her head on a large pillow covered with lace, and she was looking up at a shiny ornament in the middle of a canopy over her bead.

She heard a curious whistling noise by her left ear. When she turned her head to look she saw that a cat was sleeping next to her and snoring. It was the grey cat, Oscar, she and Harold had met in the hall.

"What a handsome cat you are," Phoebe said to Oscar, and patted him on his head. Oscar's green eyes blinked, and focused on her. He knew he was handsome.

"I'm going downstairs and look around," Phoebe told Oscar. She got up, straightened her clothes, combed her hair and put on lipstick. Then she held the door open for Oscar to follow. I think I will go down the grand staircase, she thought. I think that might be fun. Oscar followed her.

As she walked down the hall toward the staircase, she heard an odd creaking noise from above. She looked up to see a trap door open in the ceiling and a wooden ladder drop down to the floor. As Phoebe watched, a strange looking person emerged from the trapdoor and began climbing down the ladder. He (or she, for the person's gender was unclear) was covered from head to toe in white. The figure's body was encased in a sort of quilted white overall, and its head was covered over entirely by a white hat and a white veil. "How do you do," the person said in a friendly contralto voice. "I'm Alex. The bay kipper."

"Excuse me," Phoebe said. "The what?"

"The...BAY-EE... KIPPER. You know. Bay Hives. Bays. Bzzzzzz. That sort of thing. I'm Alex. Short for Alexandra. Who are you?" She pulled off her hat, and thrust out her hand.

"I'm Phoebe Snow," Phoebe said, and shook Alex's hand. Without her hat, Alex appeared to be about twenty-five, and rather pretty. She had short brown hair streaked with blond highlights.

"I'm Irish," Alex said, "but I've been here for ages. My partner works for Dr. Eads. Her name's Teresa. Are you new here?"

"Just visiting," Phoebe said

"We get a lot of those," Alex said. "I'm just come from up on the roof. To mess around with the bees. Some of ours have been sick recently, but most of them are doing fine. We're not sure why."

"I see," Phoebe said, although she really didn't. "I was just going downstairs."

"I'll be down shortly," Alex said. "To the Commons, I mean. Everyone goes there for drinks about now. Just go down the staircase and turn right at the bottom. You can't miss it. Part of the perks. The free bar, I mean. Personally, I find it's a challenge, but then I'm Irish, as I said before. Gotta go." She put her hat back on, bent over and patted Oscar, who was rubbing his head against her leg. Then she opened a door in the hallway to a utility closet, took out a box marked "BEE STUFF" in large black letters, climbed back up the ladder and through the trap door, and pulled the ladder up behind her and disappeared. Oscar looked mournfully at the trap door in the ceiling. Then he sat down next to the utility closet and curled up in a ball, presumably to wait for Alex's return.

At the end of the hallway, a balcony overlooked the grand staircase and the ballroom. From this vantage point, Phoebe cautiously peered down and examined the goings on below. To her left, the ballroom was empty except for a grand piano, a number of empty chairs and sofas. To her right, however, a line of potted palms marked out a very different scene.

Perhaps twenty or twenty-five people were standing in small groups or sitting at little tables, holding drinks and talking loudly. Their voices blended together and produced a pleasant but incomprehensible humming noise. Bees, Phoebe thought. They were clearly having —if not a party— a very good time. This must be the Commons, Phoebe decided. Feeling a little like Scarlett O'Hara (or perhaps Carol Burnett), she descended the grand staircase and joined the group below.

A tall young man wearing a bow tie and a blue and white seersucker suit detached himself from a knot of people and came toward Phoebe. "I'm Dexter Slate," he said, "Dr. Eads' administrative assistant. And you must be Dr. Snow, from University Hall. Andy asked me to tell you he'll be back soon. Come and meet some people, and I'll get you a drink."

"How do you do, " Phoebe said, and they shook hands. "I'd love a glass of water."

"Something stronger, perhaps? We have a wonderful open bar here. Part of the famous Grafton House perks. Anything you could possibly want."

Phoebe smiled. "Just water," she said. "With some ice if you have it." Free bar, she thought. Melanie would certainly be interested in that little bit of information. But I don't think I'll mention it to her.

"This is Henry Leathwood," Dexter Slate said. "He's a reporter with the *Washington Post*. And this is Teresa Morgan, Andy's personal assistant. I'd like you both to meet Dr. Phoebe Snow. She's visiting from Harvard's University Hall — they're the 'admin' people for Grafton House. I'll be right back with your water," Dexter Slate said, and hurried off. He seems nervous, Phoebe thought. I'm afraid visitors from University Hall always make research center administrators nervous.

Henry Leathwood was an inch or two taller than Phoebe, maybe 5' 9"and muscular, with a shock of blond hair, light blue eyes and an engaging smile. He looks like a wrestler, Phoebe thought. He appeared to be in his late thirties. He solemnly shook Phoebe's hand, started to say something, and then apparently thought better of it. I wonder what he was going to say, Phoebe thought.

Teresa Morgan was somewhere in her forties, a good-looking woman with long black hair and golden skin. At first glance, it wasn't clear whether she was African-American or something more exotic. She smiled at Phoebe and said, "I think you've met my partner, Alex. She sent me a text about you — she said she'd met a newcomer in the guest wing."

"I did meet Alex," Phoebe said. "She was doing something with your beehives."

"Alma's beehives are one of our proudest possessions here at Grafton House," Teresa said. "Mrs. Grafton — we always think of her as Alma— brought a beekeeper with her from Honduras when she married Mr. Grafton and he built her this house. It's a very romantic story."

"I've read about it," Phoebe said. "And it is very romantic. I wonder what Mrs. Grafton would think about Grafton House today. Do you think she had any idea that you would become such a busy place?"

"We're certainly busy, all right," Teresa said. "I saw you when you got here this afternoon. When we had such a fuss about Karim, one of our research associates, getting nauseous and passing out. Fortunately it was food poisoning. I went to the hospital with him, in the ambulance, and stayed until they were sure he was OK."

"Here's your water," Dexter Slate said, and handed Phoebe a tall glass with a slice of lemon perched on the rim. "You're sure you wouldn't like something stronger?"

"This is just what I wanted," Phoebe said, and took a long drink.

"We were just talking about Alma's bees," Teresa said. "Dr. Snow ran into Alex up in the guest quarters. She was in her beekeeper drag."

"I'm afraid our beehives may give Dr. Snow the impression — the incorrect impression — that we're not serious here at Grafton House," Dexter Slate said, looking irritated.

Teresa smiled. "No, they won't, Dexter. They're fun, and good for the environment. And they're a nice way to pay our respects to Alma and her husband."

"I suppose you're right," Dexter Slate said, "But we're about a lot more important things here as well. Andy has done a miraculous job here. He's turned his vision of what interdisciplinary research on migration policy ideally should be into a vibrantly functioning reality. Here in Grafton House, he's brought together some of the best and brightest minds in the county — no, the world — to think and converse about one of our most important phenomena — worldwide migration. And to converse civilly, cooperatively, in a spirit of comity." He paused for breath, and looked slightly embarrassed.

"Dexter's right," Henry Leathwood said. "Andy is doing something very interesting here."

As they chatted, Phoebe became aware that the couple standing behind her were having a heated argument, and that the argument was rapidly becoming overheated. "What I'm telling you," a young man with a brown beard said in a loud voice to a blond young woman, "is that Andy Eads is refusing to face the facts. I won't say he's doing that intentionally. But the reality is that some of the junior staff are getting preferential treatment. And they're all foreign-born. And I don't think that's accidental." He made a chopping motion with his hand, and the blond young woman looked alarmed.

"That's the stupidest thing, I've ever heard you say, Donald," she said. "You've had too much to drink, and you're talking nonsense. Dr. Eads is one of the fairest men I've ever met, especially in academia. Ask anyone who's ever worked with him and they'll tell you. Dr. Eads doesn't play favorites. Frankly, if he has a fault, it's that he's too forgiving. He lets people like you get away with repeating gossip that's simply untrue."

"You're wrong, Sally, and I can prove it," the young man said loudly. His face was red, and his body swayed slightly from side to side. He is drunk, Phoebe thought.

"I can prove it," the young man said again, in a very loud voice. By now, everyone in his immediate vicinity had stopped talking and was listening to him. "Al Copeland got Tobie Shaw to run an analysis of financial assistance packages for junior staff. They compared who got what by country of origin. And the median assistance package for native-born junior staff was 37.4 percent lower than the package for foreign-born staff. And the mode was even more skewed – American-born staff were 46 percent lower. What do you think of that, my dear naïve friend? If that's not overt prejudice, what is it?"

"Al and Tobie did WHAT?" the blond young woman said in a startled voice. "Are you people insane? You broke into confidential personnel files?"

Dexter Slate was the first person to say something. He carefully put his drink down on a small table, and walked over to the couple that were arguing and said, "Excuse me, Donald, I couldn't help overhearing what you just told Sally. I'm sorry but I can't ignore what you said. I'm going to report this to Dr. Eads as soon as he gets back here."

"Oh Dexter, please don't!" the young woman pleaded. "Don's just running off at the mouth. He's had too much to drink."

"I may have had a few drinks," Donald said, "but I'm in complete control of my medical facilities." Good heavens, Phoebe thought, he really is drunk. "I know the truth about this place," the young man went on, "and it's not a pretty one. Tell Andy Eads what you like, Slake, Slate, Snake, whatever you call yourself. I don't care. I'm out of here."

"Goodbye, Sally," the young man said. "Give me a call when you get back to Cambridge." He began to walk away and the crowd melted away from him like the Red Sea parting for Moses. Then he stopped suddenly. Coming toward him was an older man, tall and distinguished-looking. It's Dr. Eads, Phoebe realized.

Dexter Slate was facing Phoebe and didn't see Dr. Eads arrive. "I'm sorry, Dr. Snow," he said. "I'm afraid that confirms any concerns in University Hall about the discrimination complaint. I can assure you that it's a tempest in a teapot, but as you can see, it's had some unfortunate consequences." Then he noticed that Phoebe was looking over his shoulder towards the entrance to the room. He turned his head just in time to see the young man lunge forward and try to grab Andy Eads by the shoulder.

What happened next was confusing. Andy Eads gracefully moved to one side, and the young man stumbled and fell forward. Phoebe wasn't sure, but it looked very much as if Andy Eads' outstretched foot had played a key role in the fall. The young man certainly thought so. "He tripped me up," the young man said, sounding booth puzzled and indignant.

"Andy was a wrestler in the Army," Teresa said. She sounded very much like a proud mother. "The U.S. Army Pacific Command Wrestling Champion. He has a lovely plaque commemorating this hanging on the wall in his office. Andy says it got him out of KP duty — that's what the Army calls working in the kitchen. Donald Pike is lucky he didn't actually strike Andy. That would have been a very bad idea."

Well, Phoebe thought, there certainly appears to be enough going on to justify my visit here. I wonder what will happen next.

CHAPTER 14

Lieutenant Samuel Jeremiah Graves III sat down at his desk and opened the pizza shop takeout box containing his supper. Two slices with pepperoni, and a sprinkling of red pepper. Plus a can of Diet Coke. I should eat better, he thought, but I haven't got the time. Maybe tomorrow I'll go on a diet. Maybe tomorrow I'll have seafood at Anthony's. He took a bite of the first slice of pizza, and washed it down with some Coke. Then he pushed the pizza box to the corner of his desk and picked up a red folder labeled in large black letters: EDWARD MORIARTY CASE: MURDER/ARMED ROBBERY, CAMBRIDGE, MA, JUNE 18, 2011.

Inside the red folder were six white folders labeled: 1) Overview, 2) Ed Moriarty (Deceased), 3) Wilford "Fat Willie" Thomas, 4) Tobie Shaw, 5) George Rakylz (a.k.a. Omega), and 6) Grafton House Issues. Lieutenant Graves spread out the white folders on his desk top, took a felt tip pen from a pencil cup on his desk and wrote the names Thomas and Rakylz in block letters on a yellow pad of paper.

Sam Graves had grown up in Newport, the eldest son of a long established African-American family. He played basketball at Newport's Rogers High School, and upon graduation married his high school sweetheart and enlisted in the Marine Corps. He served two tours in Vietnam, the first in the infantry, the second as a military policeman, and then joined the Massachusetts State Police where he worked for ten years. Then his wife's favorite uncle, Jack Oliveira, was appointed Assistant Chief of the Newport police department. With Jack's help, Sam was hired by the Newport police department and moved back to his hometown.

He had prospered there, rising slowly but surely to his present post of Lieutenant. In general, he liked working in the Newport police department. Newport had plenty of minor crime — drug- and drinking-related for the most part, and an occasional domestic dispute turned violent. But in comparison to crime in the big cities, Newport was a piece of cake for the police. Everybody knew everybody else, and it usually wasn't hard to find out who had done what to whom. If you were thorough and organized, as Sam Graves certainly was, police work in Newport was very rewarding.

The Ed Moriarty case was in most respects the standard violent crime case that Sam Graves had dealt with throughout his career. The details of the incident were familiar: two incompetents try to rob a drug dealer, botch the job and wind up murdering the dealer. Nothing new there.

A botched robbery in which someone gets killed is all too common. And the Cambridge police knew exactly who did it: a petty criminal from Providence and an MIT graduate student. Nothing surprising there, either. Petty criminals and MIT grad students both smoke pot and some of them sell it, too. Neither one is likely to be a skilled robber.

But at that point, things stopped being routine. As a practical matter, Sam Graves was pretty sure how to deal with petty criminals like Wilford "Fat Willie" Thomas. As a general rule, people on the run from the law like Fat Willie usually return to their home turf. Back home, they try unsuccessfully to hide from the police, and are eventually turned in by a relative or a snitch. Fat Willie was from Providence. So Sam would normally have expected him to return to Providence and the tender mercies of the Providence police. And not bother the good citizens of Newport, RI.

Ordinarily, crimes committed in one state are of little interest to the police in other states. In this case, however, it seemed possible that Fat Willie and George might turn up in Newport. Sam Graves' interest in the case had been triggered by a call from a friend on the Cambridge police force.

Fat Willie, his friend told him, had a girlfriend named Tobie Shaw who lived in Newport and worked for "a Harvard-owned research center called Grafton House." Moreover, Tobie Shaw was definitely the ex-girlfriend of the murder victim, Ed Moriarty, and possibly a former girlfriend of George Rakylz. So Fat Willie and maybe George might come to Newport seeking money and shelter from Tobie Shaw. Sam Graves had taken several steps to deal with this possibility.

The Cambridge police had sent out a wanted notice with photos and brief descriptions of Fat Willie and George Rakylz. Fat Willie's photo was a mug shot from the Pawtucket, RI police department. George Rakylz's photo was a copy of his Facebook page. Sam had distributed copies of the notice to the patrol officers who worked in the bar district around Thames Street.

He had also given copies to the cops who had contacts in the small African-American community, and to the manager of the bus terminal at the Newport Visitor Center. For good measure, he had given copies to his counterparts in the Middletown and Portsmouth police forces — the other two towns on Aquidneck Island — and the police department in Jamestown, the island on the other end of the Pell Bridge. In addition, Sam had talked to detectives in the Providence police force.

So the only other thing that needed to be done about Fat Willie was to talk to Tobie Shaw. Sam had done some preliminary work on this already. Teresa Morgan, Andy Eads' personal assistant, was also the baby sister of Sam's high school classmate Pedro Morgan. Sam had given Teresa copies of the wanted flyers to distribute at Grafton House. And he had told Teresa about the possible involvement of Tobie Shaw. Teresa was the soul of discretion, but she had made it clear that talking to Tobie Shaw wasn't going to be easy.

"I kind of like her," Teresa had said, "but calling her difficult is a major understatement."

So talking to Tobie Shaw might not produce anything useful. On balance, Sam decided that he should try it. I'll call her in the morning, he told himself.

Dealing with Fat Willie was basically routine. George Rakylz was a different matter. Tobie Shaw was also supposed to be Rakylz' girlfriend — meaning that Rakylz might come to Newport too. And George Rakylz, a.k.a. Omega, was not just another MIT grad student with a fondness for marijuana. According to the Cambridge police, he was also a bona fide nutcase.

The Cambridge police had been unable to uncover much concrete information about Rakylz' political views. He had begun and then apparently abandoned a Facebook page. It contained his picture but few clues to his politics. None of his Cambridge acquaintances was able to tell police exactly what Rakylz believed in. But most of his Cambridge acquaintances thought he was crazy and probably dangerous. Not that he had many friends; his Facebook page listed fourteen "friends".

It wasn't on his Facebook page, but several people told police that Rakylz had renamed himself Omega — the letter that ends the Greek alphabet. Allegedly, Rakylz told people that his new name symbolized his intention to end the existing political and economic system of the United States. His acquaintances told police that Rakylz wanted to destroy world capitalism and replace it with agrarian cooperatives. A few people thought Rakylz was the leader of a group of like-minded radicals, but most people believed he was a lone nutcase with delusions of grandeur. Almost everyone commented that free love was a big part of his vision. So were free marijuana and free ice cream. The Cambridge police were very heartened by these aspects of his belief system since they appeared to ensure that Rakylz was not an Islamic terrorist.

While Sam Graves also was glad that George Rakylz did not seem to be an Islamic terrorist, the rest of the information about him was worrisome. Not only was there a possibility that both he and Fat Willie might come to Newport to seek help from Tobie Shaw. There was also the possibility that once Rakylz was in Newport, he might want to do something anarchistic. Sam Graves was not particularly worried by incompetent petty crooks. He knew how to deal with them. But he didn't have any experience in dealing with anarchists, and he didn't want to have any.

Like police forces around the United States, the Newport police department had become unwillingly aware of the problem of international terrorism after the 9/11 attacks. Assorted government agencies had flooded the Newport police department with information on potential terrorist threats and methods for dealing with them. Sam was not particularly cynical, but it was fairly clear to him that preventing terrorist attacks was going to be very difficult. The Federal Department of Homeland Security had paid Sam's way to a weeklong course on terrorism at the Naval War College in

Newport. The retired FBI agent who taught the course was blunt. The question wasn't if but when. And the only useful defense was intelligence gathering— internationally, but even more important in local ethnic communities.

Sam had taken this to heart, and for the following couple of years had devoted time to making friends with members of the Muslim community in Newport. Surprisingly, there were a significant number of Muslims. Some were African-Americans who had converted to Islam. The majority was from Pakistan, Palestine and Lebanon, almost all small shopkeepers, with a smattering of health professionals, nurses and doctors. It was Sam's hope that if a radical jihadist were to surface in his town, one of his Muslim friends would alert him to the threat. Since George Rakylz wasn't a Muslim, none of that was of much use to Sam.

Which brought him to the question of Grafton House. As a boy, Sam had worked summers on the Grafton House maintenance crew. His mother had worked as a cook in the Grafton House kitchen. Sam had fond memories of the old Director, Wolfgang Froelich, handing out Christmas bonuses for the staff, and presents for their children at the annual Grafton House Christmas party. And of Alma Grafton bringing cookies and lemonade to the grounds crew in the summertime.

In those days, Grafton House had seemed like an oasis of scholarly calm. Sam had never been quite sure what the scholars at the Institute did, but they seemed peaceful and friendly and almost never caused any trouble for anyone in Newport.

That had changed in the past few years. Andy Eads certainly seemed like a nice guy, nice enough anyway. But Grafton House was very different. Worrisome stuff was happening at Grafton House. The events of that afternoon were just an example. Sam was aware of the controversy over Dr. Gardiner's *New York Review of Books* article criticizing Islam. Islamic terrorism was a concern of all police departments these days. Naturally, reports on the Internet that Islamic groups were threatening Dr. Gardiner's life were of concern to the Newport police department.

Sam was also aware that Dr. Jack Chrysler was a favorite target of right-wing talk show hosts. His brother-in-law loved those shows and frequently told Sam that Dr. Chrysler should be tried for treason. In his brother-in-law's opinion, Grafton House was a snake's nest of radicals and Communists, and patriotic Americans should do something about it. His brother-in-law was vague about what that something should be, but it worried Sam.

Now, there were rumors that some Grafton House staff had filed a discrimination complaint with Harvard against Dr. Eads. A reverse discrimination complaint. Sam Graves had experienced remarkably little discrimination in the course of his life, but he had experienced more than enough. He was willing to believe that reverse discrimination was theoretically possible; but he thought it was pretty unlikely. Still, it looked like another opportunity for trouble.

It was clear that the peace and quiet of the old Grafton House had been swept away and replaced by a new Grafton House where controversy and conflict were encouraged. Normally, that would have been of little interest to Sam Graves. But it was becoming increasingly clear to him that there might be a little too much conflict going on at Grafton House.

The events of that afternoon were a case in point. Sam was pretty sure that the Muslim staffer who had been taken to the hospital was probably the victim of food poisoning. Still, the inflammatory words and hysterical behavior of Dr. Gardiner were worrisome.

Sam had declined to follow up on Dr. Gardiner's anti-Muslim remarks earlier in the afternoon, but not because he took them lightly. He was already aware of Dr. Gardiner's hatred of the Muslim religion. In Sam's opinion, her criticisms seemed over the top and probably dangerous. He had followed the news stories on Dr. Gardiner's work and Islamic reactions, and he knew there had been threats of violence against her. And Dr. Gardiner's husband was Paul Gardiner. This was very important. First, Paul Gardiner was Sam's friend, and someone he admired. But in addition, he was also a very important man. Rich, politically powerful, and hard-nosed. Not someone Sam wanted to offend.

And now the Institute was having a summer conference on immigration policy. Sam was pretty sure there would be protestors of various kinds who would show up and demonstrate. So that was a police problem. More worrisome was the possibility that some extremists, maybe Muslims, maybe right-wing nuts, maybe overheated liberals, might take this opportunity to do something violent. And maybe George Rakylz would be one of them.

So Sam needed to talk to Andy Eads. Eads had seemed like a nice guy earlier that day. He might be able to smooth the way in setting up a discussion with Ms. Shaw. And it might be desirable to discuss what threat, if any, Eads thought protestors, and specifically radical anarchists like Rakylz, might pose to Grafton House and the upcoming conference. Certainly, the whole question of Islamic terrorism seemed to be alive and well at Grafton House, based on what Sam had seen earlier in the day.

CHAPTER 15

Standing in a mahogany-paneled stall in the men's lounge off the Grafton House Commons, Suleiman Khan stroked his limp penis and waited for his bladder to cooperate. "Hurry up, Excalibur," he said to his penis in a low voice. "You can do it, boy. Now. Now. Do it now." He reached up and pulled down on a chain hanging from a large wooden box directly over the toilet. With a whooshing sound, a burst of water descended from the overhead water reservoir and rushed into the toilet. In response, Suleiman began to pee, finally, in a slow and halting stream. I really do not like physical problems, he thought. They are a gross bore.

Suleiman finished peeing, wiped off the tip of his penis with a sheet of toilet tissue, and replaced it inside his under shorts. He buttoned up the fly on his seersucker trousers — hand-tailored by J.Press in Cambridge — and turned around to leave the stall. But before he could do so, he heard a loud crashing noise, and then a man cursing. "Goddamit," someone said, "The bastard broke my goddamn arm. Shit."

Suleiman cautiously opened the stall's heavy wooden door and peered out. A large, bearded young man sat on the tiled floor of the men's lounge, leaning against a marble washbasin. The young man held his right arm stiffly against his chest, and was clearly inebriated. Suleiman recognized the man. It was Donald somebody, a post-doc specializing in Native American studies. Not very promising, Suleiman remembered. An odd combination of pious libertarianism and conservative religiosity. An evangelical Christian. One of the fundamentalist variety, Suleiman recalled. And one of the staff who were up in arms about Andy Eads' "discrimination" against native-born Americans.

In Suleiman's personal opinion, the likelihood that Andy Eads had engaged in some sort of politically correct discrimination was vanishingly remote. Eads had his problems, of course, major ones, but that sort of trivial mucking around with the staff was not in his line. In fact, Suleiman would guess that Andy was more likely to be overly kind to second raters like this man. Tike. No, Pike. Donald Pike, like the fish in the Minnesota lakes.

While not believing a word of it, Suleiman had not been unhappy about the staff attack on Andy Eads. If Andy got in trouble with the University, then he might have to go, and Suleiman might be, could be his successor. That was his long-term goal.

Suleiman was of course aware that a group of junior staffers had convinced themselves that they were being discriminated against. In Suleiman's personal opinion, this sort of whining was one of the great flaws in the American character. Somehow, the belief in the equality of everyone translated into indignation when everyone wasn't treated the same.

Fairness to all and equal treatment of all were— of course, Suleiman reflected — not the same. Some scholars were better than others. Inevitably, they were rewarded more than their less competent colleagues. Donald Pike was one of the less competent scholars at Grafton House, and had been rewarded accordingly. And he didn't like it. And blamed Andy Eads for that.

Suleiman Khan was, without question, the most competent and the best-known scholar at Grafton House. He had been born in Lahore, in Pakistan, a few years after the 1948 partition of India. His father had been a civil engineer, a civil servant in the pre-partition Indian government, and after partition had been appointed to a similar position in the government of Pakistan. When he was ten, Suleiman's parents died in a train crash. His father's two sisters lived in New York. Aunt Zaina was a pediatrician and Aunt Azeeza was a registered nurse. The two sisters had become American citizens, but had never married. When their brother died, the two sisters immediately flew to Lahore. With the assistance of their Uncle Hussein, an eminent and well-connected attorney in Lahore, Aunt Zaina formally adopted Suleiman as her son. After more legal maneuvering with the U.S. Immigration and Naturalization Service, the sisters were able to bring Suleiman back to their spacious house in the Bronx. And in due course, Suleiman became an American citizen.

Suleiman had attended a rigorous private school in Lahore. His parents had always spoken English at home, and English was his primary language. He had always been a hard worker and he had excelled in his studies. So when he entered the New York public school system, he was far ahead of his fellow students. His aunts were kind to the quiet boy who had lost his parents and his native land, and he tried to repay their kindness by working even harder on his studies.

At age twelve he passed the entrance examination for the Bronx High School of Science. His teachers quickly recognized that he was a gifted student. And they were impressed by his diligence and hard work, which were exceptional even among his striving immigrant classmates. He finished high school in three years and enrolled at CCNY at the age of fifteen. At CCNY, Suleiman began by majoring in mathematics, but quickly realized that he would never be in the first ranks of mathematicians. Taking a course in economics, he discovered that the economics profession valued mathematics highly, but that the level of mathematical expertise among economists was rather low. He promptly switched his major to economics.

Graduating at the top of his class at the age of eighteen, Suleiman had his choice of graduate schools. MIT offered him the largest fellowship. The Vietnam War was raging at this point. Graduate school promised the possibility of a draft deferment, but his aunts suggested that service in the Army Reserve would be less risky. With the approval of the MIT admissions office he deferred his admission to graduate school while he did his military service. After six months on active duty in the Army Reserve, he enrolled at MIT. He excelled at MIT, and earned a PhD in economics in five years. His dissertation on labor market anomalies was published by the MIT Press, and he was recruited by the University of Chicago. From Chicago, he moved back to MIT, and from MIT he had lately moved to an endowed chair at Harvard where he focused on the economics of international migration. He had published five books, each a critical success, culminating in his receiving an award generally regarded as the Nobel Prize of economics. His prestige was such that, unlike anyone else at Grafton House, he retained his tenured position in the Harvard Economics Department while spending half time at Grafton House.

This précis of Suleiman's resume describes a familiar arc: the rise of a gifted scholar in his profession. But like most résumés it fails entirely to describe the man behind the accomplishments. Until he received tenure at the University of Chicago, Suleiman's external personality was quiet. Buttoned-up. Cautious. Risk-averse. Taciturn. Inside, he was the usual mix of human emotions, but he presented a pleasant demeanor to the outside world. All this changed after Suleiman began teaching at the University of Chicago. Quite naturally, Suleiman was personally conservative, cautious about risk taking, and careful not to antagonize his professors and fellow students. Yet as he achieved success as an economist, he began to feel surer of his position in society. At MIT and Chicago, his views on economics and politics had been heavily influenced by several conservative professors. And over time, he himself became one of the prominent spokesmen for the wing of the economics profession that favors minimal government involvement in the economy. And to his surprise and pleasure, he found that many of his colleagues and students admired and respected his insights and expertise.

And, at some point, Suleiman decided that the religion of his ancestors, Islam, offered a spiritual home for him. Suleiman's parents had not been religious. They were educated and defined themselves as socialists, atheists, intellectuals. They were profoundly uninterested in the religion of their parents, which they saw as benighted and a continuing source of trouble and discord — as evidenced by the partition of India. They spoke Urdu of course, but at home they spoke English. At least in part, English was a way to associate themselves with modern society and worldly culture. Suleiman's aunts were not religious either. Unlike his parents, they had no ideological objections to Islam. They simply saw it as old-fashioned, uninteresting and improbable. Thus, Suleiman's upbringing had not been a religious one. Quite the contrary.

But Suleiman was a bachelor. Despite his growing prestige and numerous admirers, he had no close friends, no significant other to come home to. And at his core, he felt lonely. Very lonely. One day, leaving his office at MIT, he saw a small group of graduate students going by. They were smiling and seemed happy. Suleiman knew two of them, young men from Palestine. He said hello, and asked where they were going. To say our prayers, they answered. Come along with us, Dr. Khan. So he did. At first, he simply observed the students praying. Then, imperceptibly at first, he began praying himself.

Suleiman's decision to become a Muslim was an intuitive one. He was a very educated man. Much of what he initially read about Islam seemed to him a curious mixture of fantasy and folktales. But the central idea of Islam, that there is one god whose prophet is Muhammed, appealed to him. So Suleiman decided to ignore the parts of the religion that seemed illogical, and focus on what he decided was the religion's central truth. Over time, he worked out a logically acceptable (to him) set of beliefs corollary with the central truth. And after a time, he began to casually identify himself as a Muslim to his colleagues and students. He began to attend regular prayer meetings held on the MIT campus by Muslim students. He continued to do so after moving to Harvard. And at Grafton House he continued to pray five times daily, as required by the faith.

You, reader, may wonder how a highly-educated man like Dr. Suleiman Khan could suddenly adopt a religion of which he knew practically nothing. A religion that is generally unpopular in the West, and thought by many Americans and Europeans to be antithetical to Western values. Let me remind you of the great Senegalese poet and statesman, Leopold Senghar's writings on the subject of deracination. Suleiman Khan, despite all his magnificent American education and numerous accomplishments felt rootless. Uprooted. Ruth among the alien corn, so to speak. He had lost his parents and his native land. Becoming part of Islam gave him a rooted place in the world, a spiritual home that he was (he felt, and that's all it really takes, isn't it?) comfortable in. Still, it's not entirely clear that turning Muslim has really worked for him. He reminds me of Romain Gary's despairing exiles in *Les Racines du Ciel*. He is still lonely, and still feels disconnected from his present as well as the roots of his past. Perhaps this is why he feels so angry at Anettka's rejection of Islam.

Suleiman's strong dislike of Anettka Gardiner had several causes. The foremost among them was Anettka's public criticisms of Islam. Suleiman is well aware of the many ways in which modern Islamic society falls short of his vision. In his opinion, much could and should be improved. But Anettka wanted to destroy Islam, tear it apart. And that made Suleiman angry.

Anettka was also an aggressively liberated woman. Suleiman was uncomfortable with liberated women. He believed (although he was careful not to say so to anyone) that men had stronger minds than women, and therefore should lead while women followed. In short, he thought that women were meant to be subordinate to men. This aspect of traditional Islamic belief appealed to him strongly. Oddly enough, he also admired his maiden aunts, who, while modest and discreet, were also models of self-sufficiency, and seemed to get along perfectly well without male guidance. And finally, Anettka was the wife of an important man, a member of the Harvard Board of Overseers. And thus she was an impediment to Suleiman's achieving his own current personal goal, the directorship of Grafton House. Suleiman knew that as long as Anettka's husband had any position of authority at Harvard, his ambition was problematic.

With some trepidation, Suleiman pushed open the door to his stall and headed toward the men's lounge's row of massive marble washbasins. The bearded young man sitting on the floor looked up at him, and said, "Hello, Dr. Khan. I'm afraid I've had an accident."

"I'm sorry," Suleiman said, "I'll just wash up and go find someone who can help you." He rolled his shirtsleeves up to the elbow, turned on the cold water tap, picked up a cake of soap, and began to wash his face. Then Suleiman heard a retching sound behind him and felt something ominously warm and wet land on his trouser leg. He reluctantly turned around and saw that Donald Pike had vomited on his trousers, and was still vomiting convulsively. "I'll find someone to help you," Suleiman said decisively, and rapidly left the room. Outside, he saw Teresa, Andy Eads' assistant, and flagged her down. "Donald Pike is in the men's room vomiting," he said. "I would appreciate it if you could find some of the men to get him and clean him up. He is drunk, I'm afraid, and appears to have injured himself."

"Thanks, Dr. Khan," Teresa said. "I'll find some of the junior staff to go get him."

"Thank you, Teresa," Suleiman said. "I'm going to go get cleaned up. I'm late for my prayers."

CHAPTER 16

Imagine that we are sitting in my Aunt Genevieve's parlor watching a magic lantern show. Imagine further that Aunt Genevieve and her magic lantern really are as magical as they seem. If we ask them to, they will show us what the people we have met so far are doing right now.

Phoebe Snow is standing by herself in the Grafton House Commons. She is thinking about men. In particular, she is thinking about three men, each of whom interests her for a different reason. Or maybe the same reason. Anyway, she's thinking about Henry Leathwood, Andy Eads, and Juan Carlos Cisneros. In that order. She's also very hungry. She has a craving for gelato. Hazelnut gelato if possible, but vanilla will do.

Harold Cummings is sitting on a folding chair in the garage. He is changing the oil in the Lincoln Town Car and drinking a cold Budweiser. Out of a bottle, not a can. The Grafton House kitchen has located one of the rare liquor stores that sell Budweiser in long-neck bottles.

Phoebe's friend Jackie Persac and his partner Edgar Stern are eating an early supper at a small Chinese restaurant in Cambridge, and arguing about which movie to see that evening. Jackie wants to see "Jules and Jim" at the Brattle. Again. Edgar doesn't. Jackie grew up in Fall River, MA speaking French with his French Canadian parents, and he loves French movies. His driver's license says he's Jacques Persac, age fifty-two. At age two, his nickname was p'tit-Jacques. His first-grade teacher decided that p'tit-Jacques sounded too foreign and renamed him Jackie.

Juan Carlos Cisneros is having a cocktail with his wife Catherine in the living room of their house in Cambridge, and pretending to watch a discussion of agricultural subsidies on WGBH-TV. In fact, he is thinking about Phoebe Snow. Catherine is thinking about the civil-rights case she will argue in the morning.

Melanie Ferguson is working late in University Hall, and is finishing her third can of Diet Coke. The laser printer in her office has jammed, and there is no one she can call to fix it. After work, Melanie is planning to go to the gym for her weekly Pilates class. She has a crush on the instructor, who is a former rugby player from New Zealand.

Anettka Gardiner is sitting in Jack Chrysler's car. They are parked under a tree in an out-of-the-way corner of the Norman Bird Sanctuary in Middletown, RI. Jack and Anettka are kissing. Unbeknownst to them, they are being observed by a fascinated group of novice birdwatchers, a troop of Brownies who are standing on a nearby ridge looking down on Jack's Mini Cooper. The Brownies' leader, Winifred Gardiner, is Paul Gardiner's first cousin. She will shortly catch up with her charges on top of the ridge and discover Anettka and Jack kissing. We do not know now if she will tell her cousin.

Paul Gardiner is in a taxi speaking French to the pretty young woman driver. He is not thinking about Anettka.

Karim Pandit is watching the WGBH-TV story on agricultural subsidies. He is very interested in agricultural policy. He hopes the nurse will remove his catheter in the near future.

Andy Eads is pretending to listen to Dexter Slate's report on Donald Pike's misdeeds. He is thinking about the satisfying thud that Donald Pike made when he hit the floor after Andy tripped him. Dexter is of two minds, but on balance (he says) he believes that Donald will probably have to be dismissed. He hopes (he says) it won't be necessary to fire Tobie Shaw, who is difficult, but one of the few people that understand the ancient Grafton House computer system.

Tobie Shaw is slowly sipping a glass of white wine and considering the thorny issues presented by her various boyfriends. In about five minutes, Teresa Morgan is going to tell Tobie that Donald Pike has told everyone about her unauthorized search of the Grafton House personnel data base.

Teresa is standing outside the men's lounge. She is waiting for two of the youngest male staffers to collect the inebriated Donald Pike and take him to his room.

Donald Pike has just vomited on the shoes of the young men, and is resisting their efforts to remove him from the bathroom floor. His arm hurts. A lot. Later that evening, Teresa will drive Donald to the emergency room of the Newport Hospital. There, they will learn that Donald's arm is broken. In two places.

Suleiman Khan has returned to his rooms, and is scrubbing out the vomit on the trousers of his seersucker suit. He is about to take a shower. He is late for evening prayers, and he is feeling unfriendly toward Donald Pike.

Sam Graves is still sitting at his desk. He is examining the Facebook photo of George Rakylz on the wanted poster issued by the Cambridge police. In the photo, George has long, curly black hair, and a bushy black beard. Unless he's completely nuts, Sam thinks, he'll cut his hair and shave off his beard. The photo probably won't be much use. Unless he really is nuts. But he's not very old. Maybe I could locate his high school yearbook photo.

Alex, the Irish beekeeper, is up on the roof repairing a beehive. She has missed all the excitement in the Commons. From her vantage point, she can see the spire of Trinity Church. I would like to be married there, she thinks, if the Americans ever fix their silly laws. But I'm not sure Teresa really wants to get married.

Oscar is standing in the corridor outside Phoebe Snow's room. He thinks he smells a mouse in the utility closet. He enjoys catching mice, even though no one seems to appreciate it when he does. He is being very quiet so the mouse won't know he's there.

Andrew Eads, Sr., is dozing in the chair in front of the television set on the terrace of Pinewood. He is dreaming. In his dream, he is playing golf on a beautiful spring day in Mississippi. He has just hit the ball, a tremendous shot, and he is watching the ball arc through the air towards the 16th hole.

Henry Leathwood is standing by a pillar in the Commons. He is watching Phoebe Snow. What a pretty girl, he thinks. I would like to talk to her.

Ed Moriarty, or rather the lump of organic matter that was formerly Ed Moriarty, is stored inside a refrigerated metal box in the Cambridge morgue, awaiting an autopsy. The Cambridge morgue's budget has been cut, so the autopsy won't happen any time soon.

Wilford "Fat Willie" Thomas is sitting next to a dumpster behind the Stop and Shop supermarket on Bellevue Avenue in Newport. He is eating potato chips and drinking a can of Budweiser. He is trying to call Tobie Shaw's cellphone, but Tobie won't answer the phone. He doesn't know where he will spend the night if he can't get hold of Tobie.

George Rakylz is also calling Tobie Shaw's cellphone. Tobie still hasn't answered the phone. He is thinking about spending the night on the beach, but the idea doesn't appeal very much.

Peruvian Naval Ensign Arturo Cisneros-Stern is standing on the deck of the *Marte*, a twin-masted brig, used by the Peruvian Navy as a training ship. The *Marte* is anchored in Newport Harbor, where it is part of the group of Tall Ships visiting Newport. Arturo is thinking about his famous uncle, Juan Carlos Cisneros-Puglisi. He plans to call Juan Carlos later in the evening. He hopes that Juan Carlos will come to Newport to see him. He is also thinking a lot about Tobie Shaw, with whom he plans to make love during his visit to Newport.

Have we missed anyone? Now that I think of it, we have. Four very different groups of concerned, not to say agitated, citizens are gathered together in various locations in Newport, Providence, and Fall River. They are planning to demonstrate at the Grafton House immigration conference.

One group is the CMCN, the Concerned Muslim Citizens of Newport. They aren't radical in any sense of the word, but they're deeply unhappy about the news that an anti-Islamic professor will speak at the Grafton House conference. (Anettka is the professor in question.) They want to show the world that Muslims are good citizens, and they're going to demonstrate this peacefully tomorrow morning in front of Grafton House. They're meeting in the basement of the Newport Mosque. They are excited. The imam of the mosque is a little worried about their being overheated, and is planning to call

Lieutenant Sam Graves later that evening to make sure everything goes smoothly.

The second group is meeting in a Unitarian Church in Providence. This group isn't radical either. It's called CFFIP, which stands for Citizens For a Fair Immigration Policy. There are lots of birders in this organization. The group's views will be familiar to any reader of the *New York Times* editorial page. Their goal is to motivate like-minded people to press harder for immigration reform. Not really a bad goal. They are relaxed and drinking herbal tea. The sister of the Mayor of Newport is part of this group. If she doesn't forget, she will call the Mayor after the meeting.

Third, we have a small group of Hispanic immigrants, perhaps 25 in all, meeting at the Iglesia de Dios in Newport. The Iglesia de Dios is an evangelical church. Most but not all of this group are legal residents, but some are not. (They prefer the term "undocumented.") They are heatedly arguing about whether the undocumented parishioners should attend the demonstration. One of the parishioners of the Iglesia is a cousin of Sam Graves' wife, and has told her about the group's plans.

Finally, we have SNARL, which stands for Systematic National Anarchist Revolutionary League. They are certainly radical, to put it mildly. Not as radical as George Rakylz, perhaps, but almost as bat-shit crazy. It's not clear what they're in favor of, but it's clear that they don't like the way things are now.

Like George Rakylz, several members of the group have read a book that explains everything. Not the same book that George read, but that kind of book. They have decided to be profoundly opposed to capitalism, which they believe was founded by Woodrow Wilson and is probably responsible for something called free trade, which is why there are no more good jobs in Fall River. They like the idea of blowing things up. They are hoping to get a lot of TV coverage that will show people in Fall River how scary they are.

This is a new group, composed primarily of underemployed college dropouts. This will be their first public outing, so the Executive Committee is meeting in secret in the parking lot behind the Peter Pan Bus stop in Fall River. Which is three blocks from

Lizzie Borden's childhood home. One of the members of the Executive Committee is a confidential informant on the payroll of the Fall River Police Department. We can assume that he will check in with the Department after the SNARL meeting breaks up. That's how you keep getting paid in that line of work.

In short, life goes on in Southern New England in its usual fashion. Now let's take a closer look at Phoebe Snow, and see how she's doing.

CHAPTER 17

Standing alone by a marble column in the Grafton House Commons, Phoebe watched the happy-hour crowd slowly drift away. The crowd had enjoyed watching Donald Pike's meltdown but that was over now, and it was time to get back to work. They are a bit like a beehive, Phoebe thought. I wonder if someone has written a book about bee psychology, she thought. I would like to read that.

As an undergraduate at Wellesley, Phoebe Snow had spent the majority of her time studying math. She had taken other courses to meet Wellesley's Gen Ed requirements, but she didn't find most of them interesting. An exception was a course in Freudian psychology. The professor was an elderly woman whose parents had fled Nazi Germany during the 1930s. Unlike some modern psychologists, Hannah Silber believed that Freud's insights into the mind were still worth studying. In her lectures, she gave particular emphasis to Freud's writings on the unconscious. Now, contemplating her situation, Phoebe remembered those lectures and thought about her own unconscious mind.

On the evening that Phoebe forgot to insert her diaphragm, she had decided that she wanted a baby. She hoped — perhaps naïvely, perhaps not — that if she told Juan Carlos how much she wanted this, he would agree. As we know, she waited until after they had made love before she told Juan Carlos this. He refused and Phoebe told him their affair was over. What are we to make of this? What indeed does Phoebe make of this?

First, let us consider whether Phoebe was naïve to hope that Juan Carlos would leave his wife and marry her. As a matter of historic fact, Juan Carlos had, on many occasions, told Phoebe how much he loved her, wanted to be with her, cared deeply for her, etc. etc. Phoebe knew, of course, that this was lover's talk, not to be taken too seriously. Nevertheless, she had replied in kind. Thus, a kind of understanding had grown up between them that, somehow, some way, some time, Juan Carlos would leave Catherine and marry

Phoebe. In fact, Juan Carlos had often fantasized about doing just that, but had never summoned up the courage to follow through. Not yet anyway.

In her present circumstances, it is not surprising that Phoebe still hopes against hope that Juan Carlos will change his mind. And rescue me, she thinks blackly, disliking the role of damsel in distress. But how will he know that I need him to come for me unless I tell him I'm pregnant, Phoebe asks herself. A good question.

When Juan Carlos had phoned her a week before and asked her to come to New York with him, she had said yes. She was lonely, she missed him, and she wanted to be with him. She wanted to tell him that she was bearing his child. Of course she wanted to. At the same time, she didn't want to tell him she was pregnant. Because, probably, no certainly, he would think that she had done this on purpose. Left her diaphragm in the drawer by her bed, knowing full well that if they made love she might get pregnant.

In the end, pride won out over need. She spent the weekend in New York with Juan Carlos. They went to the opera. Phoebe cried when Dido and Aeneas sang "Nuits d'ivresse et d'extase infinie." And was surprised at how angry she felt when Aeneas deserted Dido and ran away to found Rome. Juan Carlos made love to her three times in their tiny room in the Pod Hotel. It didn't work for her but she didn't tell him that. They ate hot dogs in Central Park, and dinner at an Afghan restaurant in Tribeca. They talked about Juan Carlos' latest commission — another park in Johannesburg — and Phoebe's mission at Grafton House. Juan Carlos told her he knew Andy Eads. "Don't run away with him," Juan Carlos said, "If he's still the same man I knew, he'll take you out on his sailboat and try to seduce you."

"I might like that," Phoebe said. But she didn't mean it. For a brief moment, she considered telling Juan Carlos what had happened. Making a clean breast of it, as her mother would say. But she couldn't do it, and kept her mouth shut. When they parted, she refused to cry until after she had boarded the train for Rhode Island. Then she listened to Purcell on her iPod, and cried as Janet Baker sang Dido's lament: "Remember me, but ah! forget my fate."

Anyway, there it is, Phoebe is pregnant and she can't tell the man who's the father what has happened. She could have an abortion, of course. But she really doesn't want to. She wants a baby. And even if she did have an abortion, she would certainly have to tell Juan Carlos before she did it. It isn't at all clear what she should do.

When she found out that she was pregnant, Phoebe had initially felt very angry. Angry at Juan Carlos, of course, for having…well, among other things, for putting her in an impossible situation and not even knowing he was doing it. But she was angrier with herself. Having an affair with a married man is classic bad judgment. Every woman knows that. Phoebe had certainly known that when she began her affair with Juan Carlos. And she had plowed ahead anyway. So for the first weeks of her pregnancy, she had berated herself daily. Cried, felt depressed, bitten her fingernails — the whole nine yards.

As time passed, though, she began to feel remarkably calm and serene. Her gynecologist had been amused. "That's nature's way of making us happy we're having a baby," she told Phoebe. Her gynecologist was a lesbian, and the mother of two boys. "Anonymous sperm donors are really handy in that regard," Dr. Castro told Phoebe. "There's no need to worry about the father's feelings." Phoebe was not convinced.

It could have been worse, of course. Phoebe had a job, a well-paying job with high-end health insurance. And if she decided to be a single mother, lots of people — at least in Cambridge — would see this is a brave act of personal liberation and self-fulfillment. Her parents wouldn't be blissed out about it, but they would come around eventually. Juan Carlos would definitely have fathered a beautiful child, and her parents would certainly like being grandparents.

But then, what would it be like to be a single mother? The mother part would be fine, but the single part was daunting. Children needed two parents, not just one. Dr. Castro wasn't a single mom. She was a lesbian, but she had a wife. Her two boys had two parents, not one. If Phoebe was going to have a child, she didn't want to do it by herself. Her baby would need a father. Which meant that she needed a husband.

Juan Carlos was the obvious candidate. But he had said no before, and getting him to change his mind might not be possible. She really needed to find out, one way or the other. Or find someone else to be her child's father. Which meant that she probably, no definitely, needed to tell Juan Carlos what had happened. I'll call him after supper, she told herself. Or maybe I should call him in the morning. I'll see.

Phoebe Snow was essentially a cheerful and well-organized young woman. True, she was faced with difficult choices. It is fair to say that she was somewhat daunted by this, but not fundamentally dismayed. And she was fortunate. She had a concrete short-term objective that she could pursue energetically while pondering her longer-term issues. She was at Grafton House to work, not to worry. And she was grateful for that fact.

Phoebe looked around the room. Most of the people who had been in the Commons had left, presumably to go to dinner. A few feet away, Henry Leathwood, the reporter from the *Washington Post*, was standing next to a marble column, nursing a glass of wine. He was looking hopefully at Phoebe.

I wish I were an extrovert, Phoebe thought. Extroverts like talking to people they don't know. If I were an extrovert, I would want to talk to that very interesting man. I would walk over and say, "Hello, Henry," and ask him why he's here. Maybe I could become an extrovert if I worked at it. I could pretend to be one anyway.

Henry Leathwood began to walk toward her and Phoebe smiled at him. Then to her surprise, and relief, she realized that he was looking over her shoulder at someone behind her. She turned around and saw Andy Eads walking toward her. Andy smiled at her warmly and said, "Doctor Snow, Henry. Have you two had supper yet? Come and join me on the veranda and we can talk."

CHAPTER 18

Tobie Shaw had eaten a quick supper in the Grafton House cafeteria: unsweetened iced tea, mesclun salad with canola oil dressing, a small carrot, and a slice of coconut cream pie. She was sort of on a diet, but it varied depending on her mood. Right now, her mood was definitely depressed. And very worried. And right now she was having an anxiety attack. Her heart was pounding, her palms were sweating, and she wanted a cigarette desperately even though she had given up tobacco two months before.

Teresa had read her the riot act before supper. What was she thinking of when she ran that data analysis for Donald Pike? (That he was sort of cute, even though dweeby.) Did she know that she was in danger of being fired? (Yes.) Was she aware of how badly she'd screwed up? (Yes. Well, sort of. What was the big deal anyway?)

So all in all that was a mess, really a big one, which was a pain in the ass. And at a very bad time, too. The whole business with Fat Willie and that nut George was looming over her. And Arturo, the boy from Peru, was already here in Newport and she really wanted to see him.

Arturo was fascinating. He was very handsome: tall, with a good tan and blue eyes. And he was very sure of himself. And she liked the whole Peru thing, like his being an officer in the Peruvian Navy and arriving in Newport on a big sailboat— no, a sailing ship is what they call it. Plus, he was definitely rich, and even though she usually didn't think it mattered, he was Jewish.

So even though it wasn't a good idea to think about it, the idea of marriage had certainly crossed her mind. She is twenty-six, and that worries her. It might not seem old to some people, but if she was honest with herself about it, it felt like she was about to be over the hill. Or go over the hill. Whatever it was her grandmother used to say.

Tobie had left the door to her tiny office open. The air conditioner didn't work very well, and it made a lot of noise. So if it wasn't too hot outside, it was more comfortable to open the window and leave the door open. One nice byproduct of doing this was listening to the evening chamber music concert in the Commons below.

Grafton House had a long tradition of amateurs playing chamber music after supper. Many of the scholars and staff were musicians, and Alma Grafton had set up a fund to cover the cost of instruments and scores. Now, a group was playing something that Tobie decided was probably Brahms. (It was indeed Brahms, the Piano Trio No. 1 in B Major. The revised version, which Brahms rewrote thirty-five years after writing the first version.) Tobie knew it was probably Brahms because her parents loved chamber music, and played it continually— well, a lot of the time anyway — on their built-in wireless high fidelity music system. And this piece fit Tobie's mood precisely. It was both romantic and slightly overwrought.

In an effort to avoid the problem of Fat Willie and George the nut, Tobie had turned her iPhone off and hidden it in a desk drawer. Now, with a doomed feeling, she took the phone out of the drawer and turned it on. There were lots of messages and missed calls, which was to be expected: the phone had been off for hours. Most of the messages were irrelevant, but sure enough Fat Willie and George whosis had both called and left messages. And called back, over and over again. What they wanted was the same thing. They were both in Newport, although neither of them seemed to know the other one was in Newport too, and they both needed a place to spend the night, and they wanted Tobie to provide it. Which she was definitely not going to do.

Which of course raised the obvious question: what was she going to do instead? Tobie thought about this. Nothing obvious presented itself. She was already much more involved with Willie and George than she wanted to be. Waiting for inspiration to strike, Tobie began to thumb through the contents of her inbox.

There were lots of internal memos from Teresa and Andy and others about hideously boring things that were happening, or had happened, or were going to happen at Grafton House. Boring, boring, boring. And then, suddenly, something not boring. A flyer from the

Newport Police — no, two flyers from the Newport Police. Wanted posters for George T. Rakylz and Wilford "Fat Willie" Thomas. And a phone number to call. "Contact Lieutenant Samuel Graves" the flyers said, if you had any information about the two men.

That's what I can do, Tobie thought. I can call the police and tell them that Willie and George are here in Newport, and they can arrest them.

But if I do, Tobie thought, what will happen to me then? But if I don't, and I give them a place to stay, then I'll be in even worse trouble. The best thing I can do is squeal on them. Tell the cops, Willie is my ex and George is his crazy buddy and I want nothing to do with them. In a surge of adrenalin, she picked up the office phone and dialed the Newport Police. Below, in the Commons, the piano trio lurched enthusiastically into the agitated second movement of Brahms' Piano Trio No. 1 in B major, the Scherzo.

*****

George Rakylz had not intended to visit the Norman Bird Sanctuary. He had parked his stolen bicycle by the entrance to the bathhouse at Second Beach. He had taken a much-needed shower in the outdoor showers overlooking the beach, and had shaved and put on a fresh pair of socks. But when he came back to get his bicycle, it had disappeared. He felt indignant, even though it really wasn't his bike. And it put a crimp in his plans.

He had originally intended to ride the bike to Grafton House, where he assumed that Tobie Shaw would give him a place to stay. But Tobie had fallen down on the job. He had called her and called her and she hadn't responded. It was hurtful to think it, but it seemed like she just didn't want to help him. Maybe she had guessed that he was planning to use Grafton House as a demonstration project.

Destroying the fat intellectual whores at Grafton House was going to be one of the seminal events that were going to inspire other idealistic young people to join The Program. But first he had to get into Grafton House, and Tobie was how he had planned to do it.

I need to figure this out, George decided. At the front of the bathhouse, a beat-up, khaki-colored pickup truck was idling while its driver stood by the door smoking a cigarette. He was an old man, and he smiled at George. "Are you going back to town, sir?" George asked.

"Which town?" the old man replied.

"Newport."

"We're in Middletown," the old man said. "That's town to me. But yes, I'm going to Newport. Eventually. I got to take this stuff to the Bird Sanctuary first. And then I got to go to Newport. If you want a ride, you can come right along in the back of the truck." He pointed to the back of the truck, which contained a number of black plastic bags bulging with something.

"Thank you, sir," George said, and got in the back of the pickup. He noticed a peculiar smell coming from the bags and then a trickle of dark liquid slowly seeping towards his trouser legs across the bed of the truck. He decided to ignore it. After a few minutes, the old man climbed into the truck cabin and drove off. It was uncomfortably bumpy in the back of the truck. And George noticed that the truck motor sounded really odd. It would roar for a moment, and then subside, and the exhaust pipe was spouting smoke. Dark, nasty smoke.

Eventually, the truck arrived at the Bird Sanctuary offices and stopped. The driver unloaded the plastic bags and took them inside. But when he finally emerged and tried to start the truck, it wouldn't start. "I should have kept the damn thing running. Got to call my nephew," the old man said. " He can fix the damn thing. If you want to wait, he'll probably give you a ride to Newport."

"I'll walk down to the main road and see if I can catch a ride from someone," George said. "Which way do I go?" And off he went.

But cars willing to pick up hitchhikers proved elusive. Jack Chrysler and Anettka Gardiner's Mini Cooper roared by George, as did Winifred Cooper's elderly yellow school bus. And both vehicles deposited quantities of Rhode Island dust on George's person. Some of the dust had joined forces with the dark liquid from the plastic bags and formed a curious crust on George's trousers.

After a long walk, George found himself on Purgatory Road, across from St. George's School. He stopped, put his backpack down, and sat down on the side of the road. The sun was going down, and everything was deathly quiet. Then he heard a rumbling noise. Looking back down Purgatory Road toward Second Beach he saw a bus heading up the hill in his direction. He stood up, waved frantically, and magically the bus slowed, and then stopped for him. "Newport Visitors Center" the sign on the front of the bus said. George got on, sat down, and relaxed as the bus resumed speed and headed toward Newport.

*****

Fat Willie Thomas was still sitting in back of the Stop and Shop store on Bellevue Avenue. He had worked his way through one six-pack of Bud Light and had started on a second one. He was feeling very sorry for himself. He wanted to go home and be with his Mama, but he knew that the police would definitely be watching his Mama's house in Providence. So he couldn't go there. And Tobie Shaw, who was supposed to be his girl, was refusing to answer her phone.

Fat Willie was not stupid. He knew that Tobie, and girls like her, thought he was an ideal way to explore dangerous waters without really risking too much. They liked his being African-American. They liked his being a little bit of a criminal. Not too much of a criminal though. And after some messing around with him, they inevitably moved on to someone more suitable, who would be workable during the long haul of life. Fat Willie was philosophical about it. Girls like Tobie were like streetcars: wait ten minutes and another one would come along. Still, it hurt Fat Willie's feelings that Tobie was giving him the cold shoulder in his hour of need. I'll call her again, he thought, and took out his cellphone.

*****

Lieutenant Sam Graves was tidying up his desk and preparing to go home for the evening when Tobie's call came in. "Hey Sam," the cop on the phone desk called out, "There's a woman wants to talk to you about the guys from Cambridge — the ones on the wanted posters. The caller ID says the call's from Grafton House."

"Hello," Sam said into the telephone. "I'm Lieutenant Graves. How can I help you?"

"I know the guys you're looking for," Tobie said. "Wilford Thomas, and George whatshisname. Rakylz. Well, I know Willie, I'm just an acquaintance of Rakylz. And they're here in Newport. I know that, too." Her voice trembled. It was obvious that she was scared.

"May I have your name, Miss?" Sam asked.

"Do you have to know it?"

"I'm afraid we do," Sam said. "It's a formality, but it works out better that way."

"OK," Tobie said. "I might as well go for broke on this. My name is Shaw, S.H.A.W., first name Tobie, T.O.B.I.E. I work at Grafton House and Willie used to be my boyfriend. Back in Cambridge. I don't know George very well. I went out with him a couple of times a year ago. He's Willie's friend, not mine."

"I see," Sam said. "And they're in Newport now?"

"Yeah," Tobie said. "They're both in Newport. I don't know if they know the other one's here or not. But they left messages on my cell. They want a place to crash, and they think I'm going to give it to them. And I'm not. No way. I'm sorry about Willie, but that guy George is nuts. Really nuts, I mean it."

"I understand," Sam said. "You were right to call me. I can help you. Now I want you to tell me exactly what they say in their messages. That's very important. And then I'll tell you what we're going to do next. You're going to be OK. Just stay calm, and we'll work this thing out together."

CHAPTER 19

Henry Leathwood's career in the newspaper business began on March 15, 1991, at 0600 hours in Kuwait City, Kuwait on the Arabian Peninsula. Henry was eighteen at the time.

After graduating from high school at the top of his class (in Berlin, Oklahoma where his father was a school teacher and his mother worked as a secretary in a law firm), Henry went east to Tufts University. He was smart and poor and the university gave him a generous scholarship. And a large loan. And a dishwashing job in the university cafeteria. But the transition from a small Oklahoma high school to college was difficult, and Henry's grades were dismal. At the end of his freshman year, the university withdrew his scholarship and suggested that he take a year or two off. "To mature." So at age eighteen, Henry enlisted in the U.S. Army. He was just in time for Operation Desert Storm, a.k.a. the first Gulf War, the good one.

Wars are curious phenomena. On the one hand, they are scary, fearsome, disorienting events. On the other, they are exciting and interesting events. If they're not frightened out of their minds, some people actually get a certain amount of enjoyment out of wars. This is especially true of young men, whose testosterone levels are high, and whose brains are still only partially mature. And in the case of the Gulf War, there was a lot to interest a young man like Henry. Because Henry had a year of college, and could type, he managed to secure a cushy job as the Battalion Sergeant Major's clerk. This meant that Henry got a ringside view of the war without being shot at or having to fire a single shot himself.

It was an interesting war. U.S. air and ground forces were devastatingly effective in destroying the Iraqi invaders. Spectacularly successful. It was a great relief to the men inside Battalion Headquarters (and to TV viewers here at home) with unpleasant memories of Vietnam, because we were definitely winning, and the enemy was fleeing in disarray. Inside Battalion headquarters, everyone was excited about how successful we were, and about the delightful feeling of clearly winning a war.

But aside from the daily drama of the war's progress, there was lots more for Henry to see. Saddam Hussein's troops had made a terrible mess of Kuwait City, and that was interesting to look at. Scary but interesting. The coalition forces were interesting, too. Brits, Canadians, and soldiers from various Arab countries. ("Coalition forces" was a term of art intended to persuade the Arab world that the international community really was in favor of kicking Saddam Hussein out of Kuwait. It was also a fig leaf intended to disguise the fact that the U.S. was running the show. And paying for most of it, too. I don't think many people were fooled.)

And the Arabs were interesting. Very interesting. Because they were a foreign culture, very different from the cultures Henry had experienced. He had spent the first seventeen years of his life in a small Oklahoma town. A little boring, but very familiar. Then he spent nine months in a Boston suburb, surrounded by affluent New Englanders and feeling like a fish out of water. Then he spent two months in Fort Dix, NJ being yelled at in basic training for being a clueless college boy.

None of this, well maybe Tufts, had prepared him for the Arabian Peninsula. Arabs were different. They spoke a different language, the women wore different clothes, the food tasted different. And the rules the Arabs played by were very different. It was clear that the Kuwaitis didn't much like Americans, even though Americans had rescued them from the Iraqis. Vendors in markets routinely cheated American buyers. Passersby shook their fists at Americans in jeeps. That sort of thing.

Anyway, on this particular March morning, Henry was sitting at his desk in a large trailer and drinking coffee (a recently acquired taste). Then a large man wearing Staff Sergeant chevrons came in and sat down opposite Henry. "I'm with *Stars and Stripes*," the man said, "and I need a gofer."

"I know what *Stars and Stripes* is," Henry said, "but what's a gofer?"

"A gofer is somebody who runs errands for busy men like me," the man said, "and I'm told that you might make a good one. The main requirements are that you can type and spell, and that you do what I tell you to do so I can get my work done. If you're interested in the newspaper business, it's a real opportunity. I'm Tony Donato, and I've got a piece in today's issue of the paper."

And that, more or less, was that. Henry took the job with Sergeant Donato and did well. Tony Donato was happy, and Henry learned how reporters do their jobs. In his spare time, he began writing stories about American soldiers risking their lives in a very strange and foreign country. They were very good, and after a few months some of them were published in *Stars and Stripes*.

After that, Henry's progress in the newspaper business was slow but steady. When he returned to Tufts, he became an editor with the *Tufts Daily*, the student newspaper, and a stringer for the *Boston Globe*. On graduating from Tufts, he returned to Oklahoma and worked on his hometown paper, the *Berlin Advertiser*. By the age of twenty-seven, he had worked his way up to the Metro section of the *Washington Post*, covering county council meetings in the DC suburbs.

Then he got a big break. A college friend told him about a Federal prosecutor who was hanging out with drug pushers in his spare time. And whose law enforcement buddies had cut him a break — let him go with a wink and a nod —when they raided a crack house and found him inside, drunk, but (they said later) not actually smoking crack. Henry wrote the story. It was a big story, and it was well written, and it got a lot of attention on the nightly TV news programs. Henry was interviewed on CNN and Fox News and the PBS News Hour. All of this pleased the *Post*'s management. And Henry got promoted. More big stories led to more promotions. And by the time Henry was thirty, he was one of the reporters covering the Congress. Which is how Henry became interested in immigration.

Along the way, Henry also got married. Quite happily, he thought. For eight years. Whereupon his wife, Amelia, fell in love with a dashing pediatrician and left Henry. In the lurch. "You're just too normal, Henry," Amelia said in explanation. "You aren't interested in anything exciting. I'm bored, and I need more out of life. Armando is exciting." (Armando favored the hard-to-maintain "two-day-old beard" look. Young mothers found him irresistible, largely because they were bored. Amelia was not a young mother yet, but she liked the idea of having Armando's baby.)

Amelia is now history, and after eighteen months Henry is beginning to recover his equilibrium. He is here at Grafton House as part of a six month sabbatical. He's writing a book on some of the lesser-known aspects of the immigration system. And he's enjoying taking time off from daily deadlines. He and Andy Eads like each other, and Andy's given him a nice room in the Grafton House annex. And he has begun thinking about women again. The woman from Harvard's administrative office, Dr. Snow, had very graceful hands. And she didn't wear a wedding ring. (Good reporters notice things like that.) Which didn't necessarily mean she didn't have a boyfriend. But if she didn't, she looked like someone he would like to know better.

CHAPTER 20

"This is so beautiful," Phoebe said to Andy Eads and Henry Leathwood. They were eating their supper outside in the late summer sunlight on an enormous verandah constructed of pink marble. The view of Narragansett Bay was equally spectacular. The sky was a soft blue – Newport blue — dotted with small white clouds. The ocean was a darker blue, dotted with the stark white sails of a small fleet of sailboats. Andy Eads sat across from her, and Henry Leathwood sat next to him. Both men beamed at her as she ate her salad. "This is very good," she said. "Especially the tomatoes. They have a wonderful taste. It's hard to find tomatoes that taste this good."

Both men nodded emphatically. "I live in Georgetown in Washington," Henry Leathwood said. "We've got a decent supermarket, Safeway. They get good tomatoes now and then, but it's rare. And there's a farmer's market nearby, but I never get to it. I hear that Whole Foods may be opening a store near my house; that would be a great improvement."

"We have a small farmer's market here in Newport on Wednesdays, and there's another in Middletown on Saturdays," Andy Eads said. "Our cook usually buys things there. And we belong to a food-buying cooperative that partners with an organic farm in Middletown. We get a regular weekly shipment of produce from the co-op. Not too expensive, and very good quality." He smiled at Phoebe. The provenance of the neighborhood tomato supply was apparently a subject of considerable interest to both men.

"You're so lucky to live here," Phoebe said to Andy Eads. "It's so peaceful."

Andy looked amused. "Well, peaceful sometimes, anyway. As you can see from the dustup in the Commons, we have our conflicts." He paused for a second and then said, "I'm sure you're interested in the complaint that some of our staff have filed. Alleging that we're favoring foreign students over U.S. citizens. We're not, as far as I know, but nothing's perfect. I've asked Dexter Slate, who runs our admin office, to review our personnel records to make sure that we're not doing that inadvertently. I suspect that any differences are the result of our paying the travel expenses of foreign students. And the substantial legal fees that seem to accompany any dealings with Homeland Security. When we get together later this week, we can bring Dexter in to tell us what he's found. And of course you should feel free to talk to anyone you want to about this, particularly the people who signed the complaint."

"Thank you," Phoebe said. "I appreciate your being so frank. That's not the only reason I'm here, but it was definitely an issue I wanted to look into."

"Do you know much about immigration?" Henry Leathwood asked Phoebe.

"I don't really," Phoebe said. "My mother's English, and I was born in London, but my Dad's from Minnesota so I'm a U.S. citizen. Actually, I've got a British passport, too. It's kind of handy if you want to travel in the EU. I went to grad school in the UK, and I used to visit the continent on breaks, and work as a waitress. I wasn't any good at it, but it brought in some cash for my trips. I guess immigration's not that simple for most people."

"I think you'll enjoy the conference," Henry said. "And I really hope you'll find time to attend the session I'm speaking at. I'm talking about a story I wrote about what I call The Pathway to Permanent Residence. And that's directly related to the situation here in Grafton House that we were just talking about. U.S. immigration law provides a built-in preferential pathway by which foreign students come to the United States, receive preferential consideration in being hired as temporary workers, and then are funneled into admission as legal permanent residents. In other words, we've provided a shortcut to a green card — permanent legal residence in the U.S. — for foreign students. It's a fascinating process."

"Henry thinks it's a bad idea," Andy said. "He likes to quote Milton Friedman. Friedman called the temporary worker program Henry's talking about a 'corporate subsidy.'"

"Friedman meant that the companies that hire temporary foreign workers pay them lower wages than they pay domestic workers," Henry said. "So it's a subsidy to the companies."

"That's interesting," Phoebe said. "I'm looking forward to your lecture." Henry looked pleased, and both men smiled benevolently at her.

One of the pleasanter aspects of life for pretty women is the unabashed attention men of all ages pay to them. This is, of course, offset by the fact that men are reluctant to take pretty women seriously. Phoebe had long been accustomed to the admiration of the male sex, but it was still enjoyable and good for her self-confidence. Particularly since she found both men charming: Andy the distinguished scholar, and Henry the energetic newspaperman.

And it sometimes allowed her to use another aspect of the male psyche to her advantage. Men love to explain complicated things to women — especially pretty women — sometimes telling them more about penguins than they really want to know. We don't know why this is so. But if a woman really wants to know more about something, this can be a golden opportunity. Phoebe was not particularly interested in the intricacies of the immigration system — or the Grafton House tomato supply for that matter — but she did want to know more about Grafton House itself.

Based on her studies at the Harvard Business School, Melanie Ferguson, Phoebe's boss, had developed detailed guidelines for evaluating Harvard's external research institutions. Phoebe had followed these guidelines before at two other research centers, and had brought a copy with her to Grafton House. Now, she mentally turned to page one of the guidelines, entitled "Entrance Conference With Center Director", and decided not to wait for a formal meeting with Andy. She put down her salad fork, wiped her lips with her napkin and addressed herself to Andy Eads.

"I've read the Grafton House annual report," Phoebe said, "so I've got a general idea of what you do here, and what the Center's about. But it would be really helpful if you would tell me yourself what you're trying to do." She gazed respectfully at Andy.

Andy looked over at Henry Leathwood and grimaced slightly. "I'm afraid Henry's heard me on this subject a dozen times," Andy said.

"No, no," Henry said, "Go ahead. You're very interesting. Although I don't always agree with your optimism."

"Well," Andy said, "here's what I think we're trying to do at Grafton House. Immigration is certainly the focus of our work here. But what we're trying to do — what I'm trying to do anyway — is broader than that." He paused and sipped his iced tea. "What I want us to do is to develop a new model for research on public policy issues. Or maybe an old-fashioned model, depending on your point of view. There's been a huge growth in public policy research in recent years. Research centers have sprung up all over the country. Almost every university has a school of public policy. It's   probably too much of a good thing. A lot of the research isn't very good. But that's not the problem that's concerning me. What I think needs fixing is the partisan nature of the research. It reflects the increasingly partisan character of national debate. Partisanship is a major reason Congress hasn't made needed changes in immigration policy."

"Come on, Andy," Henry said. "It's much more than that. Most Americans aren't going to vote for politicians who support 'reforms' that increase the labor supply and make it harder to find work."

"You're interrupting, Henry. And oversimplifying, too," Andy said. He turned toward Phoebe. "I don't mean that it's improper to have partisan views," he continued. "I happen to have what some people would describe as liberal views about immigration policy. Jack Chrysler, one of our two deputies, is certainly a liberal — one sort of liberal anyway. Jack says I'm a conservative, probably because I think we need to place some restrictions on immigration."

"Jack has never met an immigrant — legal or illegal — that he didn't like," Henry said with a derisory snort.

Andy paused and sipped his iced tea. Then he said, "On the other hand, we have our other deputy, Suleiman Khan. Suleiman is probably, no definitely, the most eminent scholar here at Grafton House. Most people would call Suleiman a conservative. He thinks the Federal government needs to take stronger measures to prevent illegal immigration. He also thinks we need to import more foreign high tech workers with advanced degrees — like the program Henry was just talking about— and also import temporary workers who'll perform low-skill jobs. That's a legitimate viewpoint, though I don't agree with it. We do policy research so we can improve our policies. That inevitably reflects people's values."

"Suleiman's values are Wall Street's values," Henry said.

"Be quiet, Henry," Andy said. "Wait until I finish. What I'm getting at is that facts are different from values, and that policy analysts have to separate the two as much as possible. As Pat Moynihan once said, 'People are entitled to their own opinions, but not to their own facts.'"

Henry Leathwood smiled. "She's never heard of Pat Moynihan, Andy. You need to tell her who he was."

"I'm sorry, Dr. Eads, but he's right," Phoebe said. "I'm a mathematician by training. I know a lot about math, but I'm afraid there are huge gaps in my education."

"Pat Moynihan was a great man," Andy said. "He was a Senator from New York for many years, but he was much more than a Senator. He grew up a poor kid in New York City — he was white but he went to high school in Harlem. Worked on the docks as a longshoreman, served in World War II and then went to City College."

"He graduated from Tufts, though," Henry interjected. "I know because I went to Tufts, too. And he was originally from Oklahoma. Which is where I'm from."

"And taught at Harvard," Andy continued. "And was Ambassador to India. And worked for President Kennedy on the poverty program. And a lot more. But he's a perfect example of what I'm talking about. Moynihan was a liberal. No question about that. But he was also a practical man. He knew that policy analysis is supposed to produce political action. And he understood that political action in a democracy involves compromise. People have to work together. And Pat was willing to work with anyone to achieve improvements in policy."

"What Andy's talking about is Moynihan's work for President Nixon," Henry said.

"Precisely," Andy said. "Moynihan had worked for President Kennedy and President Johnson. He was a liberal, and a Democrat. But when Nixon was elected, he joined the White House staff as an advisor on domestic policy. Because he thought he could make a difference. And he did. He was one of the first people in government to raise the issue of global warming — they called it the greenhouse effect in those days."

"He wasn't perfect, though, Andy," Henry said. "He wrote that memo to Nixon about benign neglect — he suggested we could damp down racial tension by talking less about our race problems."

"I think that's a bum rap, Henry. Moynihan was dealing with the Nixon Administration. Spiro Agnew was spouting off in ways that were inflaming racial tensions. Moynihan was trying to operate in the real world. Maybe that memo was a mistake, but he wasn't standing aloof and criticizing. He was trying to make a difference. And that's what I want us to do here," he said to Phoebe. "I know we have our policy differences. But if we can separate out our policy differences from our disagreement on facts, and if we can tamp down the partisan rhetoric, we have a shot at getting something useful done. What I want us to do here at Grafton House is get policy analysts to design policy options through a consensus process. I want analysts on the left and on the right to identify points on which they can agree. That way we can move forward toward making policy changes that work."

Phoebe had been listening intently and wishing she had brought her notebook. She liked both men, and she thought what they were saying made sense. But Andy Eads was perhaps overly optimistic about the possibility of compromise. He clearly believed in what he was saying, but it seemed oddly old-fashioned. And a far cry from the political opinions of her friends in Cambridge — uncompromising liberals all of them, for whom compromise was a dirty word.

"Thank you, Dr. Eads. I admire your goals," she said. "I think I should call it a day, now. I'll work on a plan for my stay here this evening, and perhaps Dexter and I can discuss it tomorrow. This is certainly one of the most interesting research centers that I've worked with. I really enjoyed talking with both of you."

"Good night, Dr. Snow," Andy said. "I'll tell Dexter you'll be seeing him tomorrow."

"Good night, Phoebe," Henry said. "I enjoyed talking to you too. And I hope to see you tomorrow."

"See you tomorrow," Phoebe said. "Definitely."

What an interesting man, Phoebe thought.

CHAPTER 21

Jack Chrysler had cunningly parked his Mini Cooper in what seemed to be a secluded spot at the far end of a gravel access road that led to the middle of the Norman Bird Sanctuary. In the sky, the July sun was beginning its long slide into the west, but there was still plenty of sunshine on Jack's forehead. I should have put on some sunscreen, he told himself again. He was hot and sweaty, and his right arm was trapped behind Anettka Gardiner's back against the passenger seat of the Mini Cooper. And his arm hurt.

When Jack had initially pulled Anettka toward him in order to kiss her, his right arm had naturally moved around her body. Anettka had wrapped her left arm tightly around Jack's neck. They had kissed for some moments. After a bit, Anettka had tilted her seat to a 45-degree angle and relaxed against it. And of course against Jack's right arm.

Traditionally, newly minted lovers must overcome these small tests of romantic fervor. Jack was very happy to have finally managed to kiss Anettka, and very pleased that she was in his arms. But now his right arm was aching. Jerking it out from behind Anettka's back seemed like a dubious idea. On the other hand, leaving it there much longer seemed unappealing. Then his dilemma was resolved.

"Look!" Anettka said. Her body suddenly jerked forward as her seat returned to the upright position. She pushed Jack away with surprising force. "Up there, on the hill!" She pointed her long lovely index finger towards the hill. The silver polish on the nail gleamed in the sunlight. Jack looked in that direction and saw what appeared to be a group of small children. Small girls to be exact, all wearing brown uniforms and white straw hats, and peering down at Jack and Anettka through binoculars. In the middle of the girls, a tall woman, also wearing a brown uniform, held a large pair of field glasses up to her eyes. She was also peering intently at Jack and Anettka.

"That's my husband's first cousin," Anettka said. "Cousin Winifred."

"Cousin Winifred," Jack said ruminatively. "I guess that's not good. What should we do now?"

"I don't know," Anettka said. "Do you have any binoculars in the car?"

"Yes," Jack said. "In the glove compartment."

With a sudden swoop, Anettka opened the glove compartment, yanked out the field glasses and put them up to her face. She looked up at Winifred and the Brownies, and waved vigorously. "Pooh!" She shouted. "It's Annie! Come down!"

"What are you doing?" Jack asked.

"I'm not sure," Anettka said. "I think I'm going to try to brazen it out. Say we were taking a break from the conference, and you suggested a drive to the bird sanctuary."

"Jesus," Jack said. "That's pretty imaginative. Especially if she's been looking at us very long."

"In for a penny, in for a pound, as the Brits say. Maybe she didn't see us until just now."

"Maybe cows have wings, too," Jack said.

"Do you have a better idea?" Anettka said. "If not, I suggest you keep quiet and try not to say anything stupid." She calmly reached in her purse, removed a compact and a lipstick, and applied the lipstick. Then she combed her hair.

The two of them sat in silence as Winifred Gardiner slowly descended the hill towards their car. Behind her, the little girls had formed a circle and were holding hands. When Winifred turned and waved at them, they obediently sat down on the ground.

"Hullo, Annie," Winifred said when she reached their car. She came to a stop next to Anettka's side of the car, and smiled at both of them in what Jack hoped was a friendly fashion.

"Hello, Pooh," Anettka said. "This is my boss at Grafton House, Dr. John Chrysler. We're playing hooky from the Grafton House Summer Conference. Jack, this is Paul's cousin Winifred. Winifred Gardiner."

"Call me Pooh," Winifred said, "Everyone does." Jack started to get out of the convertible and stand up, but Winifred stopped him. "No, no," she said. "Stay where you are. No need to get out." She walked around to Jack's side of the car and grasped his hand.

"How do you do," Winfred and Jack said to each other as they shook hands. Then Winifred turned and pointed up the hill. "That's my Brownie troop," she said proudly. "Most of the girls are in my Sunday School class at St. Thomas' Church. We're here to look at birds. 'Watching wildlife' we call it."

"Pooh works for the Rhode Island legislature," Anettka said. "She's their budget expert."

"Annie's exaggerating," Winifred said. "I'm a budget analyst. During the week, that is. Right now I'm being a Girl Scout leader, which is more fun."

"I was a Girl Guide in Pakistan," Anettka said. "My mother was going through an Anglophile phase. I enjoyed it. It was very liberating."

"Exactly," Winifred said. "I'm convinced of that. Girls need to learn early that they're just as able as boys. The dominant culture tells us we're not as able. Over and over again. I don't — well I try not to blame anyone for that. It's built into the culture. But I want to do my bit to try to change the culture."

"I agree completely. I'm quite sure that being a Girl Guide taught me things that girls don't usually learn in Pakistan. That I didn't have to be subservient to a paternalistic culture is probably the main thing. Which helped me a lot later on."

"Yes," Winifred said. "I know." Jack noticed that Winifred's cheeks were pinkish. Maybe she's sunburned, Jack thought. But it looks like she's blushing. He looked at Anettka. She looked calm, but he noticed that her hands were tightly gripping the handles of her purse. Perhaps I had better say something.

"I love this place," he said. "When my head's messed up, I find that the bird sanctuary clears my mind."

"Oh, so do I," Winifred said. She paused. "So do I," she said again. She looked intently at Jack. "You're one of the researchers at Grafton House, then? Did you come from Harvard?"

"No," Jack said. "I went to Loyola University in Chicago, and then to Boston College for graduate work. I taught at the University of Chicago until I came to Grafton House. I was originally in the priesthood, the Jesuits, but I left the priesthood seventeen years ago." It had been Jack's experience that this information usually fascinated women. He hoped that it might divert Winifred from the subject of him and Anettka.

"Oh," Pooh said. "I dated a man once who turned out to be a Catholic priest. I only found out about it because we were having coffee at his apartment and I needed a Kleenex. He said he had some in his bedroom, and when I was looking for the Kleenex box, I saw his prayer book by his bedside. I asked him about it, and it all came out. It was just as well; we really weren't suited for each other. He wasn't a Jesuit though. I forget exactly what he was."

Winifred turned and looked up the hill towards the Brownie troop. "I should probably get back to my girls," she said. "It was awfully nice to run into you, Annie, and to meet your friend too." She leaned over and kissed Anettka on the cheek. Then she smiled at Jack. "I hope your conference goes well. I know some of our parishioners at St. Thomas are planning to be there."

"We'd be happy to have you come to the conference if it interests you," Jack said. "Just call Grafton House and mention my name, Jack Chrysler, or Anettka's, and that'll do the trick."

"Thank you," Pooh said.

"Bye, Pooh," Anettka said.

"Bye bye, Annie," Pooh said. And she walked back up the hill to the Brownies.

Jack and Anettka sat in silence for a few moments. When Pooh and her troop had disappeared, Jack said, "I guess we should go now." He moved toward Anettka as if to kiss her and she pushed him away. "Not now," she said. "I need to think. Think a lot."

"OK," Jack said, and he turned the Mini Cooper around and headed back to the main road. As they drove out, they passed a young man standing by the side of the gravel road. He carried a large backpack and had a crew cut. He waved half-heartedly at them as they came closer, obviously hoping for a ride. "I don't like that boy's looks," Anettka said. "He looks peculiar to me. Don't stop." They drove by the young man without stopping. In their wake, a cloud of dust enveloped the young man, causing him to sneeze.

"Shit!" George Rakylz said, and then sneezed again, "Bastards!" His nose began to drip, and he wiped it with the sleeve of his T-shirt. Then he heard an odd grinding noise. Turning his head towards the sound, he saw an ancient yellow school bus bearing down upon him. The bus slowed as it came nearer, and George heard a cheering noise from the little girls inside.

For a moment George thought the bus would stop and pick him up. Then the bus sped up, roaring past him and leaving an enormous cloud of dust in its wake. He scrambled away from the dust cloud and in the process fell down, landing in the ditch beside the road. His elbow hurt. "No one gives a shit about other people," George thought.

CHAPTER 22

Seated at the controls of a small yellow school bus belonging to St. Thomas' Church, Winifred Gardiner drove her Brownie troop back to Newport and thought about Anettka Gardiner and her friend from Grafton House, Dr. Chrysler. It's interesting that he's a former Catholic priest, Winifred thought. There is something peculiar about men who go into that line of work. Not homosexual exactly — pretty obviously not in this man's case. Unless he was experimenting with girls to see if he liked them, of course. No, it was more of a witch doctor sort of thing.

Not to say that the Episcopal Church didn't have its own share of peculiar people. Though they tended to be somewhat more conventional. There had been Mr. Babcock for example. He had come to St. Thomas' highly recommended, and indeed he had been a very popular minister for several years. But then it became public knowledge that he was intimately involved with the wife of a vestryman. "We fell in love," Emily had told Winifred after the affair came to light and the minister resigned. "We fell in love, Pooh," she said, "and somehow it all seemed OK until Percy found out and threatened to kill Medford." Percy was Emily's husband. Medford was Mr. Babcock's Christian name. Well, not really his Christian name, since there aren't any saints named Medford. According to Emily, Medford had convinced her that their spiritual health depended on rising above conventional morality. Higher planes of being had been cited. The language of the heart had been invoked. None of this had been sufficient to pacify Emily's husband when he found out about the affair.

That was certainly peculiar enough, even if not as odd as the Catholic priests and all those altar boys. Of course, it was important to remember that Emily herself had started out as a Roman Catholic and only joined the Episcopal Church after the Catholics threw her out for getting divorced from her first husband. Excommunicated her, she said they called it.

Possibly Emily's Catholic upbringing had made her susceptible to Medford's blandishments. That's a good word, Winifred thought, my father liked that word. Papa would have liked "excommunicate" too. Mr. Babcock had wanted the congregation to call him Father, or Father Medford, which may have had some effect on Emily. Some people had called Mr. Babcock Father, but Winifred had always called him Medford. All in all, a disturbing case.

The access road to the center of the Norman Bird Sanctuary was unpaved, and dusty in the July heat, and the school bus left a trail of dark yellow dust behind it as it rolled along. Up ahead on the side of the road, Winifred spotted a man holding his hand out. A hitchhiker, Winifred thought. Should I stop for him? she asked herself, and slowed the bus down a bit. No, not a good idea, she decided, and pressed her foot down on the accelerator. The bus sped up and rolled on past the man. A huge cloud of dust enveloped him. In the back of the school bus, the Brownies shouted merrily.

As far as I'm concerned, Winifred reflected, Anettka's personal life is her own business. She was definitely a change from Paul's first wife, Myrta, who had gone to school with Winifred. Myrta was the sort of woman who wore designer clothes. Stuffy old fashioned ones. Even Castleberry knits, for heaven's sake. And gave dinner parties. Not an outdoors person at all. No interest in sports of any kind. A good mother though. She and Paul had produced four children, all of whom appeared to be successfully launched in the world. Money helps, Winifred reflected, but so does good breeding. Bloodlines count for something.

Still Paul had apparently been dissatisfied with Myrta, or being married to Myrta, or his life in general. Who knows with men? And when he and Myrta had separated and Anettka had appeared on the scene, some people had made snarky references to trophy wives. Certainly, it was true that Anettka was a good bit younger than Paul. To be exact, she was the age of Paul's oldest daughter, Abigail. Winifred knew that for a fact, because she was Abigail's godmother. A very nice christening it had been, too. Paul's father having given the money for the renovation of St. Thomas', the rector, old Dr.

Saunders, had been eager to make it a happy occasion. A much better minister than Mr. Babcock. No Father business with Dr. Saunders.

Myrta and Paul still seemed to be friends, as far as Winifred knew. Probably Myrta had gotten past the sex stage. Some women did, for lots of reasons. Not always voluntarily, of course. But there was no question that Anettka was interested in sex. As had just been demonstrated.

Probably Paul had done what lots of people do, bitten off more than he could chew. He was never in Newport, always flying off to Europe and Hong Kong. And leaving Anettka behind at Grafton House with all those young professors. Like Dr. Chrysler.

The last time Pooh had talked to Paul, he had said he was thinking about giving the old Gardiner house to the Preservation Society, but so far he hadn't done so. So when Paul was in Newport, he stayed there. In his old room, he had told Pooh. It was a big house, and not a good place to live by yourself. Not surprisingly, Anettka stayed at Grafton House when Paul was away.

I would do that too, Winifred told herself. And if a man asked me to go for a drive in his convertible to the bird sanctuary, I wouldn't say no, either. Particularly one who looked like Dr. Chrysler. You have to use your own feeble brain. Cousin Paul will have to take care of himself. My lips are sealed.

They were on Memorial Boulevard by now, proceeding at a stately pace. For no particular reason, Winifred glanced at the rear view mirror. Behind the school bus, a long line of vehicles stretched back into Middletown. I should look in the rear view mirror more often, Winifred thought, and she steered the bus to the side of the road and stopped. Then she put her arm out the window and waved vigorously at the cars backed up behind her. When she did, a long line of cars and trucks sped by them. Goodness, Winifred said to herself, it's like worming a dog.

CHAPTER 23

Tobie Shaw was an impulsive person. She occasionally told herself she ought to do something about it. So far, she hadn't. She decided to think of herself as impetuous. This verbal sleight of hand was soothing, but it didn't really change anything.

She was impulsive, and it got her in trouble. Over and over again. She was pissed off at Ed Moriarty when she tipped off Fat Willie that Ed was planning to deliver some pot to Eliot House. She didn't think about what could happen when she did that. She just had the thought and said it out loud. With the results that we've seen. Ed in the Cambridge mortuary, Fat Willie on the run from the cops, George the nut on the loose in Newport.

Now, crouching down in the back seat of Sam Graves' sky-blue Mustang — his own car, not one of the Newport P.D.'s "unmarked" elderly black-with-black-sidewalls Ford Grand Vics, so you'd have to be a moron not to know it was a cop car —Tobie realized that she had been impulsive again. Why, she asked herself, didn't I just wait and not call the cops? Not done anything?

"Tell me again," Sam said. "What did Willie say exactly? I mean where exactly did he say he was going to wait for you to pick him up?" Sam sounded nervous.

"I told you," Tobie said. "He said he was going to be standing by the loading dock behind the Bellevue Avenue Stop & Shop. Well, he didn't say it was on Bellevue Avenue, but I asked him what he could see from where he was and he said he could see something that looked like a stadium next to the store. So I knew it was this one. This Stop & Shop, I mean. Because of the Casino's tennis courts."

"I don't see him." Sam said. "I don't see anybody."

"Well, he said he'd be here," Tobie said. She was irritated. "If he's not here, it's not my fault."

"Wait a minute," Sam said. "I think it's him. Big guy, shaved head, blue T-shirt. He's coming out from behind a dumpster. Looking around like he's looking for somebody. Yeah, I think it's him all right. Peek out the window and tell me if it's him."

Reluctantly, Tobie got to her knees and peered out the rear window. "Yeah, it's Willie," she said, and crouched back down behind the seat. Oh God, Tobie thought. This is awful. I shouldn't have done this.

"We've got ID," Sam said over the police radio. "Let's move in around the exits now. I want everything closed off. Give me a thumbs up when you're in place."

"This is One, I see him."

"Two here. I see him," a second voice said.

"Three. I see him too."

"OK," Sam said. "I'm gonna give him the announcement." He removed a portable megaphone from the floor of the Mustang, got out of the car and said, in a firm voice amplified by the loudspeaker, "This is the Newport police, Mr. Thomas. Please sit down on the ground and put your hands up over your head. We have the parking lot surrounded. There's no possibility of escape."

Tobie peeked out through the rear window of the Mustang. Fat Willie looked very unhappy, but he seemed resigned to his fate. He slowly sat down on the pavement by the loading dock and raised his hands over his head.

From all sides of the parking lot, policemen came toward Willie with guns drawn. Tobie counted them. Seven in total, plus Sam Graves. She watched as Sam approached Willie and stood next to him.

"Wilford Thomas," Sam said, "I am Lieutenant Sam Graves of the Newport Police Department. You are under arrest in connection with the death of Edward Moriarty in Cambridge, Massachusetts. You have the right ..." And Sam went on to read Fat Willie his Miranda rights.

"She turned me in, didn't she?" Willie said. "Bitch set me up. She's the one got me into this fucking mess to start with. I should have known it. I'm too fucking stupid to live."

Curious shoppers from the Stop & Shop began to appear in the parking lot to see what was going on. Tobie watched from the

Mustang as the police handcuffed Willie and escorted him to a cruiser, Willie was a big man, and he towered over the policemen, but he had a defeated air. His shoulders slumped and he walked as if his feet hurt him. The bystanders watched him closely. Tobie could hear them discussing him. "What did he do?" one woman asked.

Sam Graves stood in the middle of a group of policemen, much like a captain of a basketball team. The group broke up and Sam returned to the Mustang. "Now we go find George Rakylz," he said to Tobie Shaw.

CHAPTER 24

"Do I have to?" Tobie said unhappily.

"You don't have to," Sam said, "but it would be helpful to us if you did. Helpful to me, personally. I'm not sure his picture on the wanted poster looks like him, and it would be helpful if you could identify him. I would definitely appreciate it. And I think it would definitely be worth your while to help us."

Tobie had a sinking feeling. She knew, because Sam had told her, that she was a person of interest to the Cambridge police in their investigation of Ed Moriarty's murder. She knew what that meant. If Willie told the cops that she had told him to rob Ed Moriarty, it was going to cause trouble. So she needed all the friends she could get, particularly on the police force.

When Tobie called Sam Graves earlier in the evening, Sam had immediately driven to Grafton House and collected her. They sat in his Mustang while he coached Tobie on what to say to Willie and George. Then she called each of them on her iPhone. The call to Willie had worked perfectly. She had asked him where he was, he had told her, and she had said she would pick him up in a few minutes. The call to George Rakylz hadn't gone so well.

George, of course, was paranoid, with good reason I hasten to add. He had taken up arms against civil society as we know it, and he saw everyone — well, not everyone but most people — as enemies. Potential enemies anyway, at least until proven otherwise. A critic might have pointed out that these people were also the "people" whom George's Program was going to liberate. George didn't worry about this. The "people" were certainly out there somewhere. By definition.

Anyway, when Tobie called George and asked him where he was, a tiny little voice in the back of his brain told him, "Watch out, Georgie, don't trust this woman any more than you have to." (Georgie was what his mother had called him when he was a kid, and he tended to think of himself as Georgie. Not that he ever told anybody this.)

Where George was, was the Newport Visitor Center, across from the Fire Station. The bus had left him off there, and he had bought a doughnut from a vending machine in the bus waiting room and used the rest room. When Tobie called him, he was actually sitting on the toilet in the men's room. But he didn't tell Tobie this. What he told Tobie was that he was in the men's room at Cardines Field, the baseball field on America's Cup Avenue. Across Marlborough Street from the Fire Station. He had seen the Cardines Field sign while reconnoitering the neighborhood. There was a game going on — the Newport Gulls versus Pawtucket — and it looked like a safe place to be. When you get to the Fire Station, he told Tobie, call me and I'll leave the ballpark and meet you on Marlborough Street. You can pick me up there.

"OK," Tobie said. What else could she have said? Sam had not been pleased, but what was the alternative? Anyway, that was the situation.

"What we'll do," Sam said, "is call him when all of us get to the Visitors Center, and tell him to meet us in the parking lot there. By the RIPTA bus station. That way we won't have to deal with the crowd at the ball game."

And that is what they did. Sam drove his Mustang into the Visitors Center parking lot and parked. A police car parked at the far end of the parking lot. Two more police cars parked on the streets surrounding the parking lot. Then Sam told Tobie to call George.

Unfortunately for Sam's plan, George was sitting inside the bus terminal eating his doughnut when Sam and the police cars arrived. He could see Tobie sitting in the passenger seat of the blue Mustang, and he knew immediately that it was a trap. He didn't panic. He felt a surge of intellectual power. He and the Program would prevail.

He looked around the waiting room and noticed that the cleaning staff had left a large rubber trash container in one corner. It had two wheels and contained a mop and a broom. An orange fluorescent safety harness was draped over the edge of the container. George put on the safety harness, put his backpack in the trash container and briskly wheeled it out of the bus station.

Keeping his head down, he pushed the trash container around the corner of the Visitors Center towards America's Cup Avenue. When he was out of sight of the parking lot, he retrieved his backpack and walked quickly toward the Fire Station.

A block further up Marlborough Street, he came to a bar, filled with young people drinking beer. His cell began to ring, and he turned it off. Then he entered the bar, ordered a beer, and considered his options. Clearly, Tobie Shaw had ceased to be a possible way of getting into Grafton House. Now he needed to find a place to spend the night. Looking around the room, he saw a middle aged woman sitting by herself at the bar. He smiled at her and she smiled back. That looks promising, George thought, and moved down the bar to sit next to her. Up close she looked a little old for his taste, but in good shape otherwise.

"My name's George," George said to the woman. "I'm new in town. Are you from around here?"

The woman smiled. "I'm old in town," she said. "My name's Maureen. I'm CIA — Catholic Irish Alcoholic." She laughed and then examined George closely. "You wouldn't be interested in a temporary waiter job would you?"

"Maybe," George said. "Like when?"

"Like tomorrow? I'm working on a temp assignment over at a big mansion here. It's called Grafton House, and they're having a big dinner tomorrow. And we're short- handed. Good pay if you're interested."

"I'm very interested," George said to Maureen. "I really am. I'm your man. For the job, I mean. Can I buy you a drink?"

Sam and Tobie waited in the parking lot for half an hour. Tobie called George's cell at regular intervals. No success. Then Sam gave up. And told the other police cars to leave. Sam was unhappy but philosophical about this turn of events. He consoled himself with the fact that Willie's arrest had gone well. He drove Tobie Shaw back to Grafton House, made sure she had his cellphone number, and told her to be super careful. Then he returned to the Newport police headquarters on Broadway and addressed himself to the booking of Fat Willie.

Back in Grafton House, Tobie went immediately to her room, showered, and went to bed. She had the feeling that her troubles were just beginning.

CHAPTER 25

Peruvian Naval Ensign Arturo Cisneros-Stern finished his work on the *Marte*'s log and ascended to the deck. He had chosen to stay on board that evening in exchange for a promise of a day's liberty in Newport the following day. He debated whether to call Tobie Shaw, his sometime and hoped-for future girlfriend, and decided to call his uncle Juan Carlos Cisneros-Puglisi first. This was a realistic decision. Girls were usually happy to hear from Arturo whenever he called them. Uncles like Juan Carlos sometimes were less welcoming. And he really did want to see his uncle. He dialed Juan Carlos' home in Cambridge, and on the third ring Juan Carlos answered.

They spoke in Spanish of course. I will not bore you with a literal translation of what was said. In a nutshell, Arturo asked Juan Carlos to come to Newport to see his nephew, and also to admire the Peruvian Navy Training Vessel *Marte*. Juan Carlos, who had been mulling over ways to see Phoebe Snow again, jumped at the chance to go to Newport, and told Arturo he would be delighted.

The WGBH special on agricultural subsidies was long over, and Juan Carlos' wife Catherine was still preparing for her trial the next day. Over the years she had picked up enough Spanish through living with Juan Carlos to understand the conversation he had just finished. "That was your nephew, Arturo?" she asked.

"Yes. His ship's in Newport, and he wants me to come see it. It's a big sailing ship. Arturo said it's a twin-masted brig, which sounds interesting. The Peruvian Navy uses it as a training ship for officers. It's visiting Newport along with a number of other sailing ships. They call them the Tall Ships. Would you like to come to Newport tomorrow with me?" Since Juan Carlos knew that Catherine had an important trial the next day, this was not a serious offer. Still, he felt that saying it satisfied the demands of his conscience.

"No," Catherine said, "I've got a trial tomorrow. You know that."

"Sorry," Juan Carlos said, "I forgot." A lie, of course, but perhaps a minor one in the scheme of things.

Upon reflection, Juan Carlos decided that it would be better to wait until he was in Newport to call Phoebe. That decided, he told Catherine goodnight, went up to bed, brushed his teeth, got into bed and immediately fell asleep.

Arturo, meanwhile, tried several times, and failed, to call Tobie Shaw's cell. (Tobie had turned her cell off and put it in its charging stand.) I'll call her tomorrow, Arturo decided.

CHAPTER 26

By 10:30 p.m., most of the people that we have met in this adventure have gone to bed. Or are going to bed. Or are thinking about it. Phoebe Snow is sleeping soundly in her bed in the Hyacinth Room. She is not dreaming. Oscar, the Grafton House cat, is sleeping at the foot of the bed. Both Phoebe and Oscar are snoring softly. Oscar's contralto blends nicely with Phoebe's soprano.

Tobie Shaw, as we have seen, is also in bed. She was asleep for a few minutes, but is now half-awake. She is possessed by worries that seem much scarier in the dark. Her loquacious (and usually very irritating) roommate, Agnes Chu, is spending the night with Elmer Kip, her fiancé. They are MIT graduate students who help the Grafton House senior staff with computers and statistics. They are in Elmer's bed now, but are not sleeping. I hate being by myself, Tobie thinks. I wish Arturo was here with me. I wouldn't even mind if Agnes changed her mind and didn't spend the night with Elmer, and came back here.

Karim Pandit is still hooked up to the catheter. The room is dark and he's been given a sedative so he's drowsy. But the catheter is uncomfortable and he can't fall asleep. He is thinking about his father.

Karim's father is a devout Muslim, and Suleiman Khan has been lecturing Karim about his filial responsibilities. Among which, according to Dr. Khan, is the need to follow his father's example in religious matters. In other words, Karim is supposed to be a devout Muslim, which he's not. At the very least, he's not supposed to tell his father that he's an atheist. Or even an agnostic.

In fact, Karim has told his father that he's not a believer, and his father wasn't very worried. "I used to feel that way," his father told him, "and I got over it. Just don't go running around telling everybody that you're an atheist. You'll regret it when you change your mind."

Karim admires Dr. Khan. He's also a little afraid of him. Dr. Khan is a very important man, and his good opinion is worth cultivating. And Dr. Khan is a devout Muslim who has strong views about Islam. So Karim hasn't told Dr. Khan that his father actually isn't very worried about his religious views, or lack thereof. I need to please Dr. Khan, Karim thinks. But I'm damned if I'll pretend to believe something I don't. Of course, I may be damned if it's true and I don't believe.

"Time for your temperature," a cheerful voice says, and the lights go on. It's the night nurse, a large man with a bald head, who pats Karim on the shoulder and places a thermometer in his mouth.

Like Phoebe, Juan Carlos is sleeping soundly. Phoebe has long envied Catherine's conjugal right to sleep next to Juan Carlos in their warm connubial bed. In fact, Juan Carlos and Catherine sleep in different beds in separate bedrooms, and have for many years. Juan Carlos likes to get up early in the morning, so he goes to bed early; Catherine stays up late at night working, and sleeps as late as possible. So their schedules don't match. Moreover, Juan Carlos snores loudly, and gets up often in the night to pee. One of the beds in their house is very soft; the other is very hard. Guess which bed belongs to Juan Carlos.

Catherine is still downstairs working. She is aware that Juan Carlos is up to something he shouldn't be. He has been uncharacteristically morose of late. And there was a certain excitement in his voice when he spoke to his nephew, which certainly wasn't caused by Arturo himself. In Catherine's experience, these signs usually signal that Juan Carlos is involved with yet another woman. He is probably planning to see her in Newport, Catherine thinks for a brief dark moment. Then she shoves the unwanted thought out of her consciousness and returns to her work.

Jackie and Edgar are not asleep. Jackie is listening to a new recording of Sondheim's "Follies", and Edgar is playing a violent video game. Jackie is thinking about Phoebe, with whom he shares an addiction to musical comedies. He is wondering how Phoebe is faring in Newport.

Maybe Edgar and I should go to Newport this weekend, Jackie thinks. We could stay at the Chanler House again, and have drinks on the porch. Or we could stay at Castle Hill and have drinks on the lawn there. Cuba Libres would be nice in this weather. He makes a note on the pad of yellow paper he keeps next to his bedside table. (Jackie thinks about work at night when he can't sleep, and writes interesting ideas down on the pad. He usually can't read his notes in the morning, however, because his handwriting is terrible.)

Edgar blows up another alien invader and shouts triumphantly at the video game screen. Edgar is from Peru and has macho tendencies. Jackie loves him dearly anyway. Jackie and Edgar are partners in a small, very profitable Cambridge-based engineering firm that designs robotic probes. They met while working at MIT's Lincoln Laboratory and have been partners for twenty years. (Jackie would prefer to say "lovers" rather than "partners," but if he does it makes Edgar blush.)

Arturo Cisneros-Stern is lying in his bunk on board the *Marte*, the Peruvian Navy Training Ship. He has tried several times to phone Tobie Shaw — without success. But he is young and optimistic and confident that he will eventually be successful. I'll call her again tomorrow, he thinks.

He is pleased that his famous uncle is coming to Newport. That will go over well with the ship's commanding officer. Juan Carlos knows all the people who matter in Lima, Arturo's hometown. As he drifts off to sleep, Arturo has pleasant thoughts about Tobie. She is the only girl he has ever slept with, and he is eagerly looking forward to doing that again. She knows a lot about the world, too, and has interesting things to say about it.

Alex, the Irish beekeeper, is trying to read a mystery novel by Michael Connolly. She doesn't like it very much. She wanted to like the book because Teresa said she liked it. Alex is new at the couples/lovers/long-term relationship business. She asks herself, do happy couples have to have identical tastes in literature? Probably not, she decides, and puts Teresa's book back on the night table next to their bed.

Teresa is still in her office working, and Alex hopes she will come to bed soon. She thinks about texting Teresa and decides that she shouldn't. Then she turns on the radio and is delighted to find a heated panel discussion on WRNI: what should be done about Rhode Island's rapidly growing coyote population? Alex is basically pro-coyote but can see the other side of the issue.

Andy Eads is listening to a radio broadcast from Radio 4 in Amsterdam. They are playing a recording of a live performance by the Netherlands Opera of Tchaikovsky's *Eugene Onegin* in Amsterdam's outdoor music theater. The opera has just begun and Tatyana and Onegin have just met. Andy is not going to bed until the end of Act I.

Suleiman Khan is rehearsing the remarks he plans to make at the first session of tomorrow's conference. He has added a pithy quotation from Juvenal, *"Quis custodiet ipsos custodies?"* to his closing remarks. He intends to compare the inability of Congress to effectively regulate immigration with the unreliability of Juvenal's harem guards. And to imply that members of Congress, like Juvenal's "custodies," are eunuchs.

Suleiman is a difficult man but a very able scholar. He sometimes regrets his decision to come to Grafton House. It was an uncharacteristically optimistic decision, fueled by a desire to do something different, to become a more public person, to build an institution of his own. In reality, he finds himself surrounded by second-rate scholars, beset by crackpot troublemakers like Anettka Gardiner, and burdened with administrative duties that bore him witless. Perhaps I will accept Columbia's offer and move to New York after this conference, Suleiman thinks. Then he clears his throat and begins to rehearse his presentation yet again. He shows no sign of going to bed.

Harold Cummings is writing a postcard to his niece in Trinidad. He left home a long time ago, but he still keeps in touch with his three sisters. Two of his sisters have visited him in the United States. They were particularly taken with Walmart and BJ's, mega outlet stores that had not yet arrived in Trinidad. They had wanted to visit Costco, but there's still no Costco store in Rhode Island. After a week in the United States, they were happy to go home. They said they missed home.

That made Harold sad. After forty years in the United States, he no longer sees Trinidad as home. For better or worse, his home is now in the United States. Harold is in no hurry to go to bed; his back aches and he tends to sleep in fits and starts. As an alternative to his bed, he has purchased a large reclining chair covered in Naugahyde, the kind of chair that used to be called a lounger. So far, that seems to work better than the bed. Not yet, though, Harold thinks, and he picks up the sports page of the Newport Daily News and begins reading a story about the Gulls.

Down the street from the stadium where the Gulls have been playing, George Rakylz is getting into the passenger seat of an elderly Plymouth. He is going home with Maureen, who is drunk and horny. She probably will regret this in the morning, but now she is operating more or less mindlessly on a potent mixture of adrenaline, hormones and alcohol. She is taking George home to bed, but not to sleep. George is pleased with his luck. He is also horny, and not at all sleepy. For the time being, he is not thinking about "The Program", which is just as well.

Wilford "Fat Willie" Thomas is sitting in a small conference room at the Newport Police Department headquarters on Broadway, across from St. Joseph's Church. He and Sam Graves are being videotaped as Sam slowly recites the Miranda warnings to an unhappy Willie. "I know all that shit," Willie says at one point. "You don't have to tell it to me again. Why don't you let me tell you what happened?"

"I'm sure you do know your legal rights," Sam says, "But we have to tell them to you anyway. So there won't be any trouble in the future. We don't want to have any problems. When I'm finished, you can tell me your side of the story. There's no hurry, Mr. Thomas."

Sam doesn't say so, because it could be seen as intimidation, but he's not going to bed for a long time. Neither is Fat Willie.

This is a delicate business. Sam has called the Cambridge police and told them that he has Fat Willie. The Cambridge police will undoubtedly want to bring Willie back to Cambridge. But until someone from Cambridge arrives, Sam can question Willie. And Sam is very interested in what Willie can tell him about George Rakylz, who is worrisomely at large in Sam's hometown. He also wants Willie to tell him more about Tobie Shaw. He likes Tobie, and hopes he can figure out a way to minimize the trouble she's definitely in.

Melanie Ferguson is in bed with Robin Foreman, her Pilates instructor. They have just finished sharing a large blender full of papaya and mangos mixed with yoghurt made from goat's milk. They have made love, and Melanie is feeling sleepy. She would like to go to sleep, and is trying to decide how to broach this subject with Robin. Robin is wondering if Melanie would like to go to a rugby game in which Robin is playing tomorrow. No problem here that I can see.

Winifred ("Pooh") Gardiner is watching Antique Roadshow on WGBH -TV. The British version of the show. Filmed at Astor. Everyone is eating strawberries and cream. Pooh is eating yoghurt — a small container of blueberry goat's milk yoghurt.

Andrew Eads, Sr., is sound asleep in his upscale nursing home. He holds half of an oatmeal cookie in his left hand.

Henry Leathwood is trying to go to sleep in the small room he has been assigned for the conference. He is lonely.

Anybody else? Have I forgotten someone? Yes, of course. More about Anettka (and maybe Jack) in the next chapter.

CHAPTER 27

"O wad some Pow'r the giftie gie us/ To see oursels as ithers see us!/ It wad frae mony a blunder free us,/ An' foolish notion."
-Robert Burns

Anettka Gardiner is in her bedroom in Grafton House, working on the talk she plans to give at the conference. She is finding it difficult to concentrate on her work. She is worrying about Pooh Gardiner. Will Pooh say something to Paul Gardiner? Worse, will Pooh say something to someone else, who will enthusiastically spread the news of Anettka's infidelity?

The unfairness of this weighs heavily on Anettka. In fact, of course, she has not slept with Jack Chrysler. Flirted with him, yes. Kissed him, certainly. But not slept with him. Yet. It is certainly true that Anettka has been thinking about sleeping with Jack for some time. But she hasn't done so. Which makes it really unfair to be seen as unfaithful when she really hasn't been. Yet.

Moreover, as that "yet" implies, Anettka really hasn't made her mind up about having an affair with Jack. She cares for her husband, Paul, but she is unhappy with the lack of excitement in their relationship. (For which read love life.) But she is well aware that she likes being married to a powerful and rich man.

She doesn't want to hurt Paul, whom she admires, and who has been kind to her. But she has enjoyed flirting with Jack, and daydreaming about sleeping with him. Now, all that is suddenly a real problem rather than a pleasant fantasy. And she doesn't know what to do. Not surprisingly, she is unhappy, angry, and having difficulty focusing on her prepared remarks. If we look in through her bedroom window, we will see her in bed, propped up on pillows, and holding a clipboard and a felt tip pen. She looks tired. She has been crying, and her eyes are red.

The budding romance between Anettka and Jack Chrysler has been a topic of much interest to the staff of Grafton House for several months. Women are of course interested in romance, to start off with. The spicy implications of extra-marital hanky-panky by Grafton House's second in command with the Center's newest senior scholar, made the romance interesting to almost everyone.

On the face of it, there is nothing surprising about the romance. Anettka is young and very attractive. She is married, but her husband is away on business most of the time, and she spends most of her nights alone in a two-room suite at Grafton House. And Jack is a handsome, charismatic, single heterosexual male, who also sleeps alone in rooms at Grafton House. They work together. They hang out together after work and drink coffee, and talk. Romance is, if not inevitable, unsurprising.

Until now, Anettka has managed to keep the lid on the romance. She enjoyed Jack's attention. She flirted with him. But until today, the couple has never kissed. For whatever reason, they began kissing in the elevator at the Newport Hospital, and continued to do so at the Norman Bird Sanctuary. Continued, that is, until their discovery by Pooh Gardiner, Anettka's husband Paul's first cousin.

Well, actually, we can pretty much guess why they started kissing earlier in the day. Anettka was freaked out by Karim's sudden illness. Islam and Muhammad are demon figures in her psyche. They personify the trauma that has radically reshaped her emotions: her family's attempt to murder her. Anettka's emotions were in turmoil. It has been perhaps six weeks since she and her husband last made love. She is attracted to Jack. She would like to be comforted by a man. The question is really not "why?" but "why not?"

Of course, why not was almost immediately made apparent when Pooh Gardiner and her Brownies appeared on the hill above them in the Norman Bird Sanctuary. Anettka likes Pooh, but the two women are as unlike as chalk and cheese, and Anettka has no idea what Pooh will do now. She is very afraid that Pooh will tell Paul. Or worse, that Pooh will tell other people who will tell Paul. She is obsessed by this fear. It surrounds her with a greasy, gray coating of unease and danger. The only thing that she can think to do is to work on her prepared remarks for the conference. Which she is doing now with some difficulty. She has unearthed an ancient pack of cigarettes from a desk drawer, and is smoking one. Just one, she tells herself.

It would be understandable but unfair if you were to assume that Anettka is simply a drama queen. Drama queens are people who express their feelings in an exaggerated fashion. They are people who think they care more about anything and everything than anyone else possibly can care. Anettka is only partially like that.

It may help you to understand Anettka if we compare her to Phoebe Snow. Like Phoebe, Anettka is the product of a privileged background. As children, both women had stern but adoring nannies who imbued them with a sense of self-confidence and self-worth. Both women spent their summers at (girls only) camps in the mountains, where they rode horses and played tennis. Both women attended posh private schools (girls only). And both women were top girls at their schools: good at their studies and good at sports. They continued to excel in their studies in college, and later in graduate school. Like Phoebe, Anettka is an accomplished scholar who earned a doctoral degree from an ancient English university. Like Phoebe, Anettka is an attractive woman in her early thirties. And like Phoebe, Anettka is traversing a difficult patch in life.

But, of course, the two women are very different. Start with ethnicity. Phoebe is a WASP. Like Pooh Gardiner, she has been brought up in a culture that places a premium on avoiding excessive displays of emotion. Anettka comes from a very different culture, one that equates visible emotion with authenticity. So when Anettka has feelings, she doesn't squelch them. Instead, she expresses her feelings. This makes many WASPS uncomfortable, but it makes Anettka feel…well, maybe not happy, but better than she did before. Then of course there's religion. Phoebe is an Episcopalian. Not one of those high church Episcopalians who are always flirting with becoming Romans. And not one of the new-fangled right-wing Episcopalians who are freaked out about gay priests and thinking about becoming Nigerian Anglicans. Nope, Phoebe's an old-fashioned Episcopalian. As such, her religious beliefs are mild and not dogmatic. If pressed, she might admit to doubts about the benevolence of the Deity, but she doesn't spend much time worrying about such matters. She likes going to church, and actually does so now and then. And she's pleased with the fact that other people's different views about religion don't bother her. *Chacun à son goût*, as her mother is fond of saying. (By the way, Phoebe's mother isn't very old. She's fifty-five and Anettka's mother is a year younger. Their daughters think they're old, but they're not.)

Anettka, as we have seen, is not an Episcopalian. She has very strong and almost entirely negative views about religion. She hates Islam, the religion she grew up in. It is fair to say that Anettka is dogmatic about this. For her, Islam means the harsh repression of women, and the sweeping denial of women's rights. Her own personal experience seems to her to prove this point beyond doubt. Before her very eyes, her doting father and loving brothers became mortal enemies, monsters who wanted to murder her. They believed that Anettka must marry the man they chose for her or die. And they thought their religion, Islam, supported this belief.

We'll visit Anettka more in the next chapter.

CHAPTER 28

"Perhaps all the dragons in our lives are princesses who are only waiting to see us act, just once, with beauty and courage. Perhaps everything that frightens us is, in its deepest essence, something helpless that wants our love."
— Rainer Maria Rilke

Perhaps naïvely, I'm assuming that the reader knows that Muslims aren't any nuttier than the members of the world's other religions. They're not. But let's be clear. Almost all of the world's Muslims are peaceful. They don't murder people any more often than members of other religions do. And they don't approve of terrorism either.

And only a minuscule number would even think about murdering their beloved daughters because they wouldn't marry the men their family picked out for them. They'd be irritated, of course, pissed off, maybe, but not murderous. But that isn't Anettka's experience. And she doesn't feel broadminded. Or balanced. Or interested in forgiving her father and brothers.

No, Anettka is angry and (like Samson) wants to smite her enemies hip and thigh. Bring them to justice. Tell the world about the evil their religion is fostering. In other words, Anettka isn't feeling generous. She's not in the giving vein.

Anettka plans to discuss her own experience with "honor" killings in Pakistan at some point in the Grafton House conference. She expects to get lots of criticism; in fact, she's looking forward to it. But that's not what interests us here. What's more interesting is who Anettka has become because of her experience.

First of all, unlike Phoebe, Anettka has had a traumatic, life-altering experience. Precisely because she grew up in a loving household, showered with love and privilege, Anettka has found it very difficult to adjust emotionally to the sudden negation of all that she had known before. Her father, her brothers — murderers! The mind's natural tendency is to deny this sort of hideous betrayal. To explain it away.

But Anettka has been unable to do this. No amount of discussion—with therapists, with fellow scholars, with friends from her youth and school years — none of this has done the slightest bit of good. She hates her father and brothers. She hates Islam, the drug that she believes changed them into assassins. And not surprisingly, she is fearful. At any moment, something else horrible may happen, is almost bound to happen, just as it did to her before.

We saw this the first time we met Anettka. You will recall that she was hysterical, freaked out by Karim's sudden illness, and loudly blaming Muhammad and Islam for trying to murder him. Which, of course, is a little nutty. Having calmed down, she explained this away as overwrought, stemming from a passionate disagreement with Suleiman Khan. Whom she hates. Who feels the same way about her.

But mark what that suggests. Anettka is fearful to the core. PTSD, the military shrinks call it. Post Traumatic Stress Disorder. She doesn't trust anyone. She has a hated, implacable, and diabolical enemy: Islam. And she can't relax. If she does, her enemy will destroy her. This is not a good place to be. And it makes her present situation truly unnerving. What if she loses her husband?

Anettka met Paul Gardiner at a garden party in Cambridge given by a lady whose great-uncle was Henry James' dentist. Paul was much older than she, a tall, bony man with a slight stoop, and a white scar across his cheek. She asked him about it, and he laughed. "Most people don't have enough nerve to ask me that," he said to Anettka. "I got it in the Army, in Vietnam. I was lucky; a bullet just grazed my face. I suppose it looks scary, but it's just scar tissue. I don't really notice it anymore."

One thing led to another, and before the month was out, Anettka had moved into Paul's apartment on Beacon Hill. Paul was very rich, very important, and very sure of himself. He was a non-practicing Episcopalian, so he wasn't particularly prejudiced against Islam, but he thought Anettka had been treated badly, and he was delighted to take her under his wing. Men like to rescue damsels in distress.

So far, so good. But Paul Gardiner is a very busy man. In the course of doing business, he sometimes flies to Paris and back twice in a week. In any given week, he is (usually) out of town — *i.e.*, away from home in Boston— more than he is at home. And whether he is away or at home, he works long hours. Up at five a.m., at the office until six p.m., and in bed by nine. And, he is not a young man anymore. All of which means, unfortunately, that Anettka's love life is not all that a young woman might wish it to be.

Because Paul is away so much and so busy, Anettka has never tried to settle down with him in a permanent fashion. He has his work, she has hers. Living together full time in Boston, given his schedule and her work at Grafton House, would be difficult. So they don't. He keeps an apartment in Boston. She has a suite in Grafton House.

On most weekends, Paul comes to Newport and the two of them spend a couple of nights together. They stay in a house Paul owns, one of three in the Gardiner family compound off Ocean Drive. Paul loves this house. The happiest days of his childhood were spent there. He and Anettka sleep in his old room. It was modernized twenty years ago, with the addition of a double bed, but is otherwise unchanged from his childhood.

The room is decorated with pennants from Groton, model ships, and a painting. The painting is by his cousin, Pooh Gardiner. It is a portrait of Paul's sailboat, *Le Raquin*. The boat is named after the MFA's famous Copley portrait of Watson and the Shark. (Le Raquin means shark in French.) The French are great admirers of this picture, and Paul is a great admirer of the French. Which is one reason he spends so much time in Paris.

When Paul arrives in Newport for the weekend, the couple's first order of business is to make love. They do so in Paul's old bedroom. Afterwards, they sit outside on the flagstone terrace and look at Narragansett Bay. Paul has a glass of beer; Anettka drinks soda water. It is very serene, very sedate.

Now what if Paul Gardiner were married to Pooh Gardiner? Don't laugh. In the Nineteenth century, people married their first cousins all the time. My grandparents were first cousins and blissfully happy, too. It was bad for the gene pool but good for marital compatibility. Anyway, if Paul and Pooh were married, a sepia photograph showing the couple on the terrace would probably bear the caption "Serenity". But Anettka is not Pooh. She is much younger, she is not a WASP, and she is neither serene nor sedate. She is very fond of Paul. She admires and respects him. But she is a little bored with him — no, tell the truth — she's more than a little bored with him. And bored with their excessively sedate love life.

Which is where Jack Chrysler comes in. He is attractive, charismatic, and interested in Anettka's ideas, or so she thinks. He's really just interested in her, which is enough. Most importantly, Jack is twenty years younger than Paul. Who, regrettably, is exactly twice as old as is Anettka. Moreover, Jack is in love with Anettka, and often tells her so. This is flattering. And Anettka finds Jack very attractive. QED.

So what it boils down to is this. For some time, Anettka has been thinking about sleeping with Jack Chrysler. She knows she shouldn't. She feels guilty about wanting to. And she is very much aware of the fact that she has made a very desirable marriage to a man who can protect her and wants to take care of her. Important stuff if you've had to run for your life from your murderous father and mad brothers.

But now, her chickens have come home to roost. When Pooh Gardiner saw her kissing Jack in his convertible, her enjoyable private fantasy turned into a gnawing problem. With no obvious solution. Perhaps, she thinks, I could tell Paul that I had taken a drink of alcohol (Anettka does not drink alcohol), and that it went to my head, and that I behaved badly and I'm very sorry.

Then she feels angry and thinks, it's all Paul's fault. If he were around more often and we made love more often, I wouldn't have gotten into this position.

Looking at Anettka through the window of her suite in Grafton House, we can see her bent over a desk. With a pen in her hand, she is trying to edit the remarks she plans to make at the conference. Her mind refuses to cooperate. All of her thoughts are on the afternoon's events, and the prospect of Paul learning of them. Time to go to bed, she tells herself. I'll go for a run on Ocean Drive tomorrow morning when I get up. Before breakfast, I think. That will make me feel more rational. And after brushing her teeth with an electric toothbrush, she gets in bed and promptly goes to sleep. It's probably time for us to do the same, and leave Grafton House and its inhabitants until the morning.

PART TWO: SATURDAY, JULY 2, 2011

CHAPTER 29

The morning sun slowly emerged from behind Trinity Church and began to warm up the city of Newport. Across town, the sunshine fell on a bank of unusually dense fog surrounding Grafton House and stretching to Narragansett Bay. As the fog began to disperse, three grayish brown shapes appeared as if by magic in the hydrangea beds below Harold Cumming's bedroom window. "Coyotes," Harold said to himself.

Harold stood at his window and observed the coyotes through his binoculars. Looking for rabbits, I suppose, Harold thought. Probably the hydrangeas are a good place to look. Too many pink ones, though. We need more blues. Soil's not acid enough. I need to add some aluminum.

Harold is an early riser, and is usually up by five if not before. The aging male prostate has something to do with that. It presses on his bladder.

From her perch on top of Grafton House, tending to her hives, Alex the beekeeper also looks at the coyotes. Because she is much younger and has much better eyesight than Harold, she needs no binoculars to admire them. They look beautiful, she thinks. I wonder if there are really too many coyotes in Rhode Island. And if there are, what should we or could we do about it? Alex is a committed liberal.

Harold and Alex are among the very few people in Grafton House who are awake at this hour. In fact, most of the people we have met so far are still in bed. But of course not everyone. In particular, Andy Eads is awake and waiting for his Mr. Coffee pot to beep.

Andy is eating a large bowl of high-fiber cereal mixed with blueberries, sliced bananas, a tablespoon of flax seed, and two-percent milk. Andy has reluctantly adopted this diet at the urging of his gastroenterologist, who says it will regularize Andy's bowel movements. (Andy has an exceptionally long colon.) He does like the banana slices though, which come from a specially endowed "ripe banana fund" left by Alma Grafton in her will.

Andy doesn't always get up quite this early, but this is a very big day for Andy and for Grafton House. All year long, scholars and policy analysts in universities and think tanks around the world have been getting ready for this very day. They've been toiling away at what they hope (and sometimes pray) will be cutting-edge analyses of immigration policy. Seminal analyses. Ones that will make (or burnish) their reputations within the immigration policy community. At the very least, they're hoping to produce competent research papers that will improve their résumés, and help them get better jobs.

Because Harvard University's Grafton House Conference on International Immigration Policy (GHCIIP) is the immigration policy community's most prestigious forum. You probably have never heard of the GHCIIP, but believe me, professors and think tankers in the field see it as a sort of Mecca. Getting an invitation to present a paper at Grafton House is like winning the lottery. Only less random, because it depends on what and who you know.

So Andy is mentally reviewing the day ahead and thinking about the remarks he plans to make when the conference opens. The coffee maker beeps, and Andy gratefully pours himself a large cup of black coffee. I wonder if I should try to go to a meeting, Andy asks himself. If Harold takes me, I could get to the six-a.m. at Salve Regina for half an hour. Probably a good idea, he thinks and he picks up the phone by the Mr. Coffee and calls Harold Cummings.

"I'd like to go over to Salve for the six o'clock meeting. Part of it anyway," Andy says to Harold. "See you downstairs. Would you like some coffee? OK. Will do."

In the car driving to Salve Regina, Andy sips his coffee and contemplates the shape of the day to come. He should be back at Grafton House by seven, in time to have breakfast with some of the scheduled speakers. He will give the welcoming address, and try to focus everyone on the goal of this conference. Which has been the goal of the Grafton House conferences since their inception. *E Pluribus Unum*. From many, one. From diversity, unity. Or at least comity. Progress through spirited disagreement. A challenge to the conference to rise above partisanship, and seek the best in each other's ideas through constructive disagreement. And most importantly, openness to the possibility of change.

Openness to the possibility of change is what Andy generally thinks about when he goes to an AA meeting. Most of the time, he tries to stay at meetings for the whole hour, but he learned a long time ago that half an hour is better than none. The usual people were milling around the small college classroom where the six a.m. meeting took place. On the blackboard, an instructor had outlined what appeared to be a list of key events in the life of King David. David & Goliath was underlined. So was David & Bathsheba.

"Hi Andy," an elderly lady said. "Aren't you having a conference this weekend? What are you doing here?"

"We are," Andy said. "But I thought I'd come by for a few minutes anyway. I'm not really a morning person, and I need to ease into the day gradually." The elderly lady laughed. Then a young woman sitting at the head of the table banged a gavel and the meeting began.

I wonder, Andy thought, as the young woman shared her story, why some people are open to the possibility of change and others are not. Probably the old saw about hitting bottom explains some of that. Change may be easier if you're desperate, if you've got nothing left to lose. Not that it worked for Janis Joplin. So maybe it's just luck, or chance. Hope probably has a lot to do with it.

What I do know, Andy thought, is that you can encourage people to be open to your ideas by being open to theirs. Which doesn't mean caving in to horribly bad ideas, but does mean accepting that monopolies on the truth are rare and questionable.

"Good meeting?" Harold asked as they drove back to Grafton House.

"Always good," Andy said. "Good preparation for the day to come. Puts stuff in perspective."

CHAPTER 30

Wilford Thomas, a.k.a. Fat Willie, was miserable. He had spent a sleepless night on the cold metal cot provided by the Newport Police Department in the city lockup. Now, he sat on the cold metal (and seat-less) toilet in his cell and tried unsuccessfully to defecate. He could hear his mother's voice saying "Wilford! Don't strain at stool! You'll have a heart attack!" I am well and truly fucked, Willie said to himself. It would be just as well for everybody if I did have a heart attack.

A ray of sunshine came through the bars of his cell from a window across the hall. Willie could hear voices coming from somewhere down the hall. A man said, "Is our guest up yet?" And another man laughed loudly. Then Willie heard someone whistling cheerfully and coming down the hall towards his cell.

"Good morning, Wilford," Lieutenant Sam Graves said. "How are you doing this fine morning?"

"Piss poor," Fat Willie said. "Not good. What did you think, anyway?"

"I'm sorry," Sam said. "But this is a jail, not a hotel. Very few people enjoy their stay in our jail."

"Yeah," Fat Willie said. "I can see why." He got up from the toilet, pulled his trousers back up, and sat down on the edge of the cot.

"That bitch set me up, didn't she?"

"Who?" Sam said.

"Tobie. Tobie Shaw. Did she tell you she's the one that got me into this fucking mess to begin with? And now she's playing footsy with you guys. Is that fair, or what?"

"Fair enough. She wants to save her skin. You want to save yours?"

"How do you mean, save my skin?"

"I mean, save your ass, I mean if you work with us, we can work with you. I know you didn't get into this problem all by yourself. Tell me stuff I don't know, that helps me out, and I'll do whatever I can to help you out."

"Like what?"

"Like this guy, this Rakylz. They tell me you weren't the one who stuck Moriarty. You don't have to go down the same way Rakylz is going to go down. So what can you tell me about Rakylz? What do you know that I don't? What can you tell me that will help us find him? That's what I mean. Help me out, I'll help you out."

"I don't know where Georgy Porgy is," Fat Willie said. "But I know where he's going."

"Which is where?" Sam said.

"He's going to blow up this place where Tobie works. This Grafton something. He's going to blow the whole fucking thing up. Or shoot everybody. Or both. Something crazy, anyway."

"How do you know that?" Sam asked.

"How do you think I know it?" Fat Willie said. "Georgy Porgy told me. He was very excited about it. He said it was going to strike a blow for liberty. Something like that. He's part of some nut group that wants to blow everything up and start over. They're French. The nut group I mean. At least I think so. He calls it the Program.

"He was going to get Tobie to get him inside the place. They're having some kind of a big meeting there. Professors, scientists, people like that. George hates people like that. Which is peculiar because he was studying to be a professor himself. He was at MIT, you know. Not an undergraduate, he was a graduate student. Getting his PhD. Some kind of engineering, I think. Full ride. Very smart. But nuts. Absolutely bat-shit crazy."

"When did he tell you this?" Sam asked.

"A couple of weeks ago was the last time he said he was going to do it. He's got this TEC-something machine gun and some kind of explosive he said was made out of plastic. Go figure. Then he told me he changed his mind. That was last Tuesday. We were at my cousin's place in Fall River. She took us in for a couple of nights. We talked about coming over here to Newport to see if Tobie could help us. And I said what about your plans to blow the place up. And he said that was on hold. He said that for now, we needed a place to hide out and that Tobie was the key. I think he was probably lying. But maybe not. I didn't want to come here if that was what he was going to do, so I wanted to believe he changed his mind. Now, I think he was probably lying. I know he still had that stuff in his backpack the last time I saw him."

"What's he look like now?" Sam asked. "Has he still got the beard, and the 'fro?"

"He cut it all off," Willie said. "He got a buzz cut, shaved off his beard. Looks about sixteen. Schoolboy look."

Sam Graves stood there for a moment, thinking. He looked at his watch. It said 5:53 a.m. "Well," he said to Fat Willie, "that's very interesting information. I appreciate your help in telling me that information. Would you like some coffee and a doughnut?"

"I would," Fat Willie said.

"I'll send somebody in with it," Sam said, and quickly moved off down the hall to his office.

CHAPTER 31

Since the terrorist attacks on September 11, 2001, the law enforcement community has undergone many changes aimed at improving the nation's anti-terrorism capabilities. The Federal National Counterterrorism Center (NCC) plays a key role in U.S. anti-terrorism efforts. In essence, the job of the NCC is to coordinate the response to possible terrorist attacks. You can read about NCC on its web site: http://www.nctc.gov/

Over the years, the Department of Homeland Security has made a special effort to educate local law enforcement agencies on how to respond to threats of terrorism. In practice, this all boils down to calling the NCC immediately when a terrorist threat appears. This allows the NCC to organize an effective response.

So the first thing Sam Graves did upon returning to his office was call the NCC, on the toll-free phone number assigned to local law enforcement agencies. A pleasant-voiced woman took his name and number, asked him a few questions about the nature of the terrorist threat, and said someone would contact him shortly. After that, he called Billy Grogan, his friend in the Cambridge Police Department, and George Miller, an FBI agent in the Providence office of the FBI, on their cellphones. Both men advised him to wait for the NCC to call before doing anything.

Sam thought about this advice for a few minutes. Then he called Andy Eads.

Andy was comfortably seated in the rear seat of the Grafton House Lincoln, drinking coffee from a Thermos as Harold drove back from Salve Regina. He was thinking about his opening remarks to the conference when his cellphone rang.

It had taken Andy a long time to get used to his cellphone, and he still didn't much like it. He didn't like it partly because he had acquired it at the same time that his hearing had started to diminish. He blamed the cellphone for that. He also didn't like it because the numbers on the phone were hard for him to see without putting on his reading glasses. And he didn't like being in constant contact with the outside world.

If truth be told, Andy didn't like telephones at all. He remembered his mother's father, G.C. (for Grover Cleveland) Carstairs, shouting into the mouthpiece of a telephone at a neighbor's farm in Big Creek, Mississippi, circa 1942. The mouthpiece of the telephone was mounted on the wall of the neighbor's kitchen, and the earpiece was shaped like a large black pepper shaker.

His grandfather grasped the earpiece in his left hand and stood well away from the mouthpiece on the wall. And shouted. Standing that far back meant he had to shout, but that's probably not why he shouted. G.C. Carstairs saw telephones as unnatural. Dangerous even. On a par with flush toilets. He was dead set against flush toilets, on the grounds that running water underneath your private parts was likely to have unnatural effects. Dire consequences. Andy sometimes felt the same way about telephones.

"Hello," Andy said, holding the cellphone against his right cheek. (His right ear was marginally better than his left.)

"Hello, Dr. Eads," Sam Graves said. "This is Lieutenant Sam Graves with the Newport Police. We have a very serious problem, and I need to talk with you immediately. Can you come downtown to the station? Now?"

"This is a bad time, Sam. We're having the start of our conference in a couple of hours, and I had hoped to do some things at Grafton House before then. Can you tell me what the problem is?"

"It would be better to talk to you in person. What it's about is the problem we discussed the other day. The man involved in the robbery in Cambridge and your computer expert. I'd rather not say anything on the open phone, but there's a possibility of something very bad happening at Grafton House. Today. At the conference."

"Oh dear," Andy said. "Of course. I'm in the car right now. We'll be there in about ten minutes."

"That was Sam Graves," Andy said to Harold. "We need to go down to the police station to see him. It sounds like we have a problem. A big one probably, or he wouldn't have asked me to come down immediately."

"Okay," Harold said. The big Lincoln proceeded at a stately pace along Narragansett Avenue to the intersection with Bellevue Avenue. Harold waited patiently for the traffic signal to turn green, looked over at August Belmont's statue in front of the Preservation Society headquarters, and then turned right on Bellevue Avenue.

"I thought this was going to be a peculiar day," Harold said.

CHAPTER 32

George Rakylz was awakened by the sound of bells from St. Paul's Church. The summer sun was streaming through the open window, and the woman he had met the night before lay next to him in bed, snoring softly. Her name's Maureen, he thought. The Catholic Irish Alcoholic. The woman who's going to get me into Grafton House.

George felt wonderful. This was going to be a good day. He could feel it in his bones. Maybe it would turn out to be THE day. *Der Tag.* Judgment Day. The beginning of the end for capitalist society. And he would be the man who brought the hammer down.

It was too bad about Tobie. He had never thought she was reliable, but he hadn't thought she'd sell him out to the cops. Fat Willie had said she was trustworthy. She wasn't. She had squealed on him. Probably on Fat Willie, too. She will deserve what she gets.

But he, George Rakylz, had prevailed. He was smarter than they were. They had tried to trap him and he had escaped. And he hadn't had to chew off his own leg either. But he would have done that too, if he'd had to. Because he was on a mission. He was going to save society by destroying the cancer that was slowly killing it. *Vive la Revolution*, he whispered to himself.

He had a plan. He had thought it up the night before at the bar where he had met the woman next to him. He had originally thought that Tobie would hide him somewhere in Grafton House. Hide him until he righteously destroyed the mealy-mouthed pseudo-intellectuals whose lies prop up the rotten status quo. Who disguise society's internal rot with their bogus scholarly "studies."

But Maureen was even better than Tobie. This was going to work beautifully. Maureen was going to hire him as part of the catering crew. Give him a white uniform. Maybe a photo ID too. And drive him into the heart of the enemy camp. Where he can wreak havoc on the enemy. Mumbai only better, because not some crazy Muslim nonsense but the real deal.

He had a printout in his backpack of the floor plan at Grafton House. He had found the floor plan through Google, courtesy of the Preservation Society of Newport County. (The Preservation Society concerns itself with preserving the city's historic structures from the colonial period to the mansions of the Gilded Age. While neither, Grafton House was a related structure.)

He had already sketched out one game plan, but meeting Maureen had given him a better idea. He would begin his assault at the opening day festive luncheon on the lawn, where he would be a waiter.

He would put his plastic explosive inside a flower vase that he would place in the middle of the tables on the lawn. He would begin by opening fire with his TEC-DC9 machine pistol on the assembled scholars, and when he had exhausted two of his three magazines, he would set off the explosive, blowing everyone else up. Then he would hole up inside Grafton House with a few hostages — Tobie and Maureen would do for starters— and wait for the police and the media to show up. He would use the occasion as an opportunity to explain The Program to the world. He would speak in French as well as English so the Invisible Committee would hear and approve his message. It was all going to be a blast.

George thought of waking Maureen up. They had enjoyed a brief but passionate interlude the night before, and repeating it was appealing. On the other hand, it was early, and he felt sleepy. No need to get up this early, George told himself. I need to get a good night's sleep to be at my best today. He turned on his side, put a pillow over his head and promptly went back to sleep. We will leave him there for a while.

CHAPTER 33

Before going to bed the night before, Juan Carlos had set the musical alarm on his cellphone. One of his minor talents was the ability to make small electronic gadgets work at the height of their capacity. He liked setting his cellphone alarm. He particularly liked the playful tune that the phone alarm played. He had selected the tune from a large selection of alarm sounds offered by his cellphone provider because it sounded a bit like the chimes he had once heard on the *Queen Mary* announcing that dinner was being served.

He was dreaming when the alarm went off. In his dream, Juan Carlos, Phoebe and Catherine were standing in a crowd of people in a large amphitheater. Juan Carlos was smoking a large Cuban cigar — puzzling, since he had stopped smoking on his thirtieth birthday.

All of the people in the crowd were men except for Phoebe and Catherine. Everyone was dressed in the clothes of the 1890s, and everyone but Phoebe and Catherine was smoking. Juan Carlos realized at once that he was in a George Bellows painting of a *fin-de-siècle* prizefight. In the ring at the center of the arena, two prizefighters were slugging it out. The crowd was cheering noisily.

Then the round ended and the bell rang. The boxers stopped fighting and returned to their corners. The crowd began to rhythmically chant the words "WAN! CAR! LOS!" over and over again. That's my name Juan Carlos said to himself. The referee —a very young man dressed in a black cassock — beckoned to Juan Carlos to come up and join the fighters in the ring. Phoebe and Catherine took off their bowler hats and gestured toward the ring as if to say, "Go ahead and fight!"

"But I don't want to!" Juan Carlos shouted, and woke up. The cellphone alarm was making cheerful chimes-like sounds. He reached over to the nightstand by his bed and turned the alarm off.

What was all that about, Juan Carlos asked himself. Juan Carlos didn't usually remember his dreams, but this one seemed important. He reached over to the nightstand and made a note on the yellow pad of paper he kept there for recording midnight inspirations. The referee's cassock obviously had something to do with religion. Phoebe and Catherine were the two women he was most involved with. And the big cigar meant something phallic. That he was horny, obviously. But did it mean more? (In fact, what it meant was that Juan Carlos is in the early stages of Parkinson's Disease. In brief, the normal brain paralyzes the body during REM sleep, so that when you dream of being attacked by a bear, you don't shout "Help!" or jump out of bed. Parkinson's disables this useful mechanism. Sorry about that.) Juan Carlos put the question and the yellow pad aside for the time being and got up from the bed. Then he knelt down and said his morning prayers.

Juan Carlos' religious views were complex. Some would say muddled. He had grown up in Lima, where he attended the Colegio de la Inmaculada. The Colegio is a Jesuit-run prep school originally founded in 1582 as the Real Colegio de San Martín. Real means Royal. A very posh prep school.

Juan Carlos liked the school a lot. He admired the priests who taught there and ran the school. And unlike many of his fellow students, he liked going to church. He thought briefly of becoming a priest himself, but abandoned the idea when he reached adolescence and discovered girls. But he continued to take God seriously.

At the age of fourteen, he was introduced to the idea of urban planning. His mother, an ardent believer in world government, brought home a coffee table book that described the United Nations Organization. On the cover of the book were the big blue letters ONU (the Spanish acronym for the UN Organization) and a picture of the UN Building in New York. Juan Carlos was fascinated by Oscar Niemeyer's architectural masterpiece. It was not the first piece of modern architecture that he had seen, but it was the first one that seemed beautiful to him.

So Juan Carlos told his mother how much he liked the UN Building. His mother was thrilled. Perhaps Juan Carlos would like to become an architect, she told him. She brought home another book, an even bigger coffee table book, on Brazil's new capital city,

Brasilia. Look, Juan Carlos, she said, this is a whole city created by the same man who designed the UN Building.

And so Juan Carlos fell in love with urban planning. This is what I want to do when I grow up, he thought: be an architect and create cities. He read all he could about Brasilia and Oscar Ribeiro de Almeida Niemeyer Soares Filho. (Filho means Junior in Portuguese.) His father's brother Mauricio, who was a building contractor, had a treasure trove of old architecture magazines stored in his garage, and Juan Carlos spent many pleasant hours there searching the magazines for articles about Niemeyer and Brasilia.

On the advice of his Uncle Mauricio, Juan Carlos decided to study civil engineering at the National University of San Marcos (founded in 1551 by Charles V, a Spaniard who was the Holy Roman Empire's Emperor at the time). The University had an architecture program, but Uncle Mauricio told him that was a waste of time. Civil engineers knew how to do useful work. They could always get jobs in the building business, while most architects — at least those trained at the University — were impractical dilettantes who were typically unemployed and virtually unemployable. "If you still want to be an architect when you get your engineering degree," Uncle Mauricio told him, "do what I did and get a graduate degree in architecture in the United States. MIT may not teach you anything practical either, but an MIT degree will help you get a job when you graduate." And that's more or less what Juan Carlos did.

At the University, Juan Carlos was surrounded by many young men and women who had decided God was dead and religion was nonsense. They were puzzled by Juan Carlos. On the other hand, a few of his classmates had found an appealing new way to think about God and Christianity. They called it liberation theology.

If you haven't heard of liberation theology, there's a fascinating book that explains the idea: *A Theology of Liberation*. The author, Gustavo Gutierrez, is a Peruvian and a Dominican priest. He's a professor at Notre Dame University — the one in Indiana. And the book lays out a new vision of Christianity. (Well, not that new. Catholic socialists have been around for a long time. Think Dorothy Day and the *Catholic Worker*. Still, it was new to Juan Carlos and his classmates.) In a nutshell, it says that Jesus' teachings should be seen as calling for social justice, and for the liberation of the poor and politically oppressed.

Over the years, Juan Carlos has incorporated this idea into his work in urban design. He is far from orthodox in his views of the deity or of sin. But he believes that God wants people— wants him — to work for social justice. So in his work as an urban planner, he tries to design environments — parks, shopping centers, communities, cities — that make life better for everyone.

So liberation theology, Christian socialism if you will, has a lot to do with the way Juan Carlos thinks about himself and his role — his mission— in the world. Not so much so in his private life.

Juan Carlos is not a regular churchgoer. But he occasionally attends mass with his wife, Catherine (though he usually doesn't take Communion). And he always says his prayers. Twice a day. This had come to Phoebe's attention in their recent stay at the Pod Hotel in New York.

"What are you doing, Juan Carlos?" Phoebe had asked him when he knelt down by the ridiculously small bed in their tiny hotel room.

"Saying my prayers," Juan Carlos said. "I do that every night. Didn't you know that?"

"I've never spent the night with you," Phoebe said. "How would I know something like that?" As you can tell, this made Phoebe mad.

"I pray in the mornings, too," Juan Carlos said. "It's an old habit."

"What are you praying for?" Phoebe asked. "I mean is there something specific you're asking for? Or what?"

'I'm not exactly asking for something. Or maybe I am. I ask God for help in doing the right thing. In being better."

"What does that mean?" Phoebe said, in a tone that made it clear that she was irritated beyond belief. "Better at what you do? Better to me? You've got to be kidding. Are you really doing that? Seriously?"

"I'm sorry," Juan Carlos said. He knew he had stepped in a pothole, but wasn't sure how to get his foot out. "Don't mind me," he said. "It's a habit. I mean it's…lots of prayers I learned when I was a kid." He had started to say, "It's nothing to do with you," but then thought better of it. "It's hard to explain," he said. "It's a habit. In the morning, I think about the day ahead. What I ought to do, and what I ought not to do. In the evening, I examine my conscience and try to figure out what I could have done better."

"Oh," Phoebe said, and pulled the cotton bedspread over her head. Juan Carlos finished his prayers and got into the bed next to her. He put his hand on her thigh. "Stop it," Phoebe snapped.

CHAPTER 34

Since their weekend in New York, Juan Carlos had thought a lot about Phoebe. Not just because he was horny, though he was. But because he really is "in love," or at least thinks he is, and thinking obsessively about the beloved one is a standard feature of that particular affliction. But he had assiduously avoided bringing up the topic of Phoebe in his prayers. You might say that he was dispensing with, or prescinding from, this sticky issue. Which is understandable.

Over the years, Juan Carlos has tried to keep his romantic adventures separate from his prayer life. He is aware, of course, that infidelity to one's spouse is frowned upon by many if not most believing Christians. But he granted himself a pass on the issue, on the grounds that it was unlikely that God really cared about anyone's love life. At least if you didn't hurt anyone. Anyway, he generally didn't go there when he was praying.

In fact, Juan Carlos has hurt a number of people with his amorous adventures. To start with, he's hurt his wife Catherine. She knew about most of his affairs, and they made her unhappy. Her (so-called) friends would tell her about seeing Juan Carlos and his latest squeeze riding on Juan Carlos' Harley, and she would smile in pretended amusement. But she was not amused. Early on, she had tried to discuss the subject with Juan Carlos, but he had bobbed and weaved and avoided being pinned down. Eventually, she gave up and accepted the situation as best she could. Their sex life, though erratic, is better than nothing. She is devout, and doesn't believe in divorce, and legal separation seems like a barren alternative. And of course, Juan Carlos is an important man, a prominent member of the Harvard faculty, and an internationally famous urban designer. All of which gives Catherine a lot of status in the Harvard community, which is pleasant. Trophy husbands are just as flattering to the female ego as trophy wives are to male egos. Women on the street always look admiringly at Juan Carlos and this makes Catherine feel smug. He's mine, she would think. Anyway, she hasn't divorced him, although she thinks about it when she's feeling gloomy. Lots of women have impossible husbands, she tells herself. If she meets another man, I won't be surprised if she becomes an Episcopalian and divorces Juan Carlos.

So Catherine isn't very happy, and in truth Phoebe's three predecessors haven't been all that happy either. All of Phoebe's predecessors had worked with Juan Carlos on his various urban design projects. Over the years, Juan Carlos has become the leader, the central figure in a very successful team of urban designers. Think of it as an atelier, a major artist's workshop. Just being chosen as a member of the Juan Carlos group is a great honor, a compliment. It's not surprising that being chosen by Juan Carlos as a lover is an even greater compliment.

Think about it. There you are, a young woman in an exotic foreign country, working fourteen hours a day on an exciting and very important design project, under great pressure, and partying hard at night with your fellow designers. And your leader, the famous — and very good-looking — Juan Carlos, thinks you're wonderful, beautiful, and talented. What's a girl to do? (Juan Carlos, as far as we know, has always limited his indiscretions to young women, though some of his male associates were also smitten by him.)

Can you blame Juan Carlos for picking this ripe fruit? I don't know. I do know that all of these young women eventually left him. He was certainly exciting. Even a little dangerous, like Tobie Shaw's ex-boyfriend, Wilford "Fat Willie" Thomas. For some women, men like Juan Carlos and Fat Willie are sort of like catnip. No, I think the reason these women broke up with Juan Carlos, was that although he was "in love" with them, he was not really interested in them most of the time. What really interested him was his work. At which he was very talented. And to which he devoted almost all of his time. Being "in love" was a distant second.

In this regard, Juan Carlos is probably representative of many if not most very successful men. Or women. To get to the very top of your profession requires talent, drive and lots of luck. In Juan Carlos' case, the necessary attributes were buttressed by a passionate belief in the rightness of his cause. He wanted to do good for others. Making money was of almost no interest to him. (Partly because he had always had plenty.) Designing urban environments that improved people's lives interested him a lot.

Plus, not to mince words, Juan Carlos is good at manipulating people. Early in his career, he had realized that he didn't want to work for other people. Which meant he had to get people to work for him. He was idealistic, but he quickly realized that the best is the enemy of the good.

After graduating from the National University in Lima with a degree in civil engineering, he applied to urban planning schools in the United States. He was accepted at MIT in the School of Urban Studies and Planning. He obtained an F-1 student visa to enter the United States. Thus began his integration into American society.

Juan Carlos was a diligent student, and he impressed his professors with both his talent and his character. On his arrival in Cambridge, he began working part-time for a local homebuilder. And when he graduated, he began working for the same builder, who got him an H-1B temporary specialty worker visa. All these odd alphanumeric categories are subsections of the Immigration and Nationality Act. (You may remember Henry Leathwood telling Phoebe about this particular fast track to a green card. In fact, it's exactly the same trajectory followed by Edgar Stern, Jackie Persac's partner, when he emigrated from Peru, enrolled in grad school at MIT and then joined MIT's Lincoln Lab.)

Juan Carlos quickly became the builder's in-house designer. In that capacity, he made a name for himself as someone practical who could work with architectural firms to design housing projects that were not only aesthetically pleasing but also made money. His employer successfully petitioned for his green card. Then a rich Saudi businessman hired him to design a community in Riyadh, and his career was launched.

Now he was forty-eight, and he was feeling a little…what? Well, perhaps a little lonely. He and Catherine were not soulmates. And one of the motives behind his affairs with other women had always been the desire for a soulmate. Someone to be in love with whose heart resonated to the same melodies.

So, you may ask, what's the problem with Phoebe? If he's in love with Phoebe, and she's in love with him, why not leave Catherine and marry Phoebe? Well, there are reasons.

To start off, think about what Melville says in *Moby-Dick* about the whaling terms fast fish and loose fish:

"I. A Fast-Fish belongs to the party fast to it.

"II. A Loose-Fish is fair game for anybody who can soonest catch it."

Loose fish is a term whalers use to describe whales which don't belong to anyone, and thus are lawful catches for any whaler who finds them. Fast fish belong to someone. You can tell a fast fish even if the owner isn't around by the red flag on a harpoon that the owner has stuck in the whale. It's called a waif flag, a waif being a captured animal whose owner is not known.

What is John Bull's poor Ireland but a fast fish, Melville asks. So we must ask, is Juan Carlos a fast fish, or a loose fish? Over the years, he has posed as a fast fish, duly harpooned by Catherine, and bound to her forever. He has told each of his lovers that he cannot leave Catherine because…well you know, I mean it would be like betraying her. Something like that, anyway. But if he's really a loose fish, then he's fair game for anybody who can catch him.

Juan Carlos started to get up from beside his bed and then knelt back down. I had better ask God about Phoebe, he thought. And so he did. Then he got up, and began getting ready to go to Newport. On his Harley, of course. Heading south on Massachusetts Route 24, at a ridiculously high speed. (He actually owns two motorcycles: a Honda for running around Cambridge, and a Harley for road trips.) You can think of him as a distraught sperm whale, racing toward Newport with Catherine's waif flag still firmly attached and batting violently in the wind. Not a loose fish as yet, but not exactly a fast one either.

CHAPTER 35

Elsewhere in Cambridge, Jackie Persac and Edgar Stern are also up early. Well, Jackie is up. Jackie is an early riser. Edgar is not an early riser. He is theoretically awake, but he's still in bed, and trying unsuccessfully to ignore Jackie. Jackie has found that the early morning is a good time to get Edgar to do something new.

Edgar tends to react to new ideas by saying "No!" But Edgar is groggy early in the morning, and doesn't think quickly when he first wakes up. Jackie has brought Edgar a cup of coffee — lots of cream, no sugar — and a warm croissant. It is explicitly intended as a bribe. Edgar props himself up against three pillows and begins to eat his croissant. Brown crumbs from the croissant fall on his heavy black beard.

"You're cute," Jackie tells Edgar.

"No, I'm not," Edgar says, but he looks pleased.

"We're going to Newport," Jackie says. "This morning. Now. We can take our bikes in the truck and go for a ride on Ocean Drive. We need a vacation. Don't object. Just get up and get ready to go."

"Where will we stay?" Edgar asks, in a feeble attempt to derail Jackie's plan.

"I've made a reservation at Castle Hill," Jackie says. "You remember. It's very posh. We stayed there once. It's the one on Ocean Drive. Next to the lighthouse. They have a little beach so we can go swimming, too."

"What's it going to cost?" Edgar asks, in a last ditch effort to say no.

"We got a good deal," Jackie says. "I'm using AmEx points."

"Unh," Edgar says and swings his long legs over the edge of the bed. "What did you do with my slippers?" he asks plaintively, but Jackie has won the argument and prudently made himself scarce.

Jackie and Edgar have been partners for nearly twenty years. Edgar was twenty-six when he moved in with Jackie, and Jackie was thirty-one. So they've lived together for a long time. In the past few years, a number of the same-sex couples they know have gotten married. This has been legal in the Commonwealth of Massachusetts since May 17, 2004, as a result of a decision by the Supreme Judicial Court of Massachusetts, the first U.S. state to issue marriage licenses to same-sex couples, and the sixth jurisdiction in the world to legalize same-sex marriage. Holland, Belgium and three Canadian provinces got there first.

Jackie has thought about getting married, but Edgar is unenthusiastic. It's not that Edgar is thinking about leaving Jackie. If you want my opinion, it's the macho aspect that bothers him. Jackie has been intrigued by the terminology that their married gay friends use. To wit, the married men call each other husband, and the married women call each other wife. This is Cambridge, after all, and political correctness is rampant. What it boils down to is that Edgar simply doesn't want to call Jackie his husband. Big decisions are often shaped by similar concerns. But it's not a small concern for Edgar. When the issue comes up with their friends, Edgar is likely to blush. Since he has a bushy black beard, this is mainly noticeable on his forehead and the uppermost parts of his cheeks.

What's of interest here is that in every practical sense except the law, Jackie and Edgar are just as wedded to each other as Catherine and Juan Carlos. Or Anettka and Paul Gardiner. (Maybe more so. I have my doubts about those marriages.) They make love about as frequently as do Catherine and Juan Carlos. And a lot more frequently than Paul and Anettka Gardiner. They're joint owners of a house and share the use of two motor vehicles. (Edgar usually drives their new Audi, and Jackie drives their ancient Toyota pickup.) Their lives are organized around each other. They eat together and sleep in the same bed. Unlike most married couples, they also work together in what might be called a Pop and Pop business. I'm not sure that's such a good idea, but most of the time it's harmonious. And profitable. Robotic probes are a hot commodity in certain circles these days.

How long their unmarried state will last, I don't know. The tax advantages of marriage may suffice to overcome Edgar's reluctance if the Defense of Marriage Act is struck down.

Don't get me wrong, though. I'm not trying to tell you that Jackie and Edgar have an ideal relationship. Jackie is a control freak and Edgar can be feckless. They never fight at home, but they have horrible fights at work, and say terrible things to each other. Edgar does have a roving eye, though he hasn't done any actual roving for several years now. He seems to have more or less recovered from a bad mid-life crisis. And Jackie is still punishing him for that. So a perfect couple they're not. What I'm saying is that they're a perfectly ordinary couple, whose relationship is devoid of exotic details. It's a plain- vanilla, white-bread relationship, interesting only because Jackie and Edgar are so much like the other couples you've met here.

Anyway, they'll soon be off to Newport, driving south at a leisurely pace on Massachusetts Route 24 in a ten-year-old Toyota pickup with two mountain bikes securely tied down in back. We'll meet them again in the near future.

CHAPTER 36

Winifred Gardiner, Pooh to her friends, is also an early riser. This being Saturday, she has gone for a swim in the Bay, and is now sitting on her deck in the sun, drinking a Moroccan smoothie: half a ripe avocado, six ounces of almond milk, two tablespoons of sugar, and a cup of ice, all smooshed together in a Waring blender. Very tasty.

From the deck of her condominium in Portsmouth, Pooh can see a large white sailboat that looks a lot like her cousin Paul's boat, *Le Raquin*. I wonder if Paul thinks of himself as a shark, Pooh asks herself. She likes Paul, and feels a little sorry for him. He was foolish to marry that girl, she thinks. There's no fool like an old fool. But I can see why he did it. A lot more interesting than Myrta.

Pooh is fifty-four and still interested in men. At the age of nineteen, in her junior year at Northeastern, she made a miserable early marriage to a spoiled rich boy named Slocum Partridge. Slocum liked to smoke pot. In fact, his only interest in life turned out to be obtaining and smoking marijuana. All the time. Pooh did not like to smoke pot. In addition to its being illegal, which she didn't approve of, and obviously unhealthy, she thought it was very boring. So three months after her marriage, she told Slocum goodbye and moved back to Providence to live with her parents. She finished up her bachelor's degree at URI and took a job with the State of Rhode Island as an accountant. Where she has been for the last thirty years.

During those thirty years, Pooh has had a series of boyfriends, none of whom has worked out particularly well. The best one was a married man who worked for the Internal Revenue Service. George's main problem was that he was married and didn't want to leave his wife and children. But he was good in bed, and a lot of fun to be with. That "relationship" lasted almost twelve years, until George died of liver cancer. It was a great loss for Pooh.

That had been six years ago, and Pooh hasn't slept with a man since then. She has occasionally thought about sleeping with women, but hasn't so far. She has considered making a pass at a young woman who works at the video store near her condo, but has chickened out at the last moment. This was purely out of desperation, because the general idea didn't really interest her.

Her boyfriend George had been very taken with the idea of lesbian sex. Once or twice, he had produced pornographic magazines featuring girls doing it with other girls, and shyly suggested that they find another girl to experiment with. Pooh had found this idea ridiculous. Why would I want to do that, she asked George. In my personal opinion, she told George, sleeping with another woman would be like eating a bowl of oatmeal without any sugar or cream. Filling, maybe, but not very interesting.

Anyway, men are what Pooh wants to sleep with, and Pooh is still in the market for a man. Which is why, sitting on her deck, she remembers Jack Chrysler's invitation to the Grafton House conference. I'll go down to Newport today, Pooh thought. To the conference. I need to be with interesting people. This is getting too stuffy up here in Portsmouth. Maybe I'll meet someone like Dr. Chrysler. I'll give him a call when I get to Newport.

CHAPTER 37

The morning sun woke Phoebe. Well, the sunshine and her stomach. She felt queasy. Nauseous. Mildly hysterical. She wondered if she were going to be sick. She reached for the package of saltines next to her bed, extracted two and wolfed one down. Her stomach immediately felt better. This too shall pass, she told herself. Twelve weeks was supposedly the magic number. At least that's what Dr. Castro said. I hope she's right, Phoebe thought. She was certainly right about the crackers.

She looked at her watch. I can't call Juan Carlos yet, she thought. Assuming I want to call him. Maybe I should try to go back to sleep. She turned on her side and put a pillow over her head to block out the sunshine. It didn't work. Her mind was racing frantically from one problem to the next, and every possible solution seemed flawed.

She didn't want to be a single mother, but maybe she would have to be one. If she did, she would have to stay in her job at Harvard. And it was becoming clear to her that she didn't really like her job — the prospect of being stuck in that job made her feel frantic. I feel miserable, she told herself, which made her feel slightly better.

She got up and pulled the blinds shut. The room got darker. Back in bed, she tried counting sheep. She tried counting them in French to make it less boring. That didn't work either. Lots and lots of sheep jumped over the stile, but she still couldn't go back to sleep.

Finally she decided to get up. She took a quick shower, put on jeans, sneakers and a T-shirt, and set off to find coffee. The corridor was empty, but off in the distance she could hear dishes rattling. She went down the grand staircase, walked through the empty common room, and after some time found the kitchen. A tall woman with long blond hair was putting something in a large oven. She wore white tennis shorts and a white sun visor, which contrasted nicely with her suntan. "Good morning," Phoebe said. "Is there any coffee?"

"Good morning," the woman said to Phoebe. "I just made a small pot. Nobody's up but you and me. Have a cup. I'm heating up croissants in the oven. There's fresh orange juice in the refrigerator. I squeezed it this morning."

"Thanks," Phoebe told the woman. She poured herself a cup of coffee and opened the refrigerator. Inside she found a large pitcher of orange juice. "Where are the glasses?" she asked the woman.

"In the cabinet over there," the woman said and pointed to a wall of cabinets behind Phoebe. Phoebe found the juice glasses, poured herself a glass of juice, and tasted it.

"It's delicious," she said.

"Yes, it is," the woman said. "I squeezed it myself."

"I'm Phoebe Snow," Phoebe said, and put out her hand.

"I'm Katrina Karpovitch," the woman said and shook Phoebe's hand. "My friends call me Trina. I'm one of the fellows here. I suppose you're here for the conference?"

"Not exactly," Phoebe said. "I work for one of Harvard's administrative offices; it's called External Research Management. We're in charge of external research centers, like Grafton House, that Harvard funds. We visit each of the centers once a year, and it's Grafton House's turn. The conference seemed like a good time to visit and see what's going on."

"I assume you're here to investigate this nonsense about Andy discriminating against Americans, in favor of foreigners. Sheerest nonsense. Makes my blood boil. Bunch of malcontents, if you ask me. But of course you're not asking me." She smiled at Phoebe. "Sorry to sound so angry. But really, the ridiculous things that some people do."

A door at the end of the kitchen opened, and Henry Leathwood — clad in khaki shorts and a white T-shirt and carrying a tennis racket — came into the kitchen. "Good morning, Phoebe," Henry said cheerfully. "You're up early. I see you've met Dr. Karpovitch. Trina's an economist here at Grafton House. She's been a lot of help to me on the book I'm writing. And she's an ace tennis player. She slows down her game for me so I'm not totally outclassed — uses her left hand. She still beats me though. We're going to play some tennis before the conference starts."

"Oh Henry," Trina said. "I'm so sorry. I'm afraid I can't play with you this morning. I just got a call from one of my students. She's panicked about her presentation this afternoon, and I've got to go by her room and jolly her up a bit."

"That's too bad," Henry said. Then he looked at Phoebe. "You don't play tennis by any chance, do you?" He had a hopeful look, and Phoebe felt sorry for him.

"I play," Phoebe said, "but I'm really terrible. I haven't played a game in years. Since I was in grad school. So I can't give you much of a game."

"That," Henry said, "is no problem. No problem at all. As Trina will tell you, I'm a terrible tennis player too. But I love to play anyway. You'd be doing me a real favor if you would."

"You can find a spare racquet in the locker room by the courts," Trina said. "Henry can show you where to find them. I'd better go comfort my student. See you at the conference, Henry. And very nice to meet you, Phoebe Snow. I think you'll enjoy playing with Henry."

Maybe I will, Phoebe thought.

CHAPTER 38

It is unfortunate that people who are successful when young sometimes fail to appreciate their good fortune. Because success was easy for them in the past, they assume it will be easy in the future. They are spoiled by their own success and place too little value on what they have achieved. Since success was easy for them, they make the mistake of believing that they will succeed at whatever they try. Then, when they quit their boring job and try out a new profession, they are startled to find that success is usually very difficult, and involves hard work with no guarantees. If they are lucky, they realize before it is too late that they should conserve what they have achieved.

Phoebe Snow had succeeded in school because: 1) she was a talented mathematician, and 2) she worked very hard. She was not a genius, and none of her advisors expected that she would become an academic superstar. What they did believe was that she could become an outstanding teacher and a respected researcher at a top university. Phoebe took this assessment for granted. What she failed to understand was that this level of success is unusual. Highly unusual. If they are lucky, most people settle into their fate in life without too much difficulty. The reality of work proves less inspiring than the young student may have dreamed, but the older professional settles for the reality. She moves forward, does what is necessary and appropriate and makes peace with the world.

Phoebe had had a privileged life. She had enjoyed success early and saw no reason why she should not continue to do so in another profession. She was sick of mathematics, bored by the book she was supposed to be writing, irritated by her hyper-competitive workaholic colleagues on the MIT faculty, and uninterested in doing more scholarly research. She wanted to do something different, something interesting that involved people, interesting people. She knew — from books and the movies — that some people led fascinating lives that involved fascinating people. She wanted (she thought) to have more, much more to do with such people. Adult people, not pimply undergraduates or hairy graduate students. People who talked about literature and poetry and the theatre and music (classical music, please). Sophisticated people who went to parties in glamorous surroundings, and ate at restaurants food critics gave stars to.

When the opportunity to work in Harvard's University Hall came along, it seemed like a match made in heaven. And for a while it was. Juan Carlos was her dream come true. A fascinating man, living a life that was as glamorous as anyone could wish for. Except for the fact that he was married to someone else. Who got to do all the glamorous things with Juan Carlos. While Phoebe rode on the back of his motorcycle and ate Chinese takeout with or without him in her apartment.

Phoebe's is the usual career path followed by the baby deans who occupy Harvard's University Hall. Very good at fancy schools. Bored by teaching. Uninterested in business. Don't want to leave Cambridge. Why not be a baby dean? But if you do become one, you can get stuck.

The archetypal Harvard baby dean was F. Skiddy von Stade '38, who eventually became Dean of Freshmen. Mr. von Stade played polo. He dropped out of Harvard in his senior year to tour South America with an international polo team. He spent three and a half years fighting the Axis in World War II. After the war, he was a master at his old prep school for two years and then hired on at Harvard as a baby dean. He liked the job and spent the rest of his life there. Harvard undergraduates amused him, an advantage if you're going to spend your life watching over their antics.

Phoebe did not like being a baby dean. She had not particularly liked the Harvard boys she had dated when she was at Wellesley. Too arrogant, too stuffy, too status-conscious. She wasn't working with undergraduates, but the Harvard administration adults she worked with were also arrogant, stuffy and status-conscious. It was remarkably like a business, except it didn't pay as well. And surprisingly like MIT, two subway stops away from Harvard Square.

And it turned out that Phoebe wasn't very good at what she did as a baby dean. She wasn't bad. She was in no danger of being fired.

But the ins and outs of management and cost efficiency studies bored her silly. So, as fate would have it, Phoebe had thrown up a job she was very good at for one she wasn't very good at and increasingly disliked. Now, what should she do? Of course, if she was going to be a single mother, there wasn't any choice. She would have to stay in her job at Harvard, like it or not. Which was yet another reason why it would be better not to be a single mother.

Phoebe was a practical young woman. Whatever she decided to do, she was going to have to tell Juan Carlos that she was pregnant. But now, sitting in the morning sun by the tennis court with Henry Leathwood, eating a large warm croissant and drinking café au lait, the urge to call Juan Carlos was at a low ebb. Because she really liked Henry.

Looking down on Henry and Phoebe from the veranda of Grafton House, you can see why the human race continues to reproduce itself. Because the two of them are wonderful to look at. It's not that either one is extraordinarily good looking. It's that they are healthy, young (well, youngish) long-legged animals, sprawled out in their deck chairs, relaxed and sweating a little from a vigorous and very enjoyable game of tennis.

Henry had not been exaggerating — he was truly a terrible tennis player. Phoebe was long out of practice, but beating Henry was a piece of cake. Nevertheless, Henry was trying hard to improve his game, and he had obviously enjoyed playing with her. She had enjoyed his enthusiasm for the game. Now, sitting in the sun and talking, she enjoyed his obvious interest in her.

"So," Henry asked her, "Do you like your job?" Phoebe hesitated for a moment. Admitting that she was unhappy, or that she had made a mistake — of any kind — was something she almost never did. She had been brought up to see that sort of behavior as demeaning and dangerous. People in her family didn't do things like that. For very good reasons. Because if you did, other people would think less of you.

Then, in an uncharacteristic burst of rebellion, Phoebe broke free of that ingrained taboo, and told Henry "No, I really don't like it very much. At all." And then, much to her surprise, she began to cry.

"Oh, dear," Henry said. "I'm sorry. Tell me about it," and he reached over and patted her arm. And Phoebe told him about...well, not everything, but quite a lot. About studying math and teaching at MIT, and then leaving MIT to become a baby dean. She said very little about her personal life, only that she had been "in a relationship" that hadn't worked out.

In *Twelfth Night*, in her soliloquy after she meets and falls for Cesario (Viola in disguise), Olivia asks, "Even so quickly may one catch the plague?" Falling in love is a curious business. Sexual attraction has a lot to do with it, of course. Phoebe and Henry are young, physically healthy adults whose sexual needs are not being met. Phoebe's recent tryst with Juan Carlos in New York was a disappointment, coming as it did after a long period of abstinence. Henry? Well, Henry has been divorced for two years. Since then, his sex life has been dismal in quality and quantity. So both Phoebe and Henry are horny.

And both Phoebe and Henry are lonely. Some people like being solitary. Neither one of them does. Phoebe wants a father for her child, a lover, and a loving companion. In short, Phoebe wants and needs a husband. And Henry wants and needs a wife. He liked the one he had before, and he wants another one. He's sick of living by himself, and in particular sleeping by himself.

Anyway, sitting there in the sun by the tennis court and talking openly, Phoebe and Henry are falling in love. In Phoebe's case, there's no question that surging hormones are triggering a strong nesting instinct. As well, Phoebe has been unhappy for too long a time without telling anyone about it. Now, telling Henry about herself, she feels a rush of gratitude towards him. He seems to be a kind man. He seems to care about her, unlike Juan Carlos. Of course she's going to fall in love with him. With Henry Leathwood. What a nice name, she thinks.

As for Henry, well, Phoebe is a pretty woman who needs rescuing, who needs his help. He likes that, as men often do. And he likes her name. Phoebe. What a nice name.

CHAPTER 39

By now, the more energetic members of the Grafton House community have begun to arrive on the veranda overlooking Narragansett Bay. The sky is the same Newport blue, dotted with small white clouds, that it was twelve hours before. The ocean is still the same darker blue, but there's only one sailboat to be seen. There is, however, a large garbage scow slowly puttering past the Grafton House pier. Much further out to sea, a Russian fishing vessel, an enormous grey hulking box, lurks ominously on the horizon.

On the other side of the mansion, things are also starting to happen. As has long been the practice, Teresa Morgan has recruited the Rogers High School varsity basketball team and their coach, Bill Haggerty, to serve as parking attendants for the conference. The team has already arrived and is busily laying out yellow flags on the grounds to mark the places where cars can or can't park. Teresa has also paid three off-duty Newport policemen to direct traffic. They're sitting in a squad car (donated by the city) by the open Grafton House gates. They are drinking coffee and waiting for enough traffic to require them to direct it. So far, seven cars have arrived.

Dexter Slate and Teresa Morgan are standing in front of the main entrance to the mansion. Each of them is holding a clipboard. They are discussing logistics. By Dexter's count, approximately 123 people will attend one or more sessions of the conference. Most of them are staying in town at a hotel or a B&B. A select few are guests, with rooms in Grafton House or its annex. All of them must be provided with conference materials, food and drink. This requires much organization, and Dexter and Teresa are happy to provide it. This is one of the high points of the year for both of them, and they are enjoying it immensely.

"Where is Andy?" Dexter asks Teresa, whose job it is to know such things.

"He called me a half hour ago," Teresa says. "He's down at the police station. He said Lieutenant Graves — the detective who was here yesterday when Karim got sick - - wanted to talk to him. He didn't say what that was about, but I suppose it has to do with Karim. I'll call the Newport Hospital in a minute to make sure Karim's OK."

Down by the gate, a yellow school bus has pulled up. "That's curious," Dexter says. "I wonder who that is." Who it is becomes clearer when a young woman emerges from the bus and unfurls a banner. "What does that sign say?" Dexter asks Teresa. "I'm not wearing my distance glasses."

"It says CFFIP WANTS JUSTICE," Teresa says.

"CFFIP?" Dexter says.

Two more women emerge from the bus carrying a long banner. This one says CITIZENS FOR A FAIR IMMIGRATION POLICY WANT JUSTICE NOW! "Oh dear," Teresa says, and reads the sign to Dexter.

"I think we're OK with this," Dexter says. "It's a group of civil libertarians up in Providence. Unitarians, good government, that sort of thing. I know their President, a guy named Ben Carlsson. I'll go down and say welcome. See if Ben's here. See if any of them want to attend the conference. We can certainly let them demonstrate on the south lawn. The parking won't spill over to that part of the grounds."

A small group of demonstrators, perhaps ten of them, have now emerged from the bus and are milling about by the gate. One of the three policemen has emerged from the squad car and is eyeing the demonstrators warily. From her vantage point at the top of the hill, Teresa can see Dexter shaking hands with a tall man who is wearing a seersucker suit and a Tilley hat. Then Teresa's cell rings.

"Hi Teresa," Andy's voice says. "I'm down at the police station with Sam Graves. I'm afraid we've got a problem. Or at least a difficult situation. First of all, Sam says that we are going to get several groups of protestors today, maybe tomorrow too. He's not sure about that."

"We already have one," Teresa says. "They just got here. Two of them are carrying a sign that says Citizens For a Fair Immigration Policy. Dexter says they're OK. He knows one of them, the President. He's talking with him right now. I can see him. He's going to invite them to the conference. I think."

"Good," Andy says. Sam says we can expect at least two more. Maybe three more. There's a group of Muslims from Newport. Sam says they're good people. He says they mainly want to make it clear to everyone that they're patriotic Americans. But Sam says they're upset about rumors that someone at Grafton House is making anti-Muslim comments. I'm afraid they're talking about Anettka. I'm not sure what to do about that. Maybe I can talk to them and tell them that we don't censor people even if we disagree with them. That sort of thing.

'There's another group, too. It's Hispanics from the Iglesia de Dios, over by the Quaker Meeting House. Sam knows some of them. He says his wife's cousin is one. They sound pretty much like the Muslim group. Sam says he doesn't think they'll be a problem either.

"But," Andy went on, "there's another group that Sam's worried about. It's some kind of motorcycle gang from Fall River. Sam says that the Fall River police called about them. It's not clear if they'll actually come down to Newport, but just in case they do, Sam's sending more policemen over.

"None of this is why Sam needed to talk with me. You may remember the flyer the Newport Police sent out about two men who're wanted for murder in Cambridge. Sam arrested one of them last night and he thinks the other one is here in Newport. He's armed and dangerous, and Sam says he may be planning to do something crazy at the conference. We're trying to decide the best way to deal with this character. I'm going to let Sam speak with you and tell you what he wants us to do."

"Teresa," Sam said, "you remember I told you about Tobie Shaw and this case. Tobie's been helping me try to find these guys. She's how we picked up one of them last night. So if she acts a little freaked out, that's why. But this guy that we haven't caught sounds like a real nut job.

"The flyer we sent out before showed this guy with long hair and a beard, but the man we caught says he's shaved off his beard and got a haircut. Now he looks like a clean-cut high school student. An athlete. The MIT housing service sent us a photo that shows him when he was a new student there. Short hair, no beard, just a mustache. We've put this photo on a new flyer, and we're emailing it to you. I'd like you to distribute copies to everyone at Grafton House. Everyone who's there for the conference. This is important, so please do it right now. OK? Now Dr. Eads wants to talk to you."

"Teresa?" Andy said, "I'm afraid that this is a real problem. The demonstrators we can handle. I'm not so sure about this man. But please do what Sam said and get this new flyer out to everyone. Sam's called WPRI-TV Eyewitness News. They're going to interview Sam on the morning news, and put the man's picture on their website. We can expect the press to show up as soon as this gets out.

"I won't be here much longer. I should be back at Grafton House by 8:30. So I should be there to make the opening remarks at nine."

"That's good," Teresa said. "Tell Sam I'm going to get the wanted flyers right now. I'll station interns at the doors to pass them out when people come in."

"OK," Andy said. "See you soon."

CHAPTER 40

Arturo Cisneros-Stern is eating breakfast on board the *Marte*, the Peruvian Navy Training Ship, which is now securely docked in Newport harbor. Calling it breakfast is something of a stretch. It's coffee and two jelly donuts fetched from a nearby Dunkin' Donuts shop on shore. Which is fine with Arturo, who is young and hungry. Arturo is sunning himself on the deck of the *Marte*. He has found an ancient plastic deck chair in the hold of the vessel and has positioned it on the deck overlooking the harbor. He is very pleased with himself.

He is looking forward to the day. His rich and famous uncle, Juan Carlos, is coming to Newport to see him, and he likes and admires his uncle. Most importantly, his American girlfriend, Tobie, is here in Newport. He has been thinking about Tobie since the *Marte* left Peru six weeks ago. In particular, he has been thinking about going to bed with Tobie again, his second time ever. She is an older woman (he's twenty-three and she's twenty-six), and she's very straightforward, unlike most of the girls he knows in Lima. He likes that.

When Arturo spoke with his uncle the night before, they had agreed to meet at 10:00 on the dock where the *Marte* is tied up. So Arturo has a couple of hours free before he meets Juan Carlos. He's not sure if it's a good idea to telephone Tobie this early in the morning. On the other hand, he wants to see Tobie, and the sooner he calls her the sooner they can make plans to meet. He finishes the first jelly doughnut (raspberry), drinks some coffee (very weak by Peruvian standards), and dials Tobie's number.

In her room at Grafton House, Tobie is finally sound asleep, after a troubled and sleepless night. But she has placed her cellphone next to her bed so she'll be sure to hear it if Arturo calls. Which she does. She is dreaming that she is on an ocean liner, asleep in a double bed in her stateroom. The ocean liner is on its way to somewhere exotic, far, far away from New England. Someone is calling her. Who can it be? It's Arturo, she thinks, and half asleep picks up her cellphone and says, "Hello"

"It's me," Arturo says, "I'm here in Newport."

"I know that," Tobie says. "Are they going to let you off your ship today? Because I really would like to see you."

"Yeah," Arturo says. "Me, too. I'd really like to see you, too."

"So, today sometime do you think?"

"Yeah, today. Maybe this morning?"

"Like when do you think?"

"Well...it's a little complicated. Because my uncle, my Uncle Juan Carlos, I told you about him, he's a professor at Harvard, and he's coming to see me this morning. We're supposed to meet at ten, here on the dock where we're tied up. But that won't last that long. Maybe an hour. I want to introduce him to our Captain. But after that I can go anywhere I want. I mean we can go anywhere you want to. Is that OK?"

"Could I come now? I mean, what if I came down there now, and met you on the dock and then I could hang around until your uncle got there, and we could talk while we're waiting. And then when he comes, I could go to a coffee shop and wait while you were meeting your uncle."

"That would be great. We're docked at Bowen's Wharf. You can't miss us. Our ship is the *Marte*, and anyone down here can tell you where we are."

"OK," Tobie says, "I'll be there in an hour. I'm so glad you called. I really want to see you."

"Me too."

This is of course not the best time in the world for Tobie to disappear from Grafton House. Among other things: 1) the Grafton House conference begins today, and she will be needed to operate the Center's antiquated information system; 2) she is already in big trouble because of the data analysis she did for Donald Pike (which is really too bad because it was technically a very good piece of analysis); and 3) Lieutenant Sam Graves has asked her to stay in touch in case he needs to talk with her during the day about catching George Rakylz.

Tobie knows all this, of course, but to be honest, none of it matters to her very much. As for work, well, what can I say? She's been at this job for almost a year, which is much too long, and she's been thinking a lot about moving on anyway. If they fire her so what, and they probably won't because she's the only person at Grafton House who actually knows how the IT system works.

She has a cellphone, so Sam can call her if he needs to, but she would be just as happy if she never heard from Sam Graves again. Or anybody else connected with what happened to Ed Moriarty. For which she's very sorry, absolutely, but there's nothing she can do now to make it OK, is there? Because unless she's very lucky it's pretty clear that she's really in trouble if Fat Willie tells the police what she did. Which is very unfair, because she didn't know what was actually going to happen to Ed.

And the truth is, what she wants to do right now is go see Arturo. She has been thinking a lot about Arturo since she last saw him in Peru. His parents were out of town on vacation, and Arturo had taken her to their house in Lima. They had hung out by his parents' swimming pool and talked, a lot, because Arturo spoke really good English that he had learned at prep school. Arturo's family was rich, and he wasn't sure what he wanted to do with his life, which is why he had joined the Navy as a first step. Arturo's mother was Jewish, which is one reason he was interested in Tobie, and he asked her a lot of questions about her parents (she liked them but they were old-fashioned in some respects, like keeping kosher) and Israel (which was complicated because on the one hand it was wrong to mistreat the Palestinians, but on the other hand they kept shooting rockets at Israel and blowing up buses, so what else could Israel do but be tough?)

They had made love in his bedroom and he had been sweet, it was his first time, he confessed. She didn't tell him it was her first time, but she kind of hinted that she hadn't done it very often, which was untrue but certainly a white lie that was fully justified.

But the memory of being with him and how good it felt had lasted for almost a year and a half, and thinking about seeing Arturo again had become a kind of mantra which made her feel better when things were a mess. Which they certainly were now.

Tobie thought all these things while getting dressed and putting on a little eye makeup. She didn't usually wear makeup because it was like burqas: a tool that the male- dominated culture uses to repress women. But her eyes were her best feature and shouldn't be wasted because of some theoretical principle. Then she went downstairs to the garage and mounted her Vespa. She emerged from the garage on the side of the mansion and started down the driveway towards the main gate. There was a crowd of people down by the gate, and she could see Dexter Slate talking with an elderly man in a white Tilley hat and a seersucker suit. Everyone turned and looked at her as the Vespa buzzed by them. Dexter seemed to be saying something to her, but she couldn't hear what it was. She waved at Dexter as she drove by, and called out that she would be back in an hour. This was a white lie, but it made her feel better. I'll call Teresa as soon as I find Arturo, she told herself.

CHAPTER 41

Jack Chrysler was not a morning person. He had found this out the hard way, by missing various important meetings. Relying on his inner clock and his willpower to get him up on time in the morning didn't work. He didn't have an inner clock. What he needed was an outside clock. An outside alarm clock. He had tried setting his cellphone alarm in the past, but he was no good at mechanical things. So he had acquired an old-fashioned spring-powered alarm clock with a large bell. He faithfully wound the clock up when he went to bed, and it reliably woke him up every morning.

July is warm in Newport, and Jack's suite in Grafton House was very warm, not to say hot and muggy. It was a very nice suite, with a bedroom and a sitting room, lots of mahogany furniture and more than a passing resemblance to the residence quarters in the Vatican's Santa Marta hotel. But the air conditioning unit was elderly and was currently on the blink. The windows were stuck, and he could only get one window open a crack, so there was no real ventilation. Which meant that after a long night of fitful sleep, Jack was hot and sweaty and in a bad mood.

Really, what it all boiled down to was: what was he going to do about Anettka? Because there was no question that things had changed. Until yesterday, he had been blissfully stuck in a familiar posture. He was in love with an unattainable woman. A woman who was willing to flirt mildly with him in his preferred role of lovesick swain. But also a woman who was thoroughly in control of herself, at least as far as amorous men were concerned. In other words, Jack was able to safely moon about Anettka because Anettka wasn't going to let him get to first base. She wasn't going to let him get out of control because she was in control.

And now, oh my god, Anettka had given in. Well, not all the way — they hadn't been to bed with each other... yet — but she was definitely heading that way. And he, Jack Chrysler, was now supposed to be looking out for her interests, taking care of Anettka, making sure that she was OK, and didn't get into trouble.

Which, to be honest with himself — something Jack tried to do every morning before breakfast — wasn't exactly what he had had in mind. What was that, exactly, Jack? he asked himself. The pleasure of being hopelessly in love, he answered himself. The point was that it was hopeless. And now it's not. Which is scary, and will require more thought, he told himself, but not now. I need to get ready for the conference. I'll think about Anettka later. This, I'm afraid, is characteristic of the way Jack usually deals with difficult personal issues.

Jack Chrysler's role in Grafton House, as has been mentioned before, is supposed to be twofold: to be a senior scholar and mentor for the younger staff; and to be an assistant to Andy Eads in running the Center. He is good at the first but dreadful at the second. The senior scholar/mentor gig is a piece of cake. Jack is an accomplished scholar. He enjoys doing scholarly research and younger scholars find his advice helpful. He's an impassioned advocate for what he believes are needed reforms in immigration policy. He has published widely, in scholarly journals, in works of scholarship and in popular works. Younger scholars admire him, even if they don't always agree with him. The assistant director job is different. Jack isn't a manager. The ins and outs of making a large organization run smoothly don't interest him. He doesn't like logistics. He doesn't like bossing other people around, which is what assistant directors of research centers are usually supposed to do.

Jack likes writing op-ed pieces telling the Congress, or the Governor of Illinois, what to do about big issues. Individuals are different. Jack doesn't like telling other people — as distinct from public officials — what to do. Well, not quite. He enjoys telling competent but inexperienced young scholars how to improve their methodologies and their analyses. But telling incompetent staff that they needed to improve their performance or be fired.... Well, that horrifies him. And as a practical matter, running a large research center like Grafton House requires a great deal of telling people what to do. So Jack's title of Assistant Director is basically an honorary title. *Primus inter pares.* Well, not quite *primus*, because Suleiman Khan is also an Assistant Director. More like being a Monsignor.

Suleiman is different from Jack in many ways, but as an Assistant Director he's remarkably like Jack. He's an eminent scholar, admired by younger scholars. And he's utterly uninterested in management. The net result is that neither Jack nor Suleiman plays a positive role in running Grafton House. As a practical matter, Andy runs Grafton House with the assistance of Teresa Morgan and Dexter Slate. He sometimes asks Jack and Suleiman for their advice, but he usually ignores what they say.

Jack and Suleiman are, however, partly responsible for the ongoing ideological warfare within the Center. Jack's a liberal, in the modern American sense of the term. He likes to tell people that he's a "card-carrying member of the ACLU and a bleeding heart." He believes that government needs to play an important role in providing a social safety net and in regulating business. Like Juan Carlos, Jack is concerned about protecting the poor and the powerless.

Suleiman is also a liberal, but in the traditional European sense of the term: limited government and laissez-faire economics. He thinks people should take care of themselves, and sees big government as hampering the efficiency of the economy. He admired Margaret Thatcher.

All of which is fine, and what you might expect at Grafton House, given Andy Eads' commitment to ideological diversity. Except that Andy wants the competition of diverse ideologies to be leavened by a dedication to comity. In other words, Andy wants to work towards consensus. Suleiman and Jack say they want to do this, but they really don't.

To begin with, Jack and Suleiman feel strongly that the other one is wrong, wrong, wrong. There are reasons for the strength of their feelings. Interestingly enough, Jack's views on immigration — which may seem very liberal to the reader — are highly orthodox within the immigration policy community. And scholars who question this orthodoxy are sometimes dismissed as right-wingers, illiberal and vaguely racist conservatives. If you are one of these scholars, you are likely to feel unfairly treated and indignant, and to harbor some animosity towards orthodox believers.

We can see similar behaviors in other academic disciplines. In the 1950s, for example, Keynesian economics ruled the roost in Ivy League economics departments. Students who questioned this orthodoxy were seen as obtuse and a little difficult. Fast-forward sixty years, however, and Keynesian economists have become a heretical minority.

There are, in Grafton House, a considerable number of young scholars who no longer believe in the liberal orthodoxies that Jack Chrysler proudly supports. These scholars have naturally gravitated toward Suleiman Khan, not because all their views necessarily match his, but because he is openly critical of Jack Chrysler and the reigning liberal orthodoxy.

Naturally, scholars liking a good fight as much as the next person, the liberal contingent at Grafton House has lined up behind Jack Chrysler. This is partly because Jack is a likable guy — a lot more likable than Suleiman— but mainly because the liberal orthodoxy is the side their bread is buttered on. When it comes time to move on to greener pastures, people in positions of power will remember who challenged the received ideas of the day. Best to avoid that. Besides, Jack's positions are much more appealing to the kind of caring young person who takes up subjects like immigration policy.

Is this a real problem? Well, that's not clear. It's certainly not what Andy Eads is striving for, and it occasionally gets a little out of hand. But this is the real world, after all, even here in the bucolic groves of academe. People aren't really always nice to one another. And controversy spices things up, gets the juices running — something often desired by bored academics. Think about it. Would you really like to spend your life learning more and more about what a wag once called less and less?

CHAPTER 42

George Rakylz was awakened by the sound of a fire engine noisily proceeding down Marlborough Street towards the fire station. He turned on his side, expecting to see Maureen, the Catholic Irish Alcoholic lying next to him, but no one was there. He sat up in bed, and listened to see if she was somewhere else in the apartment. Not a sound. Then he noticed a yellow legal pad propped up on Maureen's pillow.

"Hi Jock," Maureen's note began. Jacques Derrida was what George had called himself the night before when he hooked up with Maureen. Maureen, not being an intellectual, had understood him to say Jock. George had not actually read anything by Derrida, but one evening while stoned he had sort of read an article in *Rolling Stone* about post-structuralism. The article said that Derrida had developed a "…post-modern form of semiotic analysis known as deconstruction," and George had really liked the way those words sounded, particularly the post-modern deconstruction part. So when he introduced himself to Maureen he had suddenly decided to adopt Jacques Derrida as a *nom de guerre*. Not that he was going to abandon Omega. But still, Jacques Derrida was pretty cool. The name reminded him of Jean-Jacques Rousseau, who was also cool. That's the way my mind always works, George thought, kind of flashes of genius. Maureen's note said:

I'm going over to the Y in Middletown. I've got to do some paperwork for my camp counselor job. I'll be back here around 9 to round you up for the catering gig that I told you about. I hope you'll be here because I really need the help. I've hung a set of waiter's whites in the closet by the bathroom. They belong to my brother, who's your size (☺ well NOT that way!). I had a very nice time last night and hope you'll be here.

Love, Maureen

George contemplated this note for a moment. Maybe he wouldn't take Maureen as a hostage after all. It was clear that his luck was improving. He had had a few bad days, but that was to be expected. Success demanded sacrifice and the ability to overcome adversity. He had dedicated himself to improving the world, and the vested interests of the world were naturally his mortal enemies. So, it was no wonder that things hadn't always gone perfectly.

But man's natural goodness would prevail. Things were definitely looking up. "Every prospect pleases...." Somebody famous had written that but he couldn't remember who it was right now. Anyway, the day ahead looked like it was going to be spectacular, in more ways than one. A real Fourth-of-July blast.

George got up out of bed and went into the bathroom. Maureen had left a tube of toothpaste and a new toothbrush on the lavatory sink next to a bottle of Listerine. George rinsed out his mouth and vigorously brushed his teeth. Then he wandered out into the living room and turned on the TV.

"Turning to late-breaking news this morning, WPRI has learned from law enforcement sources that an MIT graduate student wanted on suspicion of murdering a drug dealer last month in Cambridge, Massachusetts, is believed to be in the Newport area. This is a picture of the wanted man, George Rakylz, taken on his admission to MIT four years ago. Rakylz is twenty-nine years old. He is believed to be heavily armed and dangerous. Anyone who knows of his whereabouts is encouraged to call ..." and here the TV reporter read from a list of phone numbers which slowly scrolled across the screen.

Huh! George thought. The wanted picture was back on the screen, while the reporter recited details of the Ed Moriarty incident. (Incident was the way George preferred to think of that event. No real blame here except for Moriarty himself, who shouldn't have been so stupid.) George examined his picture. The photo showed a very young-looking man with lots of very curly black hair. Clean-shaven except for a handlebar mustache. George went back to the bathroom and examined himself in the mirror. He no longer had the mustache, and his hair was very short. Unless someone compared him very closely with the photo, he wasn't going to be recognized. I wonder if there's anything to eat around here, George thought and headed for the kitchen.

CHAPTER 43

Wilford (Fat Willie) Thomas was no longer in his original cell. He had been moved nearer the front of the police station, into a larger cell directly across the hall from an elderly TV set. The set was set to WPRI, and when the (very cute) anchorwoman began talking about George Rakylz, Willie put down his jelly doughnut and watched with interest. "No," he said out loud when they showed George's photo. I better tell them that photo's no good, Willie thought. I'm sorry to be a snitch, but that dude is nuts. He walked over to the cell door and called out "Hello!" In a minute or so, one of the policemen at the station appeared, a short young man wearing a T-shirt that said "Broons!"

"I gotta talk to Lieutenant Graves," Willie said. "That photo of George Rakylz — the one on TV—it's no good. He doesn't look that way any more."

"Oh!" the young cop said. "I better tell Sam," and disappeared down the corridor.

In a moment, Sam Graves appeared. "Tommy says you told him the Rakylz photo's no good. I'm sorry I didn't show it to you. That was stupid of me. I wasn't thinking. What does he really look like? I mean compared to the photo."

"No mustache," Willie said, "Plus his hair is real short, no more curls. He's got a buzz cut, you know, like he just started boot camp in the Marines."

"Shit," Sam Graves said. "Thank you." And disappeared down the hall.

"Teresa," Sam said when he reached Teresa Morgan on her cellphone. "I screwed up on the photo of Rakylz that I sent you. Do you have anybody there who can use Photoshop? The man we arrested last night says that Rakylz has shaved off his mustache and cut his hair very short. He says a buzz cut. So we need to change the wanted notice photo."

"We can do that," Teresa said. "My partner, Alex, the woman who keeps our beehives — is really good at Photoshop. I'll text her. Right now."

"Good," Sam Graves said. "Grace, my secretary, could do it, but she's on vacation on the Cape. I'll see if we can find someone around here who can do it as backup, too. Sorry to be such a nuisance."

"No problem, Sam," Teresa said. "I'll get right on it." And she promptly sent a text to Alex. Who shortly thereafter appeared in Teresa's office with her laptop and began Photoshopping George Rakylz's wanted photo.

Teresa Morgan (named after her mother's favorite actress, Teresa Wright) is 45 years old. She has worked at Grafton House for 22 years. Her title on paper is "Administrative Assistant to the Director," which doesn't sound very impressive. In fact, Teresa is one of the most powerful people in Grafton House. In tandem with Dexter Slate, with occasional guidance from Andy Eads, Teresa runs the place.

Teresa is a Newport native. Like Sam Graves, Teresa grew up in the city's long established African-American community, whose forebears came to work as servants in the city's mansions during the Gilded Age. Like Sam Graves, Teresa graduated from Rogers High School, and lacking the money to go to college, joined the Army. After three years in a Pentagon procurement office, Teresa still wanted to go to college and still didn't have the money. So she moved back in with her parents (who were delighted to have her back) and took a secretarial job at Grafton House.

Teresa prospered at Grafton House. Dr. Wolfgang Froelich, the Director who preceded Andy Eads, recognized her potential and she became his secretary. As the Director's secretary, Teresa learned all about the details of operating a research center. And when Andy Eads appeared on the scene, he found her an invaluable guide. With some difficulty —- because Teresa lacks a college degree — Andy has succeeded in getting Harvard's University Hall to pay Teresa what they pay Dexter Slate. Teresa's career at Grafton House has been very successful and almost trouble-free.

This has not always been true of Teresa's personal life. Upon her return to Newport, Teresa promptly got pregnant after a one-night stand with a friend from high school. She considered marrying the father, but decided against it. Her parents were supportive — they didn't like the father, but they were thrilled to have a grandchild — and Teresa's mother happily took over the role of baby sitter while Teresa went to work.

Teresa initially confined her romantic endeavors to men. She dated friends from high school. She dated sailors from the various Navy units stationed in Newport. She had a long affair with her dentist, an older and happily married man. None of these efforts to craft a love life was very satisfactory. Except maybe the dentist, but then again he was happily married already so that wasn't really in the cards. Then, one evening, Teresa met a professor at the Naval War College, one of the first female graduates of the Naval Academy. One thing led to another, and Teresa wound up in bed with the professor. And enjoyed it. This possibility had always been in the back of Teresa's mind, but until then she had never actually tried it on for size. Once she did, there was no going back. That was what she wanted to do, and that was what she did. From then on.

She had met Alex, the Irish beekeeper, two years earlier, when Alex applied for the beekeeping job at Grafton House. The previous beekeeper had been forced to retire because of poor health, and no one on the grounds keeping staff had wanted to take the job on.

Alex had been lucky enough to win a green card in the diversity lottery, and had worked as a waitress in Boston for several years. She had come to Newport to visit her aunt and uncle, and had seen the ad for the beekeeper job in the *Newport Daily News*. Alex had studied beekeeping in Ireland in a secondary vocational school, and Teresa hired her on the spot.

It was love at first sight and within a couple of weeks, Alex had moved into Teresa's apartment in Grafton House. Interestingly enough, no one seemed surprised by this development. Teresa's parents and friends thought, and said, well, that's our Teresa, and Andy Eads was pleased that his right-hand woman had found a nice partner. Remember, we're in a particularly blue corner of a blue state.

We'll come back to Alex later, but suffice it to say here that Alex is a genuinely nice person. Everyone likes her. Everyone thinks that she's been very good for Teresa, who — let's face it — is a workaholic with control-freak tendencies who's a little uptight. (Of course, these characteristics had a lot to do with Teresa's success.) Alex is relaxed, and enjoys working with bees, which means she's patient and painstaking. These are good qualities to have if you want to live with, and get along with, Teresa Morgan.

But to get back to George Rakylz's wanted picture. In about thirty minutes, Alex produced a photo showing George with a buzz cut and no mustache. Teresa emailed the photo to Sam, who emailed it to the newsroom at WPRI, and in half an hour, the new picture was shown on TV. But George Rakylz didn't see that, because he had turned off the TV in Maureen's apartment and had gone back to sleep.

CHAPTER 44

Imagine that you are Phileas Fogg and that you are comfortably seated in the wicker basket of a hot-air balloon floating high in the air above Audience Island. (You can pretend to be David Niven if you find that more comfortable.) You are balancing a cup of *café au lait* on your lap, and focusing a telescope on the landscape below you. Or you can pretend you're a hummingbird, temporarily hovering over Newport County. It doesn't really matter. In either case, you have a bird's eye view of the action, of everything that's going on down below. This is what you see.

At the southern tip of the island —really, the southwestern tip of the island — you can see Grafton House and the large tent on the grounds of the mansion. Zoom in for a closer look. You can see the scholars and protestors driving into the parking lot and walking across the lawn to the big tent behind the mansion. Even at this distance, it's not hard to tell the scholars in the crowd from the protestors. The scholars are either walking alone or chatting with one or two colleagues. The protestors are traveling in groups, and the groups are separate from one another. Not exactly enemy camps, but not mixing either. Never mind, everything down there seems calm and peaceful.

And look, down by the gate, we can see the Grafton House Lincoln, which has just arrived. Harold Cummings is getting out of the car to speak with two Newport policemen who are standing by the gate. We can't see Andy Eads, but he's sitting in the back seat going over the notes for his opening remarks.

Now, tell Passepartout you want to see more of the island. As the balloon moves over the center of Newport, you'll pass over a very large sailboat tied up at Bowen's Wharf.

If you zoom in closer you will see Peruvian Naval Ensign Arturo Cisneros-Stern sitting in a folding chair on the deck of the sailboat and eating a jelly doughnut. The boat's called the *Marte*, and it's a Peruvian Navy training ship — one of the famous Tall Ships. Arturo is waiting, impatiently, for his girlfriend Tobie Shaw, and his uncle Juan Carlos Cisneros, to arrive.

Look back towards Grafton House and you will see Tobie Shaw, mounted on her Vespa motor scooter, and zooming along Spring Street in the direction of Bowen's Wharf. She is traveling at an excessive rate of speed, but she's wearing a helmet and we trust that she'll get there safely.

Float a little higher and you'll have a good view of the routes from the outside world into Newport. To the west, you can see the Pell Bridge connecting Jamestown to Aquidneck Island. Travelers from the Amtrak station in Kingston and Greene Airport in Providence (really Warwick) cross the Pell Bridge to get to Newport. Nobody we've met so far is coming this way, but there are undoubtedly stragglers who will take this route —assorted scholars who are running late for the opening session or planning to skip it altogether and arrive in the afternoon.

To the North, RI 114 meanders through Middletown and Portsmouth. Pooh Gardiner left her condo in Portsmouth about 35 minutes ago and is closing in on the corner of Broadway and Miantonomi Avenue, a.k.a. the border where Middletown turns into Newport. She'll probably be a little bit late but she isn't worried. She called Jack Chrysler earlier in the morning to tell him she was coming. Jack, in turn, told Teresa Morgan that Anettka's husband's cousin Pooh Gardiner was coming. Teresa's mother and grandparents had worked for the Gardiner family, so she already knew who the Gardiners were: very important people. So Teresa immediately called Pooh and told her that a visitor's packet would be waiting for her at the conference tent. Making sure that very important people are taken proper care of is part of Teresa's job.

Eventually RI 114 runs out of island. That's about where it connects with RI 24. Slightly further to the north, RI 24 turns into MA 24, which is the road people take if they're driving to Newport from Cambridge, MA. Juan Carlos and Jackie Persac (and Jackie's partner, Edgar) are doing just that.

So, as a matter of fact, are four very excited members of the Fall River, MA branch of SNARL, the Systematic National Anarchist

Revolutionary League. They are riding motorcycles (Japanese imports) and playing very loud music on portable sound systems (Chinese imports) attached to their bikes. (Their profoundly satisfying opposition to free trade hasn't required them to stop buying imports.)

The kid on the first bike is named Pedro Murphy. His mother is Puerto Rican and his father is Irish. He lives with his parents, and neither they nor he like it one bit. Pedro's twenty-three, a graduate of URI (B.A. in Social Relations) and employed part-time at McDonald's. Pedro's usually very bored, and he's excited to be in the vanguard of The Movement. "The Movement" is the term SNARL members use to describe themselves and their somewhat fuzzy belief system. He's assumed the leadership of this expedition, although he really hasn't decided what he wants to do when his team gets to Newport.

The kid on the fourth motorcycle is a confidential informant for the Fall River Police Department: what cops call a CI. His name is Ezekiel Jones. People call him Lizard, which kind of fits his personality. He's why the FRPD knows a lot about SNARL. Right now he's sending a text to Lieutenant Grogan of the FRPD. He's using both hands to text and steering the bike with his thighs. Amazing. I'm a little worried by these guys, but probably shouldn't be. The FRPD is pretty competent, and they're keeping Sam Graves up to date on what SNARL's crusaders are doing. Right now, they've just crossed the state line and have arrived in Rhode Island.

Jackie Persac and his partner, Edgar Stern, are driving through Fall River right now in Jackie's ten-year-old Toyota pickup. They're going through the center of town because Jackie wanted to drive by Lizzie Borden's house. They're about fifteen minutes behind the SNARL convoy. Edgar wants to stop and get a cup of coffee, but Jackie doesn't want to. However, they're passing a Dunkin' Donuts shop just now, and I think Jackie's going to give in and stop. He is thinking about getting a glazed donut. Maybe two.

Juan Carlos Cisneros is already in Rhode Island, speeding down RI 114 on his beautiful Harley. He is thinking about Phoebe. He googled Grafton House when he got up this morning, and he knows that today's the start of their big conference. So it's probably not the best time to appear on Phoebe's doorstep. Still, Juan Carlos is a confident man. He generally succeeds at getting what he wants and he thinks nothing has changed.

Juan Carlos loves his Harley. It symbolizes America for him: a gorgeous piece of machinery that lets him speed through life like a knight in (or rather on) shining armor.

Nothing is perfect, though, and that certainly goes for Juan Carlos' Harley. According to some experts, there's a basic design flaw in Harley-Davidson's Twin-Cam V-I Twin engine. The design of the engine's cam drive system places soft plastic or nylon shoes over the cam chains. When the shoes wear out, there's metal-to-metal contact. This generates metal shavings that can cause a catastrophic engine failure.

Whether or not this is what happened to Juan Carlos' Harley is probably impossible to tell at this distance. Nevertheless, out of the blue, as Juan Carlos glided along, he heard a big bang and his engine died. On the spot. Kaput. Fortunately, Juan Carlos wasn't going that fast, and he managed to coast off the pavement to a grassy slope by the road.

Juan Carlos is an experienced traveler, and although he's not happy about this, he knows what to do. He has a smart phone, and he will use it to call for help. Maybe call AAA. Unfortunately, Juan Carlos forgot to charge his phone last night, and the lovely alarm music that woke him earlier in the morning was also the last gasp of the phone's battery. So he can't call anybody for help.

His next step is also automatic. Juan Carlos stands next to the highway and attempts to flag down a passing motorist. But no one stops. On and on the traffic flows past him, big cars, small cars, large trucks, buses. No one stops or even looks interested in his plight.

Then the four SNARL members zoom by on their bikes. There is a vague fellow feeling that usually links motorcycle owners together. Ordinarily, Juan Carlos would have benefited from this fellow feeling: another motorcyclist would have stopped to offer help. But the SNARL members are young men riding cheap Japanese bikes and the Juan Carlos they see by the side of the road is an old probably rich guy riding an expensive Harley. Which has broken down and serves him right. So the SNARL members ignore Juan Carlos. And don't stop. However, Ezekiel texts Lieutenant Grogan that a Harley has broken down just south of the RI border, and Grogan (an avid Harley owner) calls the RI State Police and reports the accident. People often are nice, for whatever reason.

And fortunately for Juan Carlos, the next people to come along are Jackie Persac and Edgar Stern in Jackie's Toyota pickup. "That's Phoebe's boyfriend," Jackie says to Edgar. "We probably should stop,"

"Yeah, stop," Edgar says. "I know him. He's from Peru. His brother married my cousin. He's a good guy." So they stop.

We'll get back to the three of them in a minute. But first let's take a look at Paul Gardiner.

CHAPTER 45

If you point your telescope toward Fall River you'll be able to see Paul Gardiner's silver Camry. He's heading south on MA 24, and he's just north of Fall River. He's not in a good mood.

He had intended to call Anettka on Friday afternoon before his plane left Paris. But after lunch, he developed an upset stomach — he wasn't used to eating at McDonald's — and when he got to Charles de Gaulle Airport, his stomach fell out, and he forgot about calling Anettka. Then, after his plane took off, he told himself (well, actually he sort of promised himself) that he would call Anettka as soon as his plane landed in Boston. But there was a long line at Customs and he didn't get around to it.

In the taxi taking him to his Beacon Hill apartment, he briefly thought about calling Anettka. But then he got into conversation with the driver — an interesting young woman from the Cote d'Ivoire with whom he spoke French (he liked speaking French) — and he didn't call.

When he got to his apartment on Friday night, he told himself he would call Anettka as soon as he unpacked. But then he didn't want to. He had an excellent excuse. He was still on Paris time, so it felt like two in the morning, even though the sun was just going down in Boston. And he usually went to bed by nine p.m. He told himself that he was too tired and didn't feel up to it just then and would call her in the morning. So he never called her Friday to say he was back in the States.

Now it was Saturday morning, and of course the question she was going to ask him, the obvious question, was: why didn't you call me to say you were coming home? And Paul didn't know how he was going to answer that question. So he still hadn't called Anettka. You really can't blame him, although you can be sure that Anettka will.

Anyway, here he is on MA 24 in his 1996 Toyota Camry. He has had this Camry for a long time and he likes it. Thanks to good engineering and regular maintenance it still runs well, even though it

John Vialet

has 192,007 miles on the odometer. Paul likes being frugal, and he
dislikes ostentation. So the Camry suits him to a T. He particularly
likes the sun roof, which he has just opened to let in the sun.

It occurs to him that he should call Edna, the housekeeper who
lives in his Newport house. Edna has worked for his family since
Paul was a boy, which means she's probably almost eighty by now.
Having her live at the house is convenient for Paul. It's also a nice
way to supplement the pension Paul's mother pays Edna. If I call
Edna now, Paul thinks, she can get the house ready for me. And
Anettka can join me at the house as soon as her conference is over.
Paul hasn't really paid any attention to the Grafton House
conference. Or to what Anettka is likely to want to do while the
conference is underway.

Which obviously isn't good. But Edna is very pleased to hear
from him when he phones her, and promises to make lobster salad
with coleslaw and potato salad. That was a good idea, Paul thinks,
and puts his iPhone in the glove compartment.

Paul is driving at what he thinks is the posted speed limit — fifty
mph — but is actually five mph more than the legal limit. So he's
speeding, as far as the law is concerned. And he's about to be pulled
over by a Massachusetts State Police cruiser. Which happens as soon
as he retrieves his cellphone from the glove compartment and starts
to key in Anettka's number. So he puts the phone down and doesn't
call her.

And after the State trooper — a very young man with a crew-cut
who clearly thinks Paul is ancient and slightly senile— gives him a
stern warning, Paul puts the cellphone back in the glove
compartment and turns on the Camry's elderly Sirius receiver. The
receiver is set to a classical music channel that is playing Chopin's
Nocturne Op. 9. No. 2. The pianist is Arthur Rubinstein.

I will wait until I get to Newport to call her, Paul tells himself.
The first morning of the Grafton House conference is obviously not a
good time to call one of their senior scholars. Even if she is my wife.
He's not sure why, but he feels melancholy. It's the music, he tells
himself, but he doesn't turn it off. His stomach feels acidy, and he

takes a CVS anti-gas anti-acid pill. Two of them, actually, on the theory that if one's good, two's better.

Back in Rhode Island, Jackie, Edgar and Juan Carlos are examining Juan Carlos' Harley. Remember this. They're all engineers. All three of them. And Edgar and Juan Carlos both own Harleys. So when they look at this Harley, they don't see an inscrutable malfunctioning appliance. They see a beloved and very interesting piece of machinery. They ask themselves, what's wrong with this Harley? And can we fix it?

Anyway, they have a very short but very interesting discussion about the Harley's breakdown. Various explanations are offered. Edgar's analysis prevails. As it happens, Edgar is familiar with the controversy over whether there's a basic design flaw in Harley-Davidson's Twin-Cam V-I Twin engine. "It's probably the cam chain tensioners," Edgar says. "They put nylon shoes over the chains and the shoes wear out. So you get direct metal-on-metal contact and metal shavings flying every which way. Fucks the engine up very nicely."

"So there's nothing we can do here, then," Juan Carlos says.

"Nothing except take it to a good shop," Edgar says. "I know where to take it in Boston, but not down here."

"We can ask Siri," Jackie says, and produces his iPhone. Functioning as billed, Siri finds the nearest Harley dealer. It's in Middletown. "We can take you there," Jackie says.

After the three men manhandle the remarkably heavy Harley into the Toyota's bed, Edgar gets in the rear seat of the pickup — it's got a crew cab— so Juan Carlos, the tallest of the three men, can sit in front.

It takes Juan Carlos about five minutes to recharge his cellphone — Jackie has a nifty charger installed in the Toyota's dashboard— and then Juan Carlos calls Arturo. Arturo is unfazed by the news that Juan Carlos' motorcycle is out of service. He knows his uncle will cope. And he's very pleased to learn that his uncle has been rescued by his mother's cousin, Edgar Stern. He remembers Edgar visiting his mother when he was a child. Juan Carlos tells Arturo that he'll call him later in the day, after he's taken the Harley to a repair shop.

"Okay." Arturo is sorry his uncle is delayed but he's also looking forward to seeing Tobie, who is just now pulling up to the dock where the *Marte* is tied up.

Juan Carlos is busily revising his plans for the day. If his Harley can't be fixed right away, he'll rent another motorcycle and spend a little time with Arturo After that, he'll find Phoebe. Maybe go to Grafton House and spend a little time at the conference. He's an old friend of Andy Eads and he's an immigrant — a very prominent immigrant, at that. So they'll roll out the red carpet for him if he shows up. (And in fact, Juan Carlos isn't dreaming. That's exactly what will happen if he shows up.)

Jackie and Edgar are also planning their day. Jackie has also thought about dropping by Grafton House and trying to see Phoebe. Maybe I'll phone her, he thinks. Edgar is thinking about Arturo. He's Arturo's cousin, not his uncle. But he feels like he's Arturo's uncle. And he would like to see Arturo and find out how Arturo's mother is doing. He hasn't been back to Lima for almost a decade, and he's feeling a little homesick. Which is ridiculous, because he didn't really like Peru that much when he lived there, and he much preferred living in Cambridge, MA. Never mind, people are like that.

Let's see now. Have we left anyone out? Well, the people at Grafton House come to mind. And George Rakylz. What can we say about them? Let's find out.

CHAPTER 46

First, let's take another look at Arturo and Tobie. Tobie has been thinking about Arturo for a long time, now. She had decided that she really liked him the year before when they slept together in his parents' house in Lima. And recently, given all the stupid stuff that was going on — Ed Moriarty being dead and Fat Willie in jail and the nut George hiding out somewhere in Newport, she had been thinking more and more about Arturo. Because what she needs right now is a knight in shining armor who will rescue her from a ridiculous mess that really isn't her fault. She feels bad about Ed being dead, but there's nothing she can do now to fix that.

And now, there he was, standing on the dock next to his very big sailboat and looking wonderfully handsome. He seemed to have grown taller since the last time she saw him. Really, he looked wonderful. If she described him to her parents, she thought, I could say that he was sort of an ideal combination of Spanish and Jewish. Brown hair, blue eyes, a nice suntan, but not too tan. Just right. Maybe we could get married, she thought suddenly.

Arturo is engaged in forward planning, too, which he doesn't usually do. He definitely wants to see his Uncle Juan Carlos. But Juan Carlos has just called to say he's in Middletown and his motorcycle is broken. He's trying to fix his motorcycle but it's not clear how long that's going to take. So it's not clear when Juan Carlos will arrive in Newport. And Arturo's looking forward to seeing his mother's cousin Edgar, who has just called to tell him about Juan Carlos' broken motorcycle. Edgar will be there in a few minutes. But mostly, what Arturo wants to do is 1) talk to Tobie, and 2) as soon as practical, go to bed with her. Which means it will be necessary to do some planning. And then it comes to him. I'll ask Tobie what to do, he thinks.

As a general rule, this is how successful relationships come to pass. One member of the couple needs to do something but isn't sure how to do it. And then realizes that the other member of the couple will know how to do it, and do it well in the bargain.

As Tobie's Vespa comes to a halt in front of the *Marte*, Arturo finishes his jelly doughnut and wipes his mouth with a paper napkin. Tobie takes off her blue helmet and quickly combs her hair. They walk towards each other solemnly. (They both feel shy.) Then they hug each other and Tobie kisses Arturo on the chin. He's much taller than she is, and that's as far as she can easily reach without standing on tiptoes. Then Arturo bends down and kisses Tobie on the lips and Tobie stands on her tiptoes and kisses him back. This sounds simple but is without question a great triumph."I've missed you," Arturo says.

"I've missed you, too," Tobie says. "I've thought about you a lot."

"Me, too," Arturo says.

We'll leave them alone now for a while. But hang in there. We'll be back.

CHAPTER 47

Anettka is not a morning person, either. She does her best work at night, so she usually goes to bed around two in the morning, and gets up at 9:30 or ten. She feels groggy when she wakes up. Not exactly sleepy, more like disorganized. Unless there's a crisis, she usually waits until after lunch to start working. She doesn't even try to work in the morning.

Instead, she usually goes for a run. A long run. When she wakes up, she makes herself a cup of tea (Earl Grey tea bags) and drinks it slowly. Goes to the bathroom and brushes her teeth. Puts on shorts and sneakers. And makeup. And goes for a run.

When her husband Paul is in town, they stay at Paul's family's house. The Gardiner family complex is just off Ocean Drive, so that's where she and Paul usually run. Anettka's a very fast runner and Paul's not, so most of the time Paul rides a bike instead of actually running. When she's staying at Grafton House, Anettka usually runs at Fort Adams. But this morning, she decides to run along Ocean Drive.

Each of the residence suites in Grafton House has a telephone. A landline telephone. When the house was built, the phones were connected to a central switchboard, which was manually operated by a human being –usually a woman – called " The Operator." Now the phones are connected to a computer, which does the same thing The Operator did. If you dial 5 on your room's phone, you can schedule a wake-up call. Just like you can in a Holiday Inn.

Anettka usually doesn't bother with this; she doesn't usually need to be told it's time to wake up. But this morning she knew she was supposed to attend the opening session of the conference. At 9:30. Ugh. So before she went to sleep on Friday night, she scheduled a wake-up call for 7:15 on Saturday morning.

She had gone to bed a little after one, which was rather early for her. But she found it hard to stop thinking about her impossible problems, and she couldn't fall asleep for what seemed like hours.

Eventually, she managed to coax her mind into thinking about ways to describe the technical details of her talk in colloquial English. At which point she finally fell asleep.

But not for long. She was fast asleep, had reached the REM state, and began to dream. In her dream, she was naked and lying on a large bed in a very modern hotel room. A man was taking a shower in the adjoining bathroom. She wondered: who is he? But before she could decide, the telephone next to the bed rang. She tried to ignore it, but it kept ringing. So she woke up. And went for a run.

Ocean Drive is a pleasant place to run, especially if it's early on a summer morning in July. Before it gets too hot. But this morning, Anettka does not feel relaxed. She did not sleep well, and her worries of the night before continue to plague her. So she runs at a fast pace along Ocean Drive – the app on her iPhone says she's running six-minute miles. At 8:05 a.m., she looks at her iPhone and realizes she's about two miles away from Grafton House. Which is cutting it a little too close for comfort. She's supposed to be dressed and present when the conference kicks off at 9:30.

So she picks up her pace, and just for the hell of it runs along the brick retaining wall near Brenton Point that separates Ocean Drive from a very steep slope down to the Bay. It's a little dangerous, of course, but she's agile. Sure footed. Until, all of a sudden, her right foot lands on a loose stone in the retaining wall. At which point, several unpleasant things happen. First of all, she twists her right ankle. Badly. It hurts a lot. Second, she falls off the retaining wall. The wrong side of the retaining wall. The side with the very steep slope.

This is scary. The tide is coming in and huge waves are crashing noisily on the rocky shore below. And the slope is very steep, so she immediately slides rapidly towards the shore. Which is not at all soft and sandy.

Then, suddenly, about half way down the slope, she lands on a large rock and stops sliding.

The rock juts out from the slope and forms a narrow ledge that's just wide enough for Anettka to lie on. She lies there for a few moments without daring to move. Then she peers over the edge of the ledge and sees the waves crashing on the rocks below. I almost died, she thinks. What a stupid thing to do. Why did I try to run on the wall?

Her ankle hurts. She's wearing shorts and a T-shirt, so she's covered with scratches from her fall. The slope itself is rocky and covered with thorny bushes. They're probably poison ivy, she thinks. And she feels foolish. Which actually isn't so bad, because it takes her mind off her various emotional problems and focuses it on her immediate situation. Which is very unpleasant, to be sure. But also very real.

What to do? She immediately reaches for her iPhone, which she carries in a pouch attached to a strap around her waist. It's not there. Of course. It's undoubtedly somewhere on the slope above her. On the ground. Underneath a thorny bush. "Shit," Anettka says. Which is uncharacteristic of her. She rarely swears. What am I going to do? she asks herself. A loud voice immediately responds to this question, saying:

"Anettka! Can you hear me?"

One of life's most dispiriting lessons is the fact that some people are luckier than others. This is not to say that lucky people don't have bad things happen to them, or that unlucky people don't have nice things happen to them. Still, it's unquestionably true that some people are very lucky.

Of course, you have to ask what does it mean to be lucky? When Cio-Cio-san arrives for her sham wedding to Lt. Pinkerton, Mr. Sharpless tells Pinkerton, "You're a lucky man." What Sharpless means is that Cio-Cio-san is an adolescent boy's wet dream: nubile, pretty, and fifteen years old. Sharpless thinks Pinkerton is lucky because he's getting all this at a bargain price. And he thinks Butterfly is getting screwed: Pinkerton's luck is being acquired at Butterfly's expense; QED, Butterfly is unlucky.

But is Sharpless correct? On the one hand, Butterfly is definitely unlucky in a lot of respects. Her father had to kill himself to preserve the family honor, and she had to become a geisha. Her "husband" knocks her up, skips town and leaves her in the lurch. When he does come back to Nagasaki, he brings along his American wife, making it completely clear to Butterfly that her "marriage" was a sham.

On the other hand, Butterfly has been living in a very interesting dream world. A fantasy world fueled by her own vivid imagination. In that world, Pinkerton loves her dearly. He will certainly come back to take care of her. And he will be delighted to find that he has fathered a wonderful son. And Butterfly gets to sing wonderful songs about all these things, songs that move our hearts. Isn't this lucky?

And when Pinkerton returns and finds Butterfly dying, hasn't his so-called luck turned on him? Pinkerton hates himself for what he's done. And isn't Butterfly lucky? She has kept her father's sword so she can sing a final beautiful song and then do the honorable thing.

I guess you can say it all depends on how you define luck. Still, Anettka is definitely in the lucky category. She has inherited a wonderful set of genes, which means that she is physically healthy, very intelligent, and beautiful. She is the child of a wealthy family in a country where most families are very poor. She was well loved by her parents and her nanny. She was brought up to be self-reliant and competent and well organized. She received a wonderful education at elite universities, which allowed her to make many influential and well-connected friends.

And when her father decided that he should murder her in order to avoid a stain on his honor, all these lucky things allowed her to escape death. Her mother, and her nanny and her friends, and the family house servants made sure that she knew what her father and brothers were planning.

So Anettka was able to flee Pakistan, obtain refugee status in the UK and then the US — not an easy thing to do — because of her friends in high places. And she was introduced to her husband, Paul Gardiner, because these same friends invited her to a party on Beacon Hill. And she was lucky when Paul Gardiner, who was powerful and rich, fell in love with her.

It's of course clear that these lucky things came at a price. Paul's a wonderful man, but he's twice as old as she is, and her sex life sucks. She feels nutty about her family and their religion, Islam, which is one of the world's saner religions. So nutty that she often feels hysterical. She's suffering from a classic case of post-traumatic stress. Still, on balance, you have to say Anettka's lucky. Even now, as she lies on a narrow stone ledge jutting out from the steep slope next to Ocean Drive near Brenton Point. And hears someone shout, again, "Anettka! Can you hear me?"

And gratefully shouts back "Yes! Yes! I can hear you!"

CHAPTER 48

Juan Carlos was greeted with open arms at the Harley dealership in Middletown. There are certain business transactions in which it is clear from the outset that price is not a major consideration. Or concern. Hobbies often fall into this category. The ownership of large motorcycles is such a hobby.

The owners of large motorcycles such as those made by Harley Davidson are not necessarily rich. But they want the best, and are prepared to pay for it. So when Juan Carlos arrived with his broken Harley, the owner of the dealership bent over backwards to welcome him. At the very least, Juan Carlos' Harley was going to require expensive repairs. And very possibly, Juan Carlos was going to need, and therefore buy, a new Harley.

Moreover, the dealer's owner is a snob, and the Harvard faculty parking plaque on the Harley makes it clear that Juan Carlos "really rates," as my mother was fond of saying. And Juan Carlos really does rate. He radiates confidence and charm. He expects people to like him, and they do. So he is certainly a very promising customer.

After an interesting discussion with the dealer's mechanic, an older man originally from Havana, it is decided that Juan Carlos will rent another Harley from the dealer, and use it over the weekend while the shop investigates what can be done to fix his old Harley. The dealer rents Juan Carlos a Road King, which sells for around $20,000 before taxes. He makes it clear that customization and fancier models are available at a substantial discount.

With his motorcycle problem taken care of for the time being, Juan Carlos goes to the Dunkin' Donuts shop next door, and orders a cup of coffee and two glazed doughnuts. (Not everyone likes jelly doughnuts.) What next, he asks himself.

As we have seen, Juan Carlos' decision to visit Newport was prompted by a call from his nephew Arturo. Seeing Arturo was certainly appealing enough all by itself to justify a visit to Newport.

Juan Carlos likes Arturo, and visiting him would please Arturo's parents.

But visiting Arturo in Newport also meant that he might be able to see Phoebe. With whom he thinks he is still in love. So the real question is, how to accomplish this. Without making a fool of himself. Or making Phoebe angry.

He could phone Phoebe, of course, but she didn't know he was in Newport and she wouldn't like being surprised. And she wasn't on vacation, she was working. She was evaluating Grafton House for University Hall, and she definitely wouldn't like to be interrupted.

So he had to figure out a non-irritating way to let Phoebe know he happened to be in town. Just so he could see his nephew Arturo who was there in one of the tall ships. But if, only if, she had time, he would really like to see her while he was in town. If that was convenient for her.

So maybe the best approach would be to call Grafton House and get invited to the conference they were having. And then figure out a way to see Phoebe without irritating her.

Getting invited to the Grafton House conference was easy. Juan Carlos is Dean of Harvard's Urban Planning Department. He knows Andy Eads well. He calls Grafton House, tells them who he is, and says he wants to attend the conference. Dexter Slate takes his call and makes it clear that Grafton House is honored, delighted, to have him. And Dexter gives Juan Carlos directions to Grafton House.

Now the question is, what to do about seeing Arturo. So Juan Carlos calls Edgar. Edgar and Jackie are in Newport and are about to arrive at the dock where Arturo's ship is berthed. Juan Carlos knows that Edgar also wants to see Arturo, and Jackie wants to see Phoebe.

"I just talked to the people at Grafton House," Juan Carlos tells them. "They were very enthusiastic about my visiting the conference today. What if I get them to invite both of you, and Arturo too. I know that won't be a problem. Then we can get together at Grafton House and plan the rest of the day."

Jackie and Edgar are very pleased by this idea. Juan Carlos calls Grafton House and, as expected, Dexter Slate is delighted to invite Edgar and Jackie and Arturo. Juan Carlos calls Edgar and Jackie again, and a deal is struck. They'll pick up Arturo and take him to the conference. And call Juan Carlos if this won't work out.

Juan Carlos finishes his doughnuts and coffee and walks back to the dealership. He enters the directions to Grafton House in his iPhone's Waze GPS directions app. Then he gets on his rented Harley and takes off.

This is not Juan Carlos' first visit to Newport. Over the years, he has visited Newport a number of times. So he is familiar with the city, and the directions on his Waze app are mainly there as backup. He's not in any particular hurry, and he wants to take a little extra time to think about his plans for the day. So he decides to take an indirect route to Grafton House. He rides into Newport on Broadway, and then goes out Bellevue to Ocean Drive. He takes his time, so he can get a better look at the mansions that line Bellevue. And he thinks about the ultra-rich individuals who built the old mansions, and the recent resurgence of mansion-building by the new members of the ultra-rich class.

Riding West on Ocean Drive, Juan Carlos eventually arrives at Brenton Point, the point on Aquidneck Island where the Atlantic Ocean meets Narragansett Bay. And as he rides around the Point, he sees a runner coming toward him. It's a woman, a young woman, in a T-shirt and shorts. And she's running fast along a narrow retaining wall that separates Ocean Drive from a very steep slope down to the shore.

Juan Carlos recognizes her. She's the wife of Paul Gardiner, who's a member of Harvard's Board of Overseers. She's half her husband's age and she's an Assistant Professor in the Economics Department. She's beautiful. Her name is Anettka.

As these thoughts flash through Juan Carlos' mind, Anettka suddenly vanishes. She's no longer there. She has disappeared. Juan Carlos is startled. What's happened, he wonders. And then he figures it out. Anettka has fallen off the retaining wall. Which is not good.

Juan Carlos pulls off Ocean Drive and stops where he thinks Anettka fell off. He bends over the retaining wall and looks down. Three or four meters below him, Anettka is lying on a narrow rock outcropping in the slope. And three or four meters below her, huge waves are noisily crashing on the rocky shore. Anettka is in a very dangerous position and it's not clear if she's OK. So Juan Carlos leans over the retaining wall, and calls down to Anettka: "Anettka! Can you hear me?"

He waits a second, and tries again: " Anettka! Can you hear me?"

And Anettka responds: "Yes! Yes! I can hear you!"

"Don't move!" Juan Carlos shouts. "You're in a very dangerous spot. Stay where you are and I'll get help to get you back up here. Do you understand? You must not move!"

"I understand!" Anettka shouts. "I won't move!"

"Good!" Juan Carlos shouts back. Then he calls 911.

"This is Dr. Cisneros," he says. (The "Dr." bit is a dog whistle that automatically tells people he's important. The Dr. itself is an honorary degree from Cornell.) "I'm on Ocean Drive at Brenton Point. A woman has fallen down the slope by the side of the road. She's lying on a rock halfway down the slope. I've told her to stay still. It's very steep, and she's about twenty feet down from the road. So I think you'll need a long ladder or something to get down to her."

The 911 operator transfers him to the Newport Fire Department, and he goes through all this again. Then he calls down to Anettka. "I've called the Fire Department," he shouts. "They'll be here shortly. Just stay still, and we'll get you back up here as soon as possible."

"Who are you?" Anettka asks. "How do you know my name?"

"I'm Juan Carlos Cisneros," Juan Carlos says. "I'm on the faculty at Harvard. I know your husband, Paul. He introduced me to you at a party in Cambridge."

"Oh," Anettka says. "Thank you. I'm sorry to be such a nuisance."

"No problem," Juan Carlos says. "No problem at all."

I remember her, Juan Carlos thinks. Very beautiful. From India. No, Pakistan. She was half her husband's age.

I remember him, Anettka thinks. He was a very interesting man. Charismatic. Someone who built real things. A leader.

CHAPTER 49

Paul Gardiner was not having a good morning. His stomach was acting up in an all-too-familiar way. He felt slightly queasy. He was going to have to call Anettka and tell her he was in Newport, and he wasn't looking forward to this at all. He scrabbled around in his briefcase and found a bottle of CVS anti gas/anti acid pills, and his Prilosec tablets. He took one of each with some Fiji water. His stomach immediately felt better.

It had obviously been a bad idea to come back from Paris when Grafton House was holding its annual conference. At which his wife was going to give a speech to a group of eminent scholars. An important speech about the controversial findings of her current research. He was making it clear to Anettka that he didn't take her career seriously. That he didn't take *her* seriously. She wouldn't like that at all. She would be angry with him. Justifiably angry.

So what should he do? He was on West Main Road, approaching the point at which West Main Road turns into Broadway and Middletown turns into Newport. He was in the right lane when he approached the intersection, and he suddenly realized that it was a right turn only lane. And he found himself turning right and heading down Admiral Kalbfus Road toward Narragansett Bay.

It was as if he had suddenly taken a powerful tranquilizer. He felt much calmer. He drove past the Casino and in a series of automatic turns arrived on the Claiborne Pell Bridge heading toward Jamestown. He sailed through the toll gates — he had a Newport resident E-ZPass — and followed the familiar route that led to Jamestown's Narragansett Avenue. He drove up Narragansett Avenue and stopped at one of his favorite restaurants, Slice of Heaven.

A parking space was waiting for him. He parked the Camry, went inside and ordered blueberry pancakes with bacon, orange juice and black coffee. Then he went outside with his coffee and sat down underneath an umbrella. It was a beautiful morning. The young

226

couple sitting next to him had brought their little boy and their dog, a friendly Cocker Spaniel. The dog wagged his tail, and Paul bent over and patted him. But instead of sitting back up in his chair, Paul continued to bend forward and slowly, silently fell out of his chair. He lay quietly on the floor and didn't move. At all.

The friendly Cocker Spaniel sniffed curiously at Paul's head. The young couple sprang into action. The man pulled out his cellphone, called 911, and ran into the restaurant to tell the staff what had happened. The woman knelt down by Paul and dabbed at his face with a wet napkin. "Look, Mommy," the little boy said, pointing towards the scar on Paul's cheek. "He's bumped his face." The restaurant staff rushed outside, picked Paul up and put him back in his chair. Paul didn't move.

Then the Jamestown EMT team arrived. They climbed out of the ambulance, came over and looked at Paul. One of them felt Paul's neck for a minute or so. "I'm sorry," he said, "but I'm afraid he's dead."

Paul was a regular customer of the Slice of Heaven restaurant. Dimitri, the Russian chef, knew his first name was Paul, but didn't know anything else about him. The senior EMT searched Paul's pockets and found his wallet. His Rhode Island driver's license had his Newport address, and his cellphone contact list had a number for that address.

The Jamestown police now arrived on the scene and took charge. The chief of police knew exactly who Paul was. A Very Important Person. He called the Newport Police and told them that Paul was dead. Then he called the Newport number in Paul's contact list, and got Edna, the housekeeper. Edna told the police chief that Paul's wife worked at Grafton House, so the chief called Grafton House and tried to speak to Anettka. Who wasn't there and couldn't be found. Because she was in an ambulance heading toward the Newport Hospital. More later about all this.

Not that it really matters, but what killed Paul was not your usual heart attack. It was something called "sudden cardiac arrest". What happens is that the heart's electrical system suddenly goes nuts and becomes very irregular. The heart beats much too fast, and this stops the blood flow to the brain. No more oxygen. Death.

CHAPTER 50

The Newport Fire Department's response to Juan Carlos' call was prompt and enthusiastic. In approximately fifteen minutes two vehicles arrived: a fully staffed fire truck and an ambulance. Rescuing people from steep slopes appeared to be a familiar problem. After evaluating the situation, the firemen erected a miniature crane. It consisted of a ladder extending horizontally from the fire truck and over the slope, a winch at the end of the ladder, and a bosun's chair attached to the winch. Two long ladders were arranged on either side of Anettka's ledge. Two very large firemen put on harnesses attached to ropes, and climbed down the ladders. When they reached Anettka, they helped her into a harness and placed her in the bosun's chair. Then the firemen above winched Anettka to the top of the slope and over the retaining wall to the street. The firemen and EMTs all cheered. Anettka looked rumpled but basically OK. Just as Juan Carlos had remembered, she was a very beautiful woman.

The assistant chief in charge of the team and Juan Carlos watched as the rescue was carried out. When Anettka's bosun's chair was finally over Ocean Drive, two of the EMTs placed her on a stretcher and took her to the ambulance. She waved at Juan Carlos as she passed. The assistant chief was amused. "She was wearing that same little T-shirt and shorts yesterday," the assistant chief told Juan Carlos. "Very cute, but a little excitable."

"I know her husband," Juan Carlos said. "I should probably follow you to the hospital and make sure she's OK."

"Absolutely," the assistant chief said. "Follow the ambulance. We're gonna take the truck back to the firehouse."

You may ask what Juan Carlos thinks he's doing right now. The simple answer is that he is rescuing a damsel in distress, a beautiful damsel. And as a practical matter, trying to see Phoebe looks like troubling trouble before it troubles you. Not such a good idea. And to tell the truth, his love for Phoebe is getting a little shopworn. As these things do.

Meanwhile, Jackie and Edgar and Tobie and Arturo are driving to Grafton House in Jackie's Toyota truck. Tobie's Vespa is in the truck bed, and Tobie is sitting in Arturo's lap in the back seat. Edgar is driving. They have almost reached Grafton House. Jackie and Tobie are talking.

"I saw your friend Phoebe Snow last night," Tobie says. "She seems very nice. Is Arturo's Uncle Juan her boyfriend?"

"He is," Jackie says. "But I think she's not very happy with him."

"So is that why he wants to go to the conference? To make up with her? Because she's probably going to be very busy. Everybody there is busy."

"I think that's it," Jackie says.

At the entrance gate, a junior staffer is waiting with information packets for Juan Carlos and his guests. The Toyota and its passengers are waved through the gate. "If you could leave my Vespa by the gate, I'll come back later and get it," Tobie says. "I better go inside quick and tell them I'm back." And she does just that.

Across town, on Marlborough Street, George Rakylz is sound asleep.

CHAPTER 51

The electronic chimes on St. Paul's Church were announcing that it was 8:45 when Maureen returned to her apartment on Marlborough Street. She opened the door and found George Rakylz asleep on her chaise longue. He was dressed in the waiter's whites that Maureen had borrowed from her brother, and he looked cute – just as cute as she had remembered him being. "Wake up, sleepyhead," she said, and George obligingly opened his eyes and smiled at her.

"Hi, Maureen," George said, and sat up on the edge of the chaise longue.

"Hi, Jock," Maureen said. She walked over to the chaise longue and patted George's crew cut. Then she bent over and kissed him. George pulled her down next to him and they kissed enthusiastically for a bit. Then Maureen sat up and said, "Later. Now we need to go over to Grafton House and set things up for the luncheon."

"No problem," George said. He picked up his backpack and followed Maureen down the stairs to Marlborough Street.

"This is my brother's van," Maureen said. "He's put some extra propane tanks in it, in case we run out. But mainly, we're going to use it as a trash can when we clean up after the lunch. We can park it behind Grafton House, and bring it down later."

"No problem," George said, and got into the passenger seat of the van. On the dashboard, Maureen had installed a charging outlet for her smart phone. "OK if I use this?" George asked.

"Sure," Maureen said. "Be my guest."

"Okay." George plugged his iPhone into the charging device. The iPhone made an obliging musical bleep.

"Okay if I turn the AC off and roll down the windows?" Maureen said.

"No problem," George said. They drove along Bellevue Avenue in silence for a while. Maureen was dreamily replaying the events of the night before in her mind, and George was busily running through his plan of action.

Then, shortly before they reached Ocean Drive, Maureen exited Bellevue Avenue and began a complicated set of maneuvers involving a bewildering number of narrow streets. "Where are we going?" George asked.

"The back way," Maureen replied. "They called me from Grafton House. There's apparently something weird going on. Cops at the front gate are checking everybody who tries to come in. I don't know why they're doing it, but we haven't got time for that. We're late already. So we're gonna go in the back way. Nancy says the guy they put there is an old friend of mine. He won't give us any shit." George reached around behind his seat and found his backpack. He felt the end of his assault weapon inside the backpack. If I need it, I can get it fast, George told himself. I'm going to stay cool.

"That's it," Maureen said, pointing her index finger toward an enormous mansion perched on the side of a hill. "That's Grafton House. Pretty fancy, huh?"

"Yeah," George said. "Very fancy."

"What we want to do, " Maureen said, "is go up the other side of that hill. The back way. So the cops can't see us drive in." They drove in a semi-circle around the hill and eventually arrived at a small entry gate. Grafton House was no longer visible. "Not   bad, huh?" Maureen said.

"Not bad," George said. "Not bad at all."

A short policeman stood by the gate. 'Hi, Jerry," Maureen said to the policeman. "What's going on?"

"They say some nut's threatening to blow this place up. I think they're making it up to get the publicity. But what do I know? Go ahead and park. Just make sure you've got the caterer parking license in the window."

"Will do," Maureen said and drove the van through the gate and up a steep slope. When they were almost at the top of the hill, Maureen stopped the van, set the emergency brake and said, "I'm gonna get out here." She pointed toward a brick walkway. "That walkway will take you down to the lunch tables on the other side of the hill. I've got to get down there now, or they're going to be really mad at me. Park the van over there where it says 'OVERFLOW PARKING' and then meet me at the tent. Okay?"

"No problem," George said, and slid over into the driver's seat. He watched Maureen walk up the brick walkway and over the crest of the hill. And suddenly felt overwhelmed with amazement. He, George Rakylz, had formulated The Program, a comprehensive reform of a decadent society. He had recreated himself as Omega, the Destroyer of Bourgeois Corruption. And he was now on the verge of carrying out a monumental action that would resonate throughout the world. It was amazing. It was, really, you had to admit it, funny! And George began to laugh. Out loud. Softly to begin with, and then louder and louder. Stop it, he told himself. Get serious. But he continued to laugh. He couldn't stop. Stop it! he told himself. But he couldn't.

He put the van in gear and drove toward the overflow parking lot. And he continued to laugh. Hysterically. You've got to stop laughing, he told himself. You're being hysterical. You've got to be serious. "Hey!" he said out loud. "HEY!" he shouted at himself. "You've got to get SERIOUS!" He had reached the very end of the overflow parking area. It was a perfect location. He would be completely invisible to the people on the other side of the hill. And then, without warning, the front wheels of the van fell into a large pothole. And George was startled. And George stopped laughing. And George said "SHIT!" Such things do happen.

CHAPTER 52

By the time Andy Eads and Harold Cummings pulled up to the main gate at Grafton House, peace and calm reigned supreme. The various groups of demonstrators — except for SNARL, the anarchists from Fall River, MA — had arrived and been taken in hand by Teresa Morgan and her team of junior staff. In addition to the welcome booth for conference registrants, Teresa had set up a separate welcome booth for the demonstrators.

As they arrived, conference registrants were given packets containing copies of the papers to be presented, and a conference schedule. Plus an information sheet with a map showing the location of public restrooms and water fountains. At the demonstrators' welcoming kiosk, each demonstrator was given a less fancy but still very satisfactory package containing an outline of the day's events and the information sheet.

Members of the Newport police force were stationed at each kiosk. They distributed Xerox copies of wanted posters with the updated George Rakylz photo, along with a stern warning: "If you see this man, DON'T say ANYTHING to him. Just quietly come and tell us where he is. We'll take care of it."

Signs by the information kiosks pointed the way to the enormous white tent on the lawn in back of Grafton House where the conference proceedings were to be held. Two hundred folding chairs had been provided at the front of the tent for the conference registrants. Teresa had added another 150 chairs for the demonstrators. One of Harold Cummings' assistant groundkeepers — a rock musician in his spare time —had added extra loudspeakers to the PA system, plus additional microphones for audience questions.

So things were proceeding nicely for the conference, as far as Andy Eads could tell. He had typed up the remarks he planned to make at the opening of the conference. Not that he really needed to, since they were pretty much the same remarks he had been making for the past five years, ever since becoming the Director of Grafton

House. At supper the night before, we heard him deliver the gist of these remarks to Phoebe and Henry Leathwood. Not to put too fine a point on it, Andy is an idealist. He believes that compromise and comity can facilitate good government. Necessary but not sufficient is how he would characterize these virtues.

Anyway, this year, Andy has come up with a (relatively) new approach. After he opens the conference with his initial (and familiar to most of those present) remarks, he will chair a panel of five scholars who will comment on his remarks and answer questions from the audience. The panel is made up of three Grafton House scholars — Suleiman Khan, Jack Chrysler, and Anettka Gardiner — and two visiting scholars — Peter Wood (Professor of Government, Stanford University) and Annie Schwartzkopf (Professor of Sociology, Duke University). Later in the conference, all five of these scholars are supposed to present their own scholarly papers on specific topics. Now, however, they are supposed to rise above their individual areas of expertise and talk about the governance philosophy that Andy has just enunciated. What Andy envisions, or at least hopes for, is a spirited but collegial debate. Whether he'll get what he wants remains to be seen.

According to Dexter Slate's plans, Andy's remarks and the following panel discussion are supposed to last for one hour and fifteen minutes, that is until 10:15 a.m., after which there will be a fifteen-minute coffee break. (Dexter admires Andy, but he's a little dubious about the panel idea. He anticipates trouble.) When the conference resumes, the conferees are supposed to split up into small group meetings known in the conference business as "breakout sessions". Each breakout session is supposed to feature at least three presentations of scholarly papers.

Andy Eads proceeded slowly toward the podium at the front of the tent, counting the number of demonstrators and scholars in the audience. About fifty demonstrators had found seats at the back of the tent. The different groups of demonstrators were easily identifiable. About half of the people in the back two rows were speaking Spanish. The seats in the next two rows were clearly occupied by the Concerned Muslim Citizens of Newport. Most of the women in this group wore scarves over their hair, and a distinguished-looking man with a short beard wore a round blue cap on his head. That's the Imam, Andy thought.

The Citizens for a Fair Immigration Policy were instantly identifiable. As if by right, they sat nearest the stage. They wore their ethnic garb: L.L. Bean for some, Brooks Brothers for others, and an abundance of Tilley hats and baseball caps. Judging by the baseball caps, about half of the group were Yankee fans. (Rhode Island baseball fans come in two flavors, which correspond to the two cities, New York and Boston, to which they feel most attached.) Andy recognized one of the Yankee fans, a man named Tommy Frost— Andy's late wife Joan's first husband.

"Andy!" Tommy cried out enthusiastically. "How's it going, man?"

"Fine, Tommy," Andy replied. "Good to see you." That wasn't true – Andy had never much liked Tommy – but sometimes truthfulness isn't called for.

Most of the folding chairs set up at the front of the tent for the scholars were filled, for a total of perhaps 150 scholars. That makes about two hundred so far, Andy decided. And more will definitely come.

On the stage, four of the five panel participants — Suleiman, Jack Chrysler, and the two visiting scholars — waited in folding chairs arranged in a half-circle behind the podium. Anettka wasn't there, Andy realized. I'll just not mention her. A set of stairs equipped with a handrail had been placed by the podium. Andy grasped the handrail firmly and climbed the stairs to the stage.

"Good morning," Andy said into the microphone in front of him. ("Good morning," the crowd replied in unison.) "I'm Andy Eads," Andy said. "I'm the Director of Grafton House. I'm pleased to welcome all of you to Harvard University's Grafton House Conference on International Immigration Policy — or as we here at Grafton House call it, GEE-CHIP." This reference to the conference initials — GHCIIP – was a hallowed joke in the immigration policy community. The scholars dutifully chuckled at Andy's witticism. The rest of the audience looked puzzled.

"I'm going to make a few introductory remarks this morning and try to lay out my vision of the proper approach to public policy research. Then I've asked two of our senior scholars here at Grafton House, and two distinguished scholars who are visiting us today from Stanford and Duke, to comment on my ideas. " He turned towards the panelists, and introduced each of them, beginning with Peter Wood and Annie Schwartzkopf

Phoebe Snow and Henry Leathwood have arrived early and are sitting on the aisle near the front of the audience. Since Andy was in fact repeating almost exactly what he had said the night before at supper, neither of them is paying much attention. Both of them have showered and changed clothes after their enjoyable tennis match earlier in the morning. This has not reduced their bodies' production of pheromones. The pheromones are still doing their thing. Phoebe and Henry are swathed in a cloud of general well-being and mutual admiration.

Phoebe and Henry are not alone in feeling a warm sense of well-being. In general, the audience feels swell too. Andy's remarks, I fear, while soundly based and logically consistent, also can be read as platitudes, and people like listening to platitudes. As Andy speaks, many members of the audience can be seen to nod their heads (in affirmation that cooperation is good), or shake their heads (in disapproval of excessive partisanship and conflict). Jackie and Edgar and Arturo are sitting in the rear of the audience, and they have also found themselves in agreement with Andy's views. Going to church affects a lot of people the same way.

CHAPTER 53

When Andy finished his remarks, everyone in the audience applauded enthusiastically. Andy was pleased but not surprised. He had made this speech many times before and this was the usual reaction. Then, when the applause had died down, Andy said, "As I mentioned earlier, we're going to try something new this morning. I'd like to begin by asking Professor Peter Wood, from Stanford, to come up to the podium."

You don't get to be a full professor at a university like Stanford without knowing which side your bread is buttered on. And in this particular case, the location of the butter is obvious. Harvard University's Grafton House Conference on International Immigration Policy (GHCIIP) is a must-be-at scene if you're involved in immigration policy. It's important because everyone who is anyone in the immigration policy community is invited. And Andy Eads is the person who invites you. So, not to be indelicate, you don't want to piss Andy off. Besides, as noted above, platitudes make lots of people happy. Poking holes in popular ideas can be fun, and even career-enhancing. But the safer course of action is to avoid direct attacks that will hurt people's feelings.

So Professor Wood went to some effort in his brief remarks to make it clear that he, too, prized cooperation and comity. And that having different policy goals doesn't mean that it's OK to cherry-pick your facts to support your positions. On the other hand, it was important to realize that partisanship is a fact of life in a democracy. So fighting fiercely for ones views was valuable too. And finally, in his own personal experience, it was possible to combine cooperation and partisanship and do good research. The audience nodded in approval and gave him a nice round of applause.

Jack Chrysler went a little further in defending partisanship. Yes, he said, comity was vital, but so was vigorous advocacy for unpopular views. It was important not to be intimidated by the understandable desire not to be seen as a troublemaker. And it was certainly the case that people could vary in their assessment of the importance of various facts. Not the truth of the facts, of course, but their importance. Still in all, Jack concluded by saying that he thoroughly agreed with Andy about the importance of sincere and wholehearted cooperation in the conduct of scholarly research. Jack also got a decent hand, but it was clear that some in the audience weren't sure about him.

Annie Schwartzkopf, the Duke Professor of Sociology, seemed to have a bad cold. She spoke for a minute and a half in favor of cooperation and comity and then said, "Thank you." The audience liked that a lot, and clapped heartily. Many were getting tired of high-minded rhetoric and were looking forward to the coffee break.

Suleiman was the last of the panelists to speak. Andy's introduction of Suleiman was particularly fulsome. "Our distinguished colleague," Andy said, "a scholar whose contributions to the study of immigration policy have been groundbreaking in their depth and incisiveness …," and a good deal more of the same.

"The Imam says this man is a devout Muslim," one of the Newport Muslims whispered to her husband.

What's going on here, of course, is the opposite side of the coin from what was going on when Professor Peter Wood (Stanford) made his remarks. Professor Wood wanted to make Andy Eads happy. Andy controls something that Dr. Wood cares a lot about: being invited to speak at Harvard University's Grafton House Conference on International Immigration Policy (GHCIIP). Suleiman controls something Andy Eads cares a lot about: Suleiman's future presence or absence from the group of scholars who are the life-blood of Grafton House. This is not to say that Andy likes Suleiman; he doesn't. Or that Suleiman is very useful in his role as Deputy Director; he isn't. But Suleiman is definitely the jewel in the crown of Grafton House. He is a truly distinguished scholar, and is universally recognized by other scholars in the immigration policy community as such. And Andy wants him to stay at Grafton House.

"Good morning!" Suleiman said to the audience in an authoritative voice (the audience enthusiastically replied, "Good morning!"). Suleiman was pleased. It had been some time since his last public speaking assignment, and he had missed that. He missed classroom teaching. He had enjoyed teaching undergraduates throughout his career. But there aren't any bright undergraduates at Grafton House. Only deadly-dull graduate students. So Suleiman spends a good deal of his time mentoring boring graduate students. Many of whom are not only boring but also second-rate. Which is one of the reasons Suleiman is thinking about leaving Grafton House. Anyway, Suleiman isn't particularly interested in pleasing Andy. As he sees it, it's up to Andy to please him. This is an accurate reading of the situation. So Suleiman doesn't feel called upon to be overly politic in his remarks.

"Thank you, Andy," Suleiman began. " I think we can all agree that your call for civility and cooperation is spot-on." Suleiman was very fond of British slang, especially Oxbridgisms. "But what I'd like to do today is say a few words about partisanship. Certainly, there can be excesses of partisanship in scholarly endeavors just as in the world as a whole. But partisanship is also a valuable tool. Some of the scholars here today would probably say that I'm a conservative, and that my colleague Dr. Chrysler is a liberal. In fact, I would argue that the reverse is a more accurate description. I would classify myself as a liberal and Dr. Chrysler as a conservative. Let me explain.

"For some reason, the term liberal in the United States has come to stand for political views which are left of center. In the rest of the world, the term liberal is used in a different way. In this earlier usage, a liberal is one who favors limits on governmental involvement in daily life. The proper role of government in the historic liberal view is that government defends against foreign threats and enforces the country's legal system. Old-fashioned liberals believe that too much government stifles individual initiative and in the long run causes more problems than it cures. Interestingly enough, the original liberals were seen as radicals by the conservatives of their day.

"The United States of America is not part of the United Kingdom today, in large part because the conservatives in Great Britain at the time of the American Revolution overregulated the economies of their American colonies. Remember the tea tax and the Boston Tea

Party." (Suleiman smiled winningly at the audience and a substantial number of them laughed appreciatively. "He's talking about the Tea Party," various spouses whispered to their significant others.) "And on the Indian sub-continent, where I'm from," Suleiman went on, "the British did almost exactly the same thing. Some of you may know that Mahatma Gandhi began his campaign for Indian self-determination in the 1930s with a non-violent protest against the British tax on salt. That's right, an onerous and ridiculous tax on salt, imposed by an out-of-touch Imperial government in far-away London. A government led by the same kind of conservatives whose overreaching led to the Boston Tea Party.

"You may ask what this has to do with partisanship. In my opinion, it has a great deal to do with partisanship. Sometimes, compromise is a pragmatic solution to a partisan conflict. Yes, the best is sometimes the enemy of the good, as Voltaire is reported to have observed. But too much compromise can mean that important, needed reforms remain unaccomplished. Benjamin Franklin, the oldest of our nation's Founding Fathers, tried for years to reach a workable compromise with the conservative know-nothings in the British Government. He hoped to convince them that their over-regulation of the American colonies was counterproductive. He searched for a middle-ground compromise, which would persuade the American colonies to remain in the United Kingdom. He failed in this endeavor, and eventually decided that revolution — violent revolution— was the Colonies' only acceptable course of action. He did so reluctantly. His son remained a Loyalist. But Benjamin Franklin, a realist to the core, understood that sometimes the extreme, the partisan is the only viable course of action. Too much moderation, too much compromise, too much concern with gaining consensus can sometimes be the opposite of realism. As Senator Barry Goldwater said half a century ago, 'Extremism in the pursuit of liberty is no vice.'"

"Oh my God," Henry Leathwood whispered to Phoebe Snow. "He's quoting Barry Goldwater!"

"Who is Barry Goldwater?" Phoebe whispered back. Not surprisingly. Phoebe's mother wasn't born when Goldwater said this. It's ancient history to her. As is much else, I fear.

Andy Eads pondered this *aperçu* by Suleiman's hero Barry. He successfully stifled the urge to shout, "That's pure bullshit!" But Suleiman isn't just being politically incorrect. He's obviously taking a shot at Andy. This worries Andy, because it may mean that Suleiman is thinking about leaving Grafton House.

At the podium, Suleiman has moved on from a defense of partisan politics to an erudite discussion of immigration policy, with particular reference to the economic effects of various legal immigration policies. In brief, Suleiman wants to admit more high-skilled immigrants, and establish a large temporary worker program for low-skilled, low-wage workers. The usual stuff, Andy thought to himself. Eventually Suleiman came to the end of his remarks, which were warmly applauded by many of the immigration reform demonstrators. Most of whom probably hadn't understood what Suleiman was saying but liked the way he said it.

In general, the scholars in the audience were less enthusiastic. Lots of them disagreed with Suleiman's proposed changes in immigration policy. And a goodly number weren't pleased by Suleiman's insinuation that their liberalism was really King George III's blind conservatism. At this point in the proceedings, Professor Schwartzkopf pulled herself together, blew her nose noisily, and responded to the subtext of Suleiman's remarks.

"Suleiman is absolutely correct. Great Britain's American colonies revolted because they wanted and deserved more autonomy. King George was pigheaded. Here in the United States traditional liberals like me can also be pigheaded. We often refuse to recognize the bad effects of too much government. And we have to acknowledge that.

"But Suleiman suggests that government – not just government regulation but government itself — is inherently bad. He repeats the same disastrous mantra that President Reagan, and the Republican Party and all too many academic economists hold sacred. Government is bad. Dismantle government and the country will thrive. It's the same Voodoo Economics that Bush the Good correctly called Ronald Reagan's economic policy. It's the same Social Darwinism that Herbert Hoover believed in — the fittest survive on their own; government assistance weakens the moral fiber of the working class and encourages sloth and dependence.

"We have seen in this country over the decades since Reagan was elected a disastrous widening of the income gap between most Americans and a small upper class. It may well be the case that the reasons for this gap have to do with changes in technology and the economy's labor requirements. But our government has not tried to do very much about this gap. It could have tried but it didn't. Instead, the 'free market' devotees have focused on cutting taxes on the rich and cutting social safety net programs like Medicare and Social Security to make up for the lost tax revenue.

"And the reason government didn't try is that Suleiman's anti-government stand says that you shouldn't try to fix the problem — except by cutting rich people's taxes and hoping their riches will trickle down. Or by cutting regulations so employers won't have to worry about polluting the environment, and Wall Street won't have to worry about too much oversight restricting their freedom of action.

"To be fair, many of us liberals here at this immigration conference have failed to recognize that too much immigration can have disastrous effects on working class Americans. We liberals need to rethink our views on this issue.

"But," and here she slammed her hand down on the table by her chair, "don't be taken in by academic ratiocination that justifies too little government." She slammed her hand down again, and when she did, the tent was filled with the sound of an explosion. A very big explosion.

CHAPTER 54

One of the most interesting technological developments in the 21st century has been the smart phone. Apple's iPhone has changed everyone's life in amazing ways. One of the most amazing ways is Siri, the iPhone's interactive voice-activated software system. Siri can and does do lots of interesting things, and one of them is voice-activated dialing of phone numbers. The iPhone owner puts a phone number on her contact list and gives it a name: whatever she wants — Cleopatra, or Michael, or even Open Sesame. Then she presses a small button on the bottom of her iPhone, and holds the button down. This activates Siri, and the owner then can say "Call Mother," and Siri will call Mother's number.

The owner doesn't even have to say "Call." If she says "Mother," Siri will dial her mother's phone number without further ado.

Moreover, if her iPhone is charging, she doesn't have to hold the button down. She just has to say "Hey Siri," and Siri will wait for her instructions. And if she thinks for a bit and then says "Mother!" Siri will dial her mother.

Unfortunately, mistakes will happen from time to time. And so when George couldn't stop laughing and shouted at himself "HEY! Get SERIOUS!" Siri heard him. And Siri was activated. And Siri waited patiently for further instructions.

George had devoted considerable thought and attention to developing a method for detonating his explosive device at a safe distance from himself. He had attached a cheap cellphone from the drug store to a detonator inside the explosive. He had tested out the performance of a sample detonator in advance. Calling the cellphone activated the detonator and caused the bomb to explode. And he had programmed his iPhone to automatically dial the cellphone. All he had to do was turn on Siri, and say "Shit!" When Siri heard this instruction, she would automatically dial the cellphone detonator and the bomb would go off. "BOOM!" Life being what it is, George was startled when the front wheels of the van suddenly fell into a large pothole. And so George said "SHIT!" And Siri did her thing.

Which was really amazingly destructive. All by itself, George's IED was capable of demolishing the van and its contents, including George. And it did do that. But it also did something that the propane gas industry wants you to think is nearly impossible: when George's IED exploded, it destroyed the vapor-return valve on one of the two tanks of propane gas in the van. The result was truly spectacular, although invisible to the people at the Grafton House conference on the other side of the hill. Each of the propane tanks contained approximately thirty liters of propane. This is equivalent to 750 megajoules of energy, which is roughly the equivalent of 160 kilograms of TNT. That is equal to the amount of energy needed to melt 2.25 tons of ice, or raise nine fully-loaded semi trucks one kilometer in the air. That's just one tank. Two tanks exploded. Making a very loud noise. And distributing tiny fragments of George around the parking area and beyond.

CHAPTER 55

When Maureen heard the explosion, she climbed to the top of the hill and found that the van had disappeared. Very small bits of the van and its contents were scattered around the parking area. Maureen returned to the main gate and told the police that it was probably her van that had exploded. She said that she had left the van with a man she had hired to work on the catering crew. It wasn't hard to figure out that the man in question was George Rakylz. Andy and the Chief of the Newport Police Department discussed the incident and decided that there wasn't any reason to stop the conference. So they didn't.

EPILOGUE

After the conference was over, Henry asked Phoebe if she had ever thought about getting married. She said she had, and asked him if he was saying he wanted to marry her. He said he was, and she told him she had a problem. That she was pregnant. Henry said that was fine with him. They spent the next two weeks interviewing staff and reviewing records at Grafton House. They wrote a detailed report on the Center's management and sent it to Melanie Ferguson. Conclusion: Alpha, with a few minor problems that could easily be fixed. Then they got married and moved to Washington, D.C. Phoebe quit her job at Harvard and went back to teaching math. At American University, which wasn't as prestigious as MIT, but so what.

Anettka inherited a great deal of money from Paul, all of which she invested in Treasury bonds. She did not sleep with Jack Chrysler. She had a short affair with Juan Carlos, but dumped him when it became clear that he wasn't the marrying kind. She accepted a teaching position at Stanford, and used some of her inheritance to buy a modest but very expensive house in Palo Alto. House prices in the Bay Area are insane. She is working with a therapist to understand and better cope with her anxiety about Islam and her father and brothers.

Juan Carlos is currently having an affair with a young woman from New Zealand. She is enchanted with the fact that he is five years older than her father. He is not similarly enchanted. Catherine and Juan Carlos are still married, but Catherine is thinking about getting a divorce. She has lunch once a week with a woman friend who is an Episcopal priest and teaches at the Divinity School. And the Vatican seems to be softening its position on communion for divorced Catholics. Juan Carlos is worried about this.

Tobie and Arturo got married. Fat Willie's mother turned out to be right: straining at stool can be fatal. He did; he died. So there was no real evidence that Tobie was connected with Ed's murder. Tobie's parents and Arturo's parents were both delighted by their marriage. Arturo is thinking about going to business school.

Suleiman Khan has accepted a position at Columbia. He likes being back in New York. He is working with Muslim young people in an effort to prevent them from becoming radicalized.

Jack Chrysler is still at Grafton House. He and Pooh Gardiner are sleeping together. There's not that much difference in their ages, and frankly, Jack is getting a little too old for chaste romantic love.

Alex the beekeeper and Teresa also have gotten married. They went to Fall River, MA for the legal part and then had a big wedding at Grafton House. Andy Eads gave Alex away, and Teresa's father did the same for her. Teresa has been promoted to Assistant Director. She does the same things, but gets more money and has a nicer title.

Jackie and Edgar have not gotten married. They have been a couple for a long time, and they are firm believers in the who-cares-most rule. In this case, Edgar cares more than Jackie; he's freaked out at the prospect of calling Jackie his husband. On the other hand, the tax advantages of marriage still may change his mind.

Andy Eads is nearing eighty and says he's going to retire soon. But he hasn't.

Harold Cummings hasn't retired either. He is pleased with the colors he's getting in his rhododendrons.

Sam Graves has gone on a diet that requires him to eat a great deal of seafood at Anthony's in Middletown.

Oscar is also thriving. He found two mice last month. Alex was pleased and gave him a treat.